THE BLIND AFFECT. Copyright © 2021 by Michael Poeltl.

Cover photo by Justin Hamilton. Cover design by *MP*

FIRST EDITION
ISBN 978-0-9952885-2-2

Realistic Fiction 2. American Literature 3. Substance Abuse 4. Family Life Fiction 5. Coming of Age

Trigger Warnings: alcoholism, kidnapping, drug use, domestic violence, childhood sexual slavery, human trafficking

Michael Poeltl

Acknowledgments

There is a conscious stamp we put on an act that we are aware of, and often, we will experience the impact of that act immediately. So, what of the impacts of our actions that go without notice? Do these, too, register influence?

A blind affect describes the emotional response upon learning of your action or inaction on a person, place, thing, or event.

How did I arrive at *The Blind Affect?* As it happens, one of the characters in the novel explained the process so succinctly that I was prompted to make the phrase the title of my book. It summed it up perfectly.

Thank you to my peers; your suggestions and corrections are always welcome. Deciding whether to go forward with the title alone was a complex (grammatical) equation that I'm happy we satisfied in lengthy threads on social media as Poetic license.

Thanks again to you, the reader. That an indie author can find an audience is inspiring, but what's more so is that indie readers are out there mingling with conventional readers and consuming books like this.

Always grateful to you. Sincerely;

Michael Poeltl

Michael Poeltl

FOR ANNE

"Life can only be understood backwards, but must be lived forwards."

Soren Kierkegaard

Michael Poeltl

CHAPTERS

1.   2021, February, Jonah at 61
2.   1970, The Suburbs
3.   1973, The Sting of Love
4.   2020, May, Severn at 59
5.   1974, The Fox & Ferret
6.   1973, Grandma Anne
7.   1974, The Love Letter
8.   1975, The Happening
9.   1973, The Reveal
10.   1973, A Victory of Conscience
11.   1973, Puberty
12.   1976, It's a Blur
13.   1977, The Black Tar
14.   1977, Rehab, Relapse, Rehab
15.   1979, The Invisible Man
16.   1980, Five Years Gone
17.   1984, Funerals. Jonah, 24
18.   1986, Leaving on a Jet Plane
19.   1988, 13 Years Gone
20.   1993, the Shrink and the Shooter
21.   1992, Seventeen Years
22.   1993, Tattoos
23.   2020, December, Darnell
24.   1993, Inner City
25.   1993, The Culling
26.   1993, Freedom
27.   1994, The Return
28.   1995, Lost Time
29.   1994, A New Beginning
30.   1994, Out of the City
31.   2020, December, Severn at 60
32.   2020, Severn & Darnell
33.   1994, Talking it Out
34.   1994, A Walk in the Park
35.   1997, Christmas
36.   1999, Dinner
37.   1999, They Say They Come in Threes
38.   2001, Of Loss and Lessons
39.   2003, An Attempt at a Normal Life
40.   2003, Dr. Sturgis
41.   2013, Doing Good
42.   2017, The Beginning of the End
43.   2020, Remembrances
44.   2020, August, Severn's Awakening
45.   2020, October, Group
46.   2021, The Diagnosis
47.   2021, Walking the Talk
48.   2021, A Reunion of Sorts

Michael Poeltl

2021, February
Jonah at Sixty-One

In time, I've come to believe man is a canvas, brushed by those he's known and those who knew him. Tenderly painted by some or stroked harshly by those he's wronged. While some would include bright hues to offset the dark corners, mine would surely be a thousand shades of gray, save the one black stroke that blankets the only bright spot my canvas ever knew.

As he lies on his deathbed, regret wrenches him into the past. Like a disoriented time traveler caught in a vacuum, Jonah is forced to recount the losses in his life. The loss of innocence, the loss of purpose, the loss of the one person who had made life bearable. It's all very dismal, but the pull is absolute as he relives a plethora of painful memories. Ancient emotions compel him to believe they're happening in the present rather than decades ago. Still, he hasn't lost all sense. He knows these are only memories. But the pain causes his nervous system to live them as though they are real, one final time. The heart monitor spikes next to his head. *Take me.* He begs the universe, hoping this time it's a full-blown heart attack. *Take me.* A nurse rushes in to check the machine and listens to his heart. He senses he is in no danger as she mops a considerable amount of sweat from his brow. Suddenly, she notices something unusual. It is his trademark scent, which he labeled the "pong." Her conditioned smile instinctively fades from her round face, reacting to the sharp waft of body odor. It soaks his gown under the arms. It is an embarrassing trauma he's lived with since he was thirteen, but there's nothing to do about it now. She adds something to the cocktail, feeding his body nutrients with a quick push of a plunger. Jonah feels an immediate sense of calm rush over him. His eyes feel fuzzy. He turns his head toward the windowed wall. Tears escape his glazed eyes over the false alarm. He feels the light touch of the nurse's hand brush his shoulder as she leaves the room, mumbling something reassuring.

The smell of the hospice, midwinter. The food. The cleaning solution. The blood and urine and feces and death. The sweat. It all amasses to a particular scent, he deliberates. *I wanted to die in the summer.* The view outside his window is dismal but fitting. The universe *would* place him in this dreary season at the end of life. Icicles drip from his window where water gathers from a hole in the gutter, freezing overnight and melting during the day. Spring is two months away. He may yet make it to summer, depending on how long he is to suffer. He wishes he wouldn't.

Jonah shifts slightly in his bed, careful not to dislodge the tubes, keeping his sixty-one-year-old body tethered to the present in a morphine dream. The burn of addiction enters his chest as the scent of tobacco lingers in his room. Some of the nurses smoke. In another hour, he would be wheeled to the open-air balcony by Mav, who would join him for his twice-daily constitutional. It was nowhere near enough for his addiction, but it was about all he could manage in his current state. The hacking cough that assails him for the hour to follow is most unpleasant.

He hates being chained to this existence, waiting for death. His mother drank herself to an early grave while his father worked himself there. Both were dead before ever facing old age. Perhaps there was some dignity in it - dying before they'd been given a chance to choose. *Choose or lose.* But with today's treatments and medications, a person could easily outlive their usefulness by decades, it would seem. Jonah remembers when he'd turned fifty. *"For what,"* he'd asked himself.

No matter. He's no one to visit him at sixty-one, no one to care. He has made sure of that. He's been hard on himself these last fifty years, and that kind of internal torment is his friend, his partner, his child.

It's not how he imagined it in his youth, dying. He'd envisioned children and grandchildren gathered around his deathbed. Or no, maybe he'd track a slow walk as he follows his family out of the driveway after a Thanksgiving to remember, waving goodbye. In this universe, he blows a kiss, and there it is, the image they remember of him: a happy man who had lived a full life and had loved and been loved in return. That even he would die in his sleep with a smile. But that's a fairy-tale ending reserved for those worthy of such an end.

"You can't do that." His mother meant to protect him, of course. After his twin died in childbirth, he was it, and his mother at first seemed adamant he would survive. He couldn't climb a hill or walk across a stony creek without an ever-scrupulous eye. Everything boys did, everything that seemed normal, was off limits. *Nothing* was safe. Everything was terrifying to his mother. He hadn't even learned to ride a bike. Still, he had loved her through all of it. He had felt confined but protected.

Later, he understood her sickness; reality was unbearable. She'd mistaken him for his dead brother, and he'd corrected her and was slapped so hard his glasses flew across the room. He was startled. She was never the same after that. A few weeks later, strange men started accompanying her home from the bar. This was when he considered his first drink. At thirteen, he found one of his mother's hidden bottles of vodka and forced himself to drink. It was awful, but drinking it made him feel closer to her. The burn in his abdomen made him feel safe and warm. The delirium, the pain, the vomiting, and the rush of love. He now wished he'd never brought up her alcoholism.

And now, at the end of a life unlived, one born of sadness, dragged along on the coattails of depression, Jonah waits to close his eyes for good.

* * *

Another day breaks. He's never been a morning person. He's always hated mornings. But to function in society, one must have a job to go to, like it or not, or so one was told. Money earned to afford the life everyone else wanted for you. Jonah didn't want for much. He would have been quite content to avoid life altogether. People especially. Morning people the most. Now, there is no job and no reason. The start of another day begs the question of whether it is even worth the effort. Should he just pull the IV out of his arm and let nature take its course? The IV is for the pain, hydration too, he'd heard them say. Jonah doesn't deal well with pain. *Why go out in pain?* He'd lived in pain.

He glances at the tattoos on his left forearm. Each is a reminder of an event in his life. His skin is still smooth. He reaches over his narrow frame to run a slow finger over one of the words imprinted on his flesh. *FORGIVENESS*, in Beyond Wonderland font. He coughs out an ironic laugh. He remembers his mother's voice urging him against the 'dangerous' practice of inking. *"Not in this lifetime, Mister,"* she would have said. She was dead so soon, long before his first, but still, her voice rang true in his head. He often whispered this mantra to himself when he sensed a choice might take him in a direction his mother would disapprove of—the woman who had robbed him of adventure.

Jonah had always wished he'd been named Jack rather than his twin brother. Jack was a name used in so many nursery rhymes and fairy tales. Not all had happy endings, but Jonah always imagined himself in their place. Jack and Jill, Jack Sprat, Jack and the Bean Stock, Jack B. Nimble, Little Jack Horner. Jack wasn't even a real name. It was a nickname. As though his mother naming him something unreal had created his destiny. Maybe if Jonah had been named Jack, his life would have been fuller, less dull, or shorter.

Christ, I could use a drink. "Clean" for three years. No alcohol, and still, he gets struck down with this. Sepsis. *How many organs are failing right now? Did they say three?* Two weeks in the hospice and still not dead. *Why do I linger?* Meanwhile, they've carted four bodies out of the place. He has a spectacular view from his front room window as the ambulances pull up, lights on, but no sirens. Too late. But that's the idea behind a hospice: to die in plain sight of those being paid to wait you out. He swore he could make out singing or humming and whispers to the dying in adjoining rooms before the declaration of death was handed out. DO NOT RESUSCITATE. It was a choice he'd made after his latest trip to the hospital when he'd received the grim news. The kidney infection had led to sepsis, and any odds of surviving seemed to deteriorate daily as symptoms worsened. The short-lived series of antibiotics further damaged his kidneys and liver. The news would almost have had Jonah smiling if it weren't for the pain in his abdomen. He took the doctor's recommendations, finished his Will, and checked himself into this hospice. It's nothing close to luxurious, but it had an opening. He had his lawyer arrange for a local charity to pick up his worldly belongings and rent his apartment to someone else. Just like that, he'd never existed. He imagines that's how he will leave the world, too. His story lost to the larger lives being lived. Someone will pick up the rent where he left off. Someone will eventually fill this bed, too. His body will soon be ash. *Who will spread his ashes? Who cares?* Just throw them into the wind in a celebratory "*Hooray.*" Like a handful of confetti, his final farewell to a world he'd never been a part of.

1970

The Suburbs

It was a difficult pregnancy. That's how his mother described having Jonah and his brother Jack in her womb. "The two of you were always play-fighting in there," she explained, her slender hand motioning to her now trim waistline, her tone more cheerful than usual. "It was very uncomfortable, but I put up with it. I told you both to get it out of your systems before I came in and smacked you." She placed her cigarette on the edge of an empty beer can and picked up a glass of something more potent than beer. She took a hard swallow, picked up the smoke and sucked the end, held the smoke in her lungs a moment, then exhaled, the sadness given room by her escaping breath. Jonah watched the smoke fill the kitchen. He liked how it swirled around and even how the smoke continued to fall out of his mother's nostrils. He could take or leave the smell, but everything he wore smelled like his mother, which was comforting. The little breakfast nook was lit by the sun pouring through the kitchen window and the white lace valance that made oblong circles on the floor. His mother picked a rogue bit of tobacco from the end of her tongue and studied it. *Spirit in the Sky* by Norman Greenbaum came on the radio. The radio was always on at a low volume. It kept her from thinking too much, she'd said. She turned it up. A smile and a far-away look accompanied her, humming the song.

"How long was I in there?" Jonah asked, seated on a wooden chair, pulled close to his mother's, their knees practically touching. She looked at him disapprovingly. "You were *both* in there nine months, Jonah. You *and* Jack." She never forgot about Jack. Jonah forgot on purpose. He wanted his mother to himself. She always brought up stupid old Jack. Jack, Jack, dead old Jack. "*He's dead!*" He wanted to scream this in her face as if she didn't know. Wasn't it enough they visited his grave every Sunday, took a picnic, and stayed there for three stupid, wasted hours at a time? Meanwhile, Jonah couldn't do anything right, and he certainly wasn't allowed to do anything fun. Homework at the green laminate table, pencil sharpening's, and eraser bits dotting the swirly pattern. Then, less lucid, T.V. and dinner, mostly shoveled down or scraped away. Then, the inside of his room, the escape. The posters on the wall are the only spark to his imagination and the only essence of the outside world. He was real, but he didn't feel real when she was alone with her glass, and he was alone, alone. He would sneak peeks at the street beyond the window and see boys racing their bicycles up and down the road or maybe climbing the large maples that lined the boulevard. A world of fun and exploration awaited anyone bold enough to venture outdoors. *What if I fell out of one of those trees? What if the wheel came loose from the bike? What if, what if, what if, what if.* It was exhausting to think about. But she was his mother, and he loved her for many other reasons, like when she would trace her fingers along his small face, ending at the tip of his petite nose, telling him what a handsome little man he was. That was a favorite for him. He felt loved and safe and warm under her playful eyes.

Jonah's mother had been like this for as long as he could remember. Frazzled. It made him anxious for her, and he wanted to help her but sometimes didn't see how. He had been home-schooled for the first few years until she enrolled him in grade four at the school three blocks from their home. She'd told him she couldn't teach at that level. He felt scared to leave her alone but excited at the possibility of having friends outside the house. By the following year, he still hadn't made any. He didn't know how to make friends when he didn't feel normal. He couldn't have them over to his house or play after school. His mother didn't mingle with the other mothers at drop-off or pick-up. And her behavior was becoming his behavior. He kept to himself in class, not participating in group activities, and never raised his hand even if he knew the answer. He stayed in his head with his thoughts, where he was safe. His daydreaming was becoming an issue with his teacher.

"The school wants you to take a test, Jonah," his mother told him, lighting another cigarette. Her fingers were like gold where they held the filter. (Jonah found this appealing. Imagine having golden fingers! *What were they worth?)* "They're concerned about your progress."

"I do my work. I'm just not as smart as the other kids." He watched the smoke slip out the open window. It was spring now. The last snow had melted into a gray sludge on the lawns and the road.

"You have to try harder, Jonah. You have to *talk*. Just say *something* once in a while." A long drag, a disinterested look, a frown on her forehead. She might yell, but he hoped not.

"It's okay, mommy. I don't need friends. I've got you." His mother laid a hand on his and squeezed.

"I love you. But I've got things to worry about, things you wouldn't understand. I'm not your friend. I'm your *mother*." He nodded up at her. She was a pretty woman, he thought. Short, dark hair framed a pale complexion. Full lips and wide eyes blinked away the smoke as it caught up in her lashes. He lifted a small palm to his mother's cheek. She leaned into it and stubbed out the cigarette. She wrapped her golden fingers around his hand, and Jonah instantly felt richer.

"You're my friend, Mommy. My *best* friend." His smile was genuine.

She didn't smile. She looked away.

"Is Grandma coming tonight?"

"Soon, actually, Mommy is helping Daddy at the pub again," she said. She loved to get out and help at the restaurant. Other than him, Jonah thought it was her favorite thing. He liked seeing his mother happy, though he occasionally wondered whether she was happy to leave *him* or happy to get out of the house.

After dinner, Grandma rang the front bell, and Jonah rushed to let her in. A big hug. She smelled of flowers, lemons, and something else he couldn't place but was probably just an old lady smell. They would play board games, and she would let him stay out of his room until late. Jonah's mother kissed him on the top of his head and slipped on her high heels. He couldn't understand why anyone would wear such ridiculous shoes. Grandma didn't. His mother looked extra pretty every time she went out of the house. Make-up, hair and nails done, and a dress he thought she might suffocate in. A fur coat completed the ensemble. *Why didn't she go out like this in the day, only at night? What happened out there?* It was a world he would never see, which made him jealous.

"I'm just going to have a chat with your mommy before she goes, Jonah. Why don't you pull out a few of your games and get ready to lose at Monopoly," Grandma said with a wink. Jonah nodded enthusiastically and headed for the living room, but he knew he'd be listening to the conversation. A clue to the mystery of his mother.

"This is becoming a habit. *Every* night? You're turning into your father, Lucinda."

There was a pause. Jonah felt the tension.

"I'm going to help Luca - my *husband* - at the pub. I'm not just sitting at the bar drinking wine." His mother's voice was terse.

"Be sure you don't. They say it runs in families; you know." Now Grandma's words were short and staccato.

"I'm doing my best, mother. But being home all day and night with just him is not easy. I need something else."

Jonah sat down hard on the carpet. He heard his mother stumble to the door,

"Look at you. You've already been drinking! And around *Jonah*." She lowered her voice and turned to point at the living room. Jonah sat stock still. He didn't think he was even breathing.

"Thank you for coming to watch Jonah." His mother slammed the door shut. Jonah jumped a little in his skin. So, this was all his fault. Now he understood. Grandma probably knew this, too.

"Be a good boy, Jonah. Just let me sit for a while." Grandma lowered herself slowly onto the couch and let out a sigh. The television was playing a western, and its light cast a cruel shadow over her face. She suddenly looked mean and sad, not loving and kind. It was his fault his mother was how she was; everyone knew it and hated him. "We all *love* you, Jonah. We want the best for you." *Lies.* The western made loud, banging sounds.

1973

The Sting of Love

A week after turning thirteen, Jonah sat on the front porch, watching men cut down a dead tree. They were sawing and hacking with relish at the misshapen branches. The old relic stood askew under the electrical lines running miles along the sidewalk. It was July, and school was becoming a distant memory. His mother had left him to run errands, so he sat in the noisy chaos of chippers and saws, awaiting her return. There was the sweet smell of fresh sawdust in the air.

The metallic blue '69 Chevy Nova squealed into the driveway, and his mother emerged, hair electrified, dress sideways, arms flailing, screaming terrible words. She grabbed him by the collar of his shirt and dragged him into the house backward. Jonah stumbled and fell on the laminate floor, banging his head hard. His mother's behavior dumbfounded him. She continued to scream at him even as she kneeled to tend to his head. Jonah thought she must be as shocked at her actions as he was, but it was difficult to tell. She began to replace the screams with sobs and moved her small body into a ball beside him. A paper bag, clinking with bottles, rattled under her head, where she had somehow managed to set them carefully.

"Why would you do that, Jack?!"

His head pounded. He knew yelling back at his mother didn't help. Yelling, "I'M NOT JACK," would only make it worse. Slowly, gently, he reached for her. Her golden fingers no longer fostered the innocent curiosity they once had. He knew now they were tinted yellow from habitually drawing the foul-smelling nicotine into her lungs. He sat in astonishment, looking at his mother with new eyes. One hand rubbed at the pain exploding from the back of his head. The other hand steadied him as he rose to his feet.

"Why can't I sit on the porch?! They're a *hundred* feet away!" His voice cracked with the apparent signs of puberty and his crumbling sense of self as he pointed at the men and the noise through the open door. He was angry. It was a culmination of things. He was lonely. He was afraid. He was sick of being safe.

His mother reached out to him with trembling fingers, shaking her head. "I'm so sorry, baby," she said, her voice now soft from the screams and the realization. "I didn't mean for you to fall." Her face was shiny and wet with tears.

"Yeah, well, I don't *need* you to protect me anymore. I'm *thirteen!*" Jonah pulled his hand away from the warmth collecting on his palm at the back of his head. Bloodstained fingers. His mother cried out and leaped to her feet. Jonah backed away instinctively, and his mother burst into tears again. He didn't like seeing her like this, but enough was enough. The increasingly erratic behavior had come to this. He was bleeding, and it was her fault, not his.

He knew how much she'd hate herself now, how sorry she'd feel, how bad it was. A pang of sympathy entered him and then just as quickly fled.

"Just calm down," he said. She was shaking. He helped her up and brought her to a chair.

"I've tried so hard to keep you safe," she began. "You're the only thing in my life that makes sense, Jonah. I *need* you." She held his hands, which were becoming red as she entwined her fingers in his and kissed them. She had his blood on her lips. The scene disoriented Jonah. He felt weak. He felt sick. Nauseous.

"Can you look at my head?" He knelt at her feet and bent his head to rest on her lap. Her fingers carefully navigated his thick, brown hair to inspect the damage. "It's just a small split," she whispered. "I can fix this for you." She released his hair and looked Jonah in the eyes. "I love you, Jonah." The words, the fingers in his hair, and the look of desperation on her face were too much. Jonah stood and feigned a smile. She stood, too, and picked up her bag of bottles. "I'll get you a wet cloth, and we'll clean you up." She slinked down the hall to the kitchen. Jonah heard the lid twist off one of the bottles. Then the tap ran as he sat, wanting to be sick. A damp tea towel. He took it from her without touching her hand. She gulped thirstily from the cup.

"You're not so breakable after all."

She turned on the television. They sat in silence for an hour.

2020, May

Severn at Fifty-Nine.

Severn hates how an event can be tracked so easily back to that one decision or experience as if life were something so wholly unchangeable. As though that distinctive moment where your action or inaction - already written in the stars - would inevitably play out a specific event. Are our lives simply destiny? Does everything have a beginning, middle, and end? It's the middle she labors over.

Severn's life to this point has been anything but rosy. Her 12-year-old self could never have predicted that this would be how it would end up. From thirteen to thirty-one, she had no real memories to hold onto. They were essentially gone. She'd visited psychiatrists for years, but something was keeping those memories locked away. Something kept them from surfacing and, perhaps, causing her enormous grief. That's how Dr. Sturgis described it to her. But now was apparently the time to get them back. Let the chips fall where they may, she thought.

"Severn, are you ready to experience your lost memories?" Dr. Sturgis, a woman of retirement age herself, opened today's session frankly.

Severn flinches, hands folded in her lap, seated on the worn, leather couch. The room smells of lavender, as it always has, meant to promote calm. To Severn, today, it wasn't having that effect.

Severn looked at the woman before her and thought she must have been striking thirty years ago.

"I ask because I no longer want to dance around the subject. We've done everything we can to manage your day-to-day concerns. You've done remarkably well with your cognitive behavioral therapy, but forever avoiding the real trigger is keeping you from experiencing a full life. I liken it to someone who a dog bit at a young age. They avoid dogs altogether, feeding their anxieties, fearful of a potential run-in with a dog at a park or when out for a walk. Soon, they don't leave the house because of their fear of dogs and their anxiety around the thought spikes. Seems a little irrational, right?" Severn nods reluctantly. "But that's learned behavior from a traumatic event. Knowing where the fear is coming from is easy in this case: the dog bite. Your case doesn't offer us a point of reference to your issues. When this person avoids dogs, they avoid the fear but build the anxiety around it. What's driving your fear is a mystery to you. So how can you ever truly free yourself of it and its consequences?"

"Knowing?"

The doctor raises her eyebrows, places her clipboard down, and removes her heavy glasses. "Right, your thoughts feed your feelings, which create the behavior. Your thoughts just so happen to be buried at a subconscious level. There are ways to access them. It's been seventeen years, and I want to get to the root of your symptoms. You're so anxious over knowing your lost past that you've backed yourself into a corner. Tell me again, what's stopping you?"

"I just... I get *blocked.* I can't access memories from that time in my life. Also, I made promises."

"To yourself?"

"No, to Mary, my friend, and my mother." Severn feels a chill travel up her spine.

"The only person you need to make promises to is *yourself,* Severn. Promise yourself that you will get better."

"I want to get better."

"Then let's begin." Dr. Sturgis leans forward, pressing the subject. Severn had been to therapists before her. None of them did anything but try to treat Severn's immediate issues. None ever sought to visit her event horizon. "What do you recall from 1974?"

Severn takes a deep, trembling breath. Maybe this time, it will all come back to her. Maybe she can handle it.

"My mother... my father had died... and my mother was a wreck." Severn's brow tightens as she struggles to remember.

"And what about your mother in 1994, twenty years later; what do you remember about her then?"

"Not a drunk. Not anymore. She was constantly calling me after I moved out. I was thirty-four."

"Did she never mention your life from '75-'93?" Dr. Sturgis was baffled by this. She knew what had happened to Severn when she'd agreed to take her on as a patient. She had worked with her for seven years. They had made progress with her related issues, but now she felt it was time to get to the root of it. "Others know what you were doing, even if you don't."

"Everyone walks on eggshells around those two decades. They always have and still do," Severn explains calmly. "As I mentioned when we started, I was originally counseled to leave it alone for fear of what it would do to me. They said I had forgotten to protect myself."

"You've enjoyed a purposeful life since then. A career in social work. A house of your own. A relationship with your mother. By all outward indicators, you have a *normal* life."

"So why would I want to ruin that by knowing?"

"Because holding trauma back, even hidden in the most secure places in your mind... it's still *in* you. You can't always see the damage it's causing, but there it is, influencing you negatively."

"I'm happy." Severn nearly chokes on the phrase. "Excuse me." She picks up her water glass and drinks. Severn's face hints at the missing decades: the frown lines, the damaged skin, the tired eyes. She had been through something awful. The stress had turned her once blonde hair into a nearly translucent grey. Still, she was a pretty woman.

"Your life has been manageable through the work we've done, but our progress could disappear altogether if we don't break down those walls and recover your memories. I won't press if you don't want me to, but I think you have the tools you need to cope now, and so I feel my work with you is nearly done unless we press on further."

"No, please!" This revelation visibly shakes Severn. "I *love* coming here."

"And I enjoy your company, Severn, but there is a waiting list of people to see me, and I can't help them if you and I are just going to reaffirm the work we've done."

Severn remains seated in silence at the shock of the doctor's statement. What would it do to her to unravel the mystery of eighteen years unaccounted for?

The question has weighed heavily on her mind for years. She takes a deep breath and calms her mind. "If you think I need to do this, then... okay."

Dr. Sturgis leans forward to address Severn delicately. "You're a courageous woman. You've been brave for a very long time. I have a simple technique to draw out your memories. It should start to happen within moments of our beginning and will take as long as it takes. Your subconscious mind will reveal itself to me under hypnosis. I will give you time to process what we find in a safe environment. Whatever it is, Severn, we'll get through it together."

1974

The Fox & Ferret

Severn gripped her mother's hand as they crossed the busy intersection. She was twelve and dressed in her Sunday best. The light on her milky-white face forced her eyes closed while her high cheekbones and forehead took the brunt of the July afternoon sun. Her mother maintained her quick pace as Severn's much shorter legs scrambled to keep up. High heels were far from Severn's favorite choice of shoe. She could barely balance on them standing still, and being hustled across a crosswalk when the hand was blinking for her to stop was altogether ridiculous. "I can see the sign, Mommy," Severn complained, nearly biting her tongue as she navigated a pothole.

"Okay, then, get a wiggle on, young lady!" They reached the sidewalk, narrowly escaping a delivery truck's determined attempt to make the corner.

The Fox & Ferret was Severn's mother's favorite pub to visit after Sunday service. The moment they entered the double doors, she asked the hostess for a glass of chardonnay.

"Thirsty? Could you have ordered me a soda while you were at it?" She sat abruptly and removed both shoes to stretch her toes. She knew her mother was an alcoholic. Everyone did. Though Severn wasn't entirely sure what this meant, she was certain it wasn't good. Her mother had repeatedly forgotten to pick her up at friends' homes. She hadn't gotten up with Severn to get her ready for school in over two years. She hadn't cooked a meal in just as many. Severn had heard the whispers. After her father died, she found her mother slowly disconnecting from everything. A massive life insurance payout had kept the family in good standing. Severn still went to a private school, and someone who was hired made sure the kitchen was always stocked, and they kept their handsome home. Severn felt they went to church to remind the congregation that everything was fine. It was all an illusion. She knew it. Her mother knew it, but the liquor seemed to dull her mother's senses. Liquor was awful stuff. Severn had sampled it at her friend's house one weekend at a sleepover. She couldn't imagine drinking it at the rate her mother went through it.

"Good afternoon! You ordered a chardonnay?" The pub's owner, Luca, passed the large glass to her mom and winked at her. Severn's mother's cheeks colored slightly. Severn liked him. He always doted on the two of them. He produced a 7up for Severn from behind his back, complete with lemon and lime wedges. She smiled and accepted the treat with gratitude.

"Let me guess," Luca said, feigning confusion. He pointed at Severn first. "Grilled cheese with tomatoes and a side of fries." She nodded with a grin. "And for the lovely mother... a Cobb salad."

"Just a small one, please, Luca," she reminded him. "Thank you." Luca nodded and navigated the growing crowd to place the order.

"Isn't he a lovely man?" Severn's mother put the smudged glass to her lips. She looked at Severn without really looking. Severn wondered if Luca was married. Maybe having someone like Luca in her mother's life might help her.

"Do you come here on days other than Sunday?" Severn drank from her 7up and burped. Her mother seemed to take exception to the question and the burp.

"So, what if I did?"

"Just a question, Mom," Severn returned. "Don't get so *offended*."

"Adults are allowed to do whatever they want, Severn." She took another long sip of her wine. "So, yes, I come here without you occasionally."

"For what? Lunch?" Severn narrowed her eyes at her mother.

"Yes, sometimes I come for lunch while you're at school." Her tone softened. "Sometimes, if there's someone to talk to, I stay until you come home from school."

"Sometimes longer," Severn said spitefully. She'd been a latch-key kid for the last year, taking herself to school and home and preparing meals. It was getting old.

"Don't be *horrible*, Severn," her mother replied harshly. "Do you think that I can just sit at home all day? I don't have any help. It's not like I have a husband.

It's just me. I have a lot to do. And I need adult company sometimes." She drained her glass.

"Well, if you can sit here all day, then I guess you could sit at home." Severn asserted, having never spoken to her mother this way before. She questioned why she was doing so now.

"I won't be interrogated by my twelve-year-old." Her mother put her face in her hands. She rubbed her eyes. Was she crying?

"I'm sorry. I don't know why I said that." Severn knew full well why she had said that. She was tired of having lost a father *and* a mother to the same accident. She was tired of being alone. Thankfully, the moment was broken by the arrival of Luca with their food. He unceremoniously placed their food in front of them. They both smiled appreciatively at him and, without speaking, began eating.

When they finished their lunch, Severn was delivered an ice cream sundae with a wink from Luca while her mother went to the bathroom. It was probably the fifth time she had made this trip in as many lunches. Severn allowed it. Luca was nice. Her mother should date him, she thought. A song by Barry White played over the pub's noisy diners. She liked this one: *You're the First, The Last, My Everything.* His voice reminded her of her father's, deep yet soothing. Severn sipped at the dregs of her 7up, staring into the sea of people moving through the pub's door, her body reacting to the music while her mother enjoyed her time in the bathroom. She picked up her napkin from her lap and wiped her face. She suddenly realized she'd spilled strawberry syrup on her white dress. Her mother would be upset. Lifting her dress to see how far the stain went, Severn noticed a larger stain on her underpants. It was much redder than the strawberry syrup. She felt the humiliation rise from her neck to her cheeks in a crimson heat. The shame hurt physically. Panic set in quickly, and Severn surveyed her surroundings. How much blood would seep out of her? *Would it collect on the floor?* How would she get out without everyone staring? What could she wrap around her waist? Where was her mother? It was hardly a surprise she was absent for this. Severn hoped against hope that her mother would have a simple fix for this unannounced event. *Why in a pub, of all places?* She peeked again under her dress, lifting it cautiously. The blood had stained the back of her dress where she sat. She would be exposed both front and back. Her mind raced. *Please come back, Mom, and don't fuss about it.*

A moment later, her mother had returned with a suspicious glow to her cheeks. That would have to take a backseat for now. Severn leaned over the table, ushered her mother forward with a frantic wave, and explained the event. Her mother looked around at the crowded tables and stood to pull on her light jacket. For a brief, terrifying moment, Severn thought she would leave her there and spare herself any embarrassment. Then, her mother carefully lifted Severn's jacket from the chair back. "Stand up, and I'll cover you." Severn obeyed, and her mother quickly placed the coat around her daughter's waist. Suddenly, Severn felt a rush of love for her mother. It had been a while since this feeling had invaded her body. It felt both comforting and unfamiliar. It reminded her of simpler times. She loved her mother, not as the drunk she had become, but as the woman who had once made her a priority. It saddened her to think this moment would vanish like other good memories.

"You ladies are leaving so soon?" Luca caught up with them at the door, and Severn noticed his face was also flushed.

"Emergency," her mother explained. "Sorry to rush off, Luca. I'll see you tomorrow."

1973

Grandma Anne

At thirteen, Jonah had made one friend, and when Grandma Anne came to watch him on Friday nights, he was allowed a guest. This was Mort, an awkward kid whose primary interests were model airplanes and insects. Mort and Jonah had little in common except for their lack of friends. Still, this was progress in his grandma's eyes, and she was happy for him.

Grandma Anne often nodded off after a board game under the hypnotic drone of the television. On this particular night, Jonah surveyed the house for his mother's stash of booze and cigarettes. Mort was an impressionable kid who only wanted to please Jonah and would do whatever that took. Jonah would be fourteen soon. Mort was already fourteen. He was overweight and wore too-tight T-shirts. He seemed unfazed by his apparent weirdness, and instead of feeling embarrassed, Jonah was proud of his friend.

"What is *vodka?*" Morty asked as he took another swig from the bottle. His round face went sour as the alcohol filled his virgin mouth. His nose shrank back into the shadows of his cheeks, and his eyes squeezed shut. Then he coughed.

"Well, it's booze. My mom's favorite." Jonah accepted the bottle back. He put it down quietly and lit a cigarette for both of them. The kitchen was dark, save the streetlight dimly illuminating their secret. Jonah took a drag and blew it out, handing the smoke over to his friend.

"My parents don't smoke," Mort said matter-of-factly. "I'd be kicked to kingdom come if they ever found out." Mort had confided in Jonah before that his father wasn't afraid to let his son know who was in charge. Jonah had seen the bruises, but they didn't talk about it. It explained why Mort treasured his time alone, putting models together or pinning new insects to his board. He knew more about bugs than anyone. Mort took a long draw of the cigarette, and the smoke slipped down his windpipe, forcing him to cough again.

"Don't inhale it, Mort." Jonah took the butt from his friend. "Just let it hit your tongue and blow it out." He'd done this twice now and remembered the ordeal of inhaling. He pushed another swig of the vodka down and felt suddenly ill. His stomach churned, and his throat opened. The vodka, his dinner, and other stragglers in his digestive system suddenly burst from his mouth in a torrent. It splattered all over the linoleum floor. Mort pulled back, but too late. The hot sick dripped from both of his feet. The smell was enough to make him suddenly gag. Mort's stomach rumbled, which quickly elevated into an unstoppable force. The foul, fiery liquid spewed from his mouth with fervor. With Jonah still doubled over in front of him, Mort tossed hot chunks all over the back of Jonah's head and neck. The scene would have been comical to both of them if they'd seen it on T.V., but this wasn't fiction. It was real, and it was disgusting.

Mort's face grimaced as they gathered their wits and surveyed the damage. He stood on rubbery legs and lifted his feet as if pulling away from a spider's web. His socks squishing.

"I need a shower," said Mort with a flat voice. Jonah just nodded and pointed to the stairs.

"Jonah!" Grandma Anne stood at the threshold between the living room and kitchen and glared at him. Her eyes were red around the edges. Jonah looked up as fear took its place next to nausea, and he quickly put out the cigarette.

"Into your mother's "stash?" Her tone was accusatory, and her fists were clenched. "Damn, fool, kids!" Mort ran the rest of the way to the bathroom, leaving a trail of footprints along the linoleum - slipping once. Jonah tried to stand, stretching the tired muscles in his stomach.

"I'm sorry, Grandma," he said, vomit dripping from his chin. "I didn't know what it was."

"You knew well enough to sneak off to drink it, though!" He wasn't going to pull the wool over her eyes. "I take a cat nap, and you two proceed to drink... what is this?" She picks up the bottle and reads. "Vodka." Another hard look in Jonah's direction sends his stomach turning. "This is poison, Jonah! Poison!"

Was she being serious? Had he actually mistaken poison for his mother's *favorite drink? Poison! He ran to the bathroom to join Mort, who was* running the shower. He climbed in with his friend, both fully clothed, and they rinsed their sticky bodies and muddied minds.

"Your grandma scares the shit out of me, Jonah," Morty confided while gulping air into his lungs. "I'm staying in here." He toweled off his head and nearly crashed into the sink while Jonah did the same.

"We can't stay in here forever, Mort. We'll have to go to bed." Jonah opened the door just enough for the boys to watch as Grandma Anne's arm thrust them each a housecoat.

"Come out when you have these on. Hang your wet things on the shower rail." Her voice was no-nonsense. They were in real trouble. Jonah knew he had disappointed her. The boys changed and emerged from the steamy bathroom in short order.

"Please don't tell my parents, Mrs. Gilchrist," Morty begged, his wet head still dripping on his housecoat. Grandma just pointed to the couch for the boys to sit on.

In the living room, they listened to Grandma Anne's rant as she paced the length of the couch. *"No excuse"* was repeated often. That and *"What's gotten into you, Jonah?"* When she'd finished, the boys were ordered to Jonah's room to sleep. *"Never again!"* they heard her affirm as Jonah softly closed his door.

1974

The Love Letter

Severn was becoming concerned over her mother's self-isolation in November of 1974. In November of 1972, Severn's father had gone away. It was a car accident; the details of which Severn was never really made aware and tried hard not to imagine. A horrible image would sometimes pass through her mind on sleepless nights, but she quickly tried to quell it with mundane thoughts of boys or movies or stories from school. November, that cruel month where winter-like cold began to settle into your bones, would forever be an unwanted shift; gain becomes loss, happiness becomes melancholy.

Severn had loved her father for his gracious manner, comical faces, and loving way he put her to bed when he was home. A book, a story, and a few minutes lying next to her as she dozed off after a smattering of questions designed to keep him with her longer. Their relationship was nothing short of perfect in her young mind. She missed him more than she could stand some nights, and while her mother sat in front of the television, finishing her wine, she ached to sit with her and talk about him.

"I know you miss him, baby," her mother would say when Severn crawled onto the couch and laid her head on her mother's lap. Her fingers would gently stroke Severn's long, blonde hair. "I miss him too. We're managing, though, aren't we?" Severn's head would nod. "We'll be alright, Severn. He made sure of it. Daddy made sure of that."

But Severn knew something had changed in her mother. The drinking had taken on an epic nature. Severn would sometimes come down dressed for school, and her mother would watch static on the TV screen with a glass of wine still firmly in her grasp. That scared her, but she didn't know what to do about it.

It was rare they would cry together over their shared loss; Severn could count on one hand how many times it had happened. She had lost count of how often she cried herself to sleep over losing her father. The absence of his presence was felt in every room and through every proud moment she experienced. Not being able to share these with him was crushing. Not to find him in his study when she walked past on her way to bed was eerie. She would tell herself stories he had once told her at bedtime to fill the void, sometimes hearing his voice in hers. She would kiss her stuffy, imagining it was him, and accept a kiss from the brown bear. It was tragic, but her counselor had recommended she do this to keep Daddy in her heart and her memory.

Luca, the man from the pub... Severn wondered whether he might love her mother. Maybe he would leave his wife and come live with them. She wasn't prepared to replace her father but was willing to allow it for her mother's sake. She considered many scenarios where the charming man rang their doorbell and entered with a bouquet for her mother, a box of chocolates, and a wink and a smile for her. Severn's heart raced at the idea. But her mother was in no shape to date anyone. Whatever was happening at the pub was one thing, but to present herself as the woman she was outside the pub or church might be impossible for her mother.

Still, it was worth a try.

Severn rifled through her mother's purse on the front table while she watched the evening news with that faraway look in her eyes. Severn was searching for a card or coaster with a number to the pub so she could call it, ask for Luca, and explain her intentions. It scared her to speak on the phone to a man, but she thought if her heart were in the right place, he would take it as a compliment and her approval of what they were already doing. Clearly, he wasn't happy at home, and God knew Severn's mother wasn't happy.

As Severn searched the deepest depths of her mother's messy purse, her hands encircled a small bottle she had brought into the light. The label read *Valium*, and she wondered if her mother was sick. Severn placed it on the table. Next, a crumpled note appeared between Severn's fingers, and she carefully pulled it free of the cluttered contents. She watched her mother a moment, still motionless on the couch, while the T.V. glared back. Severn flattened the note on the front table and then retreated to her father's study to read it. The note was from her father. Her heart skipped a beat. She felt she shouldn't read a letter from her father to her mother. It seemed wrong. (*But he was her father*

31

every bit as much as he was her mother's husband. With that reasoning, she read on.)

It was a love letter. He told her mother how much she meant to him - how much he loved their life together and their daughter. Severn smiled at this. He reminded her that the following weekend would be their eleventh anniversary and conveyed his plans. The letter was dated the week before he'd died. Severn's hand covered her mouth.

Her mother had carried this letter in her purse for over two years. The thought made her cry. Had she been too hard on her mother? Had her father's death destroyed her? She knew it had been difficult, but after reading about the love they'd shared, plans for the future, and how happy they were together, her mother's pain seemed amplified.

"Oh, Mommy," she whispered, folding the crumpled paper gently. She returned to the hall and slid it back into the purse. She watched her mother for another moment and then joined her on the couch. She laid her head on her mother's lap and hugged her. The fact was her mother had been very strong for her and herself. She drank too much, but maybe that would change.

"I'm so sorry, Mommy," she said, squeezing her around the waist more firmly. Her eyes shut tight. Perhaps no man could replace her father as a husband to her mother. "I love you."

Her mother didn't respond save a soft hand on her head. She began to stroke her hair, and this was enough for Severn, for now.

1975

The Happening

At 11:30 pm, Friday night, Severn awoke to her mother pounding on their front door. This was beginning to happen more and more lately. Her mother often left her keys at the bar or dropped them along the way. They were on her seventh set of keys for the house in six months. Severn had sworn she wouldn't let her mother in the next time this happened, but it was a cool May evening, and the sky threatened rain. *But wouldn't she deserve that?* Wouldn't she deserve the humiliation of having the neighbors find her on the front porch, soaked through and passed out?

Instead, owing to her forgiving nature, Severn opened the door to her mother's incoherent blathering. There was a thank-you buried among it somewhere. She sat her mother on the foyer bench and helped strip her of her footwear and light jacket. Then she proceeded to walk her upstairs and drop her on her bed. She pulled the unkempt bedding over her mother and placed a glass of water at her bedside.

Immediately after, she called her friend Maribel. It was late, but Mary's family were night owls, and she knew it wasn't any trouble calling after ten. Mary picked up the phone.

"Mary, it happened again," Severn began, "I just put her to bed."

"I'm sorry, Severn," Mary replied earnestly. "You're doing great. You'll be a great mom one day." Severn could make out *Someone Saved My Life Tonight* by Elton John on the other side of the call. Fitting, she thought, Mary had always been her saving grace.

"I'm getting worried about what people might think," Severn continued. "Do you think if other adults knew, they might call child services?"

"You just need to get through high school, and then you'll be an adult. Do you think you can do that?" Mary always tried her best to find solutions.

"That's six more years," Severn said, her hand rubbing her forehead. "I'm afraid she'll be found out, and someone will come to the door and take me away."

"No one's going to take you away," Mary assured her. "Just keep doing what you're doing, and everything will be fine."

There was a moment of silence between them, and Severn admitted, "I'm worried about her. It hasn't been getting better. If anything, it's worse than ever." Severn's voice cracked as she cried into the receiver to her best friend.

"Do you think you would want to live with me?" Mary asked. "With my family?"

Severn hadn't dared to consider such a solution. "That would be amazing, wouldn't it? Best friends and roommates and we could get bunk beds and share a room."

"And we could talk all night and share clothes!" Mary joined in on the fantasy. "Could you do it?" Mary's question was the end of the dream, however, as Severn realized her reality. Leaving her mother to fend for herself seemed insensitive in light of her inability even to manage her keys.

"It's a nice thought," Severn replied, reluctant to let the fantasy die altogether. "Would your parents agree to it?"

"If they knew what we know about your mom, I think they would."

"Because it's not like she's abusive..." Severn realized she was defending her mother and stopped herself. "Or maybe she is, I don't know,"

"Let's just pretend like maybe this *could* happen," Mary replied, leaving Severn open to the idea while still considering her mother. With that, they said goodbye for the night, visions of something better dancing dangerously in Severn's head.

* * *

The following evening, thirteen-year-old Severn had been invited to a party. With no one to ask whether she could or couldn't go, she decided to attend. There would be older kids there, she knew that, which made her nervous, but she would have two friends with her, Alicia and Maribel. The event had been hyped up as the party of the year, with absent parents and all that. She called Maribel and planned to meet her and Alicia at the corner.

"Do you think there will be alcohol there?" Severn wondered nervously over the phone. "Or drugs?" She knew she would never try anything like that after seeing the effects.

"We don't have to join in if there is, Sev. Let's show up so people know we came. If we don't like it, we can always come back here and watch a movie."

Severn agreed and promised to relay the same to Alicia. They would meet at the corner of Sherborne and Main, just two blocks from the party and twelve blocks from Severn's home.

Severn showered and feathered her long, blonde hair in the style of Cheryl Tiegs, who had recently graced the cover of her mother's Bazaar magazine. Rooting through the makeup boxes in her mother's vanity, Severn applied a bright coral lipstick labeled "Abstract Orange" on the smeared label on the bottom of the sticky black tube and a robin's egg blue eye shadow. At the last moment, she streaked a dark red blush across her pale cheeks. It left two lines of crimson in a way that made her appear far more like her mother than she'd ever observed before. She blinked into her reflection, feeling even more adult than a moment before. All of this was going to help. There was a good chance Chuck may be at the party, the boy she'd suddenly felt an aching attraction to. A grade older. She'd decided she would like to experience something with him. A kiss or a touch. Something that made her feel akin to being alive and cared about and loved or just liked or nice to look at or anything noticeable.

So many changes that she couldn't account for or discuss with her mother. Her breasts required more than a training bra. They had grown plump, and the nipples had become dark and sensitive. They billowed out of her flat-chested support and created lines and creases in her shirts. It embarrassed her that her breasts might be noticeable. Still, she didn't know whether she should hide them or give in to the attention they occasionally garnered. She was as tall as most of the boys in her class but inevitably forced into the "cult of likeness" too shy to return their glances. What she wanted was what most girls wanted. She wanted someone to like her in that attraction-and-love kind of way. Not the creepy way she felt she was being ogled in. Boys who still pinched her and threw dirt at her didn't make her feel good about herself. And there were still plenty of those. She wanted someone to make out with her. She wanted someone to tell her they liked her. Someone more mature. She wanted handholding and phone calls. She knew her feelings that went beyond the innocent version she was told of boy-girl relationships was something to hide. Still, she often imagined someone making her feel that feeling she had created in private. But she had no grasp of how this would ever be real with no one to tell and no one who would comment or care. She somehow feared none of it would feel real unless she could tell her mother. Her mother wouldn't ask, so there was nothing to reveal, and even worse, her mother's version of anything like this made her feel like it was wrong and dirty. The usual separation in the understanding of love and attraction between the generations was trumped by a mother who had presented a version of complete detachment. The simplicity of being told it was normal but to watch out was missing. The careful attitude that came with the knowledge someone was watching and cared about the outcome didn't exist. A tear ran down Severn's cheek as she pulled on her sneakers, cutting a line through the newly applied blush. Severn wiped at it, not realizing it would leave a trace of her maturity being compromised with a child's simple gesture.

In the family room, she looked at her father's portrait and leaned into the photograph, placing her lips on the kind face that stared back at her.

"Love you, Daddy," she told him. "Wish me luck."

It was almost 8:00 pm, and the twilight sky was transitioning to dark. Severn embraced the evening air with a deep breath as she stepped out the door. The damp warmth hit her face as a momentary breeze moved through her hair. She had ten dollars, her school ID, and her house keys in her small, over-the-shoulder purse. She felt this weight on her hip as she strode purposefully towards her friends. The streets seemed quiet - as if whispering her presence without wanting to awaken her surroundings. To wander through the dark, completely unknown, was the dreamlike quality of adulthood she longed for in the moments she knew she was no longer a child but, as of yet, unable to control her destiny.

To say this was a quiet and predictable neighborhood was, without fail, the only way to define it. Severn had been out alone many times in daylight, and her mother had allowed this. So, when she noticed a van in front of the park, she told herself to stop being stupid and move on. It was strange how the park looked menacing tonight. The van sitting idle in front of the tennis courts offered a jarring juxtaposition to the playground she had frequented only a few years ago. She was just being dumb. Just because it was dark didn't mean anything was wrong. She could do this herself. She didn't need her drunken mother to drive her to a party. So stupid. Just the same, Severn picked up her pace, moving quickly past the dark van, a sense of unrest filling her stomach with nausea.

She just kept walking. *See? Nothing.* Several cars drove past her, crawling along the residential street. She flinched slightly as each approached from behind, but they passed unceremoniously. *Only a few more blocks. So stupid.* The purse bounced more rapidly against her side. She grabbed it and held it still. The fake leather felt soft, almost like a hand, and she felt safer—another car. Expecting to see her shadow move across the passing lawn as it had with the other vehicles, Severn realized this one had no headlights. With a sudden, quick response, she strode up the front walk of a random house to appear as though she were home. The vehicle passed, and as she turned to look, it was obvious it was the same van she'd passed moments ago.

She forced the rising anxiety she was experiencing from her mind. *Who was this little girl? Who was this child who couldn't walk a few blocks without being afraid of the Boogeyman? She* was the one who took care of things. *She* took care of herself and her mother and their outcome. Severn returned to the sidewalk with this assertion and continued her path to meet her friends. Tonight was going to be a *good* night.

All of this rapidly drained away. At the next stop sign, she froze in terror. She saw the van parked on the cross street from the corner of her eye. It seemed alive with a malicious focus. Why did her body stop? Why did she know? How did she have the instinct? It could have just been a van. A driver lost. A tire flat. Parked for the night. She managed to summon the strength in her legs to cross the street, continuing her path until she connected with her friends. *It's just a van, silly.* But she knew.

On the other side of the street, two men emerged from behind a line of shrubs. *Why were they in the shrubs?* She couldn't see, as dusk was now dark. They were faceless. Big. Surprising. One was grabbing her as if hugging her. He held her, and her face was tight against his jacket. It felt rough, like old wool. She didn't have time to fight before there was another body behind her. Encircled. There wasn't any sound. Suddenly, something was in her mouth. No way to scream. She kicked a little but somehow also knew it was fruitless. It was only a moment before they were under her arms and legs. It was bad, and no one would know, and no one would care. She was going in the van. And somehow, she blacked out.

1973

The Reveal

Jonah and Morty lay in bed in Jonah's room, pretending to sleep but unable to kick the nausea, horror, and excitement of the night's events. Nicotine and vodka still crept in trace amounts through their virgin veins as they contemplated the consequences and relished the glory of their daring attempt. It all ended sadly with the sounds of his mother returning.

"Lucinda," Jonah heard his grandmother yell from the kitchen, "You've got a real problem on your hands now."

Stumbling could be heard from the foyer as shoes were kicked off and a thump as someone landed hard into a kitchen chair. Then, another body and another thump. *Dad?*

"Who's *this?*" Grandma's tone was tight and sounded like a fist punching a heavy bag. Jonah assumed the second person wasn't his father. The time was just about 11 pm. His father would still be another couple of hours closing up the pub. Jonah was confused. His mother didn't bring friends home. He rolled quietly out of bed, motioning for Morty to stay put, and crept as silently as possible to the bedroom door, slightly ajar. He wanted to hear.

"Don't wake Jonah," his mother hissed.

Then, a male voice, incoherent to Jonah. Gibberish.

"Get out." Jonah had heard anger in his grandmother's voice before, but nothing like this.

A chair pushed back on the linoleum floor. "You can leave now mother. Thank you for staying with the boys. Chad, sit down." His mother sounded calm. Strangely calm.

"Is Chad a friend of Luca's?"

"Ugg, what a *grueler!* Chad drove me home. *Obviously.*"

"Couldn't drive yourself? You're a *disgrace.*" The bitter words spewed from her throat.

"Listen, what I do is *my* business. You don't have a clue what I deal with. You don't have a CLUE. You're lucky I'm here at all." His mother's voice remained steady, contrasting his grandmother's rising emotion. It was almost eerie.

"What you do is *not* your own business, Lucinda. Not while you're still a mother!" Grandma was in fine form, Jonah thought. He'd never heard her so angry. He hadn't suspected she even had this in her. It seemed so opposite to how he viewed his home's dynamic. Someone was angry, and it was the wrong person, and it didn't feel very good. It felt like the things he depended on were disappearing.

"Do you know your son found your booze and drank it tonight?" *Grandma!* Such betrayal.

A chair fell back, and Jonah could hear footsteps and a cupboard open. "Shit," he heard his mother whisper. "And you *let* this happen?" Her tone was incredulous.

Grandma was furious. "I fell asleep momentarily and woke to find them smoking and drinking from your pantry! You have set a *terrible* example for your surviving son!" That was going to hurt his mother, and the pause immediately following reflected the stinging horror of what his grandmother had just hurled her way.

"I'm gonna leave." The strange man's voice was weak—an awkward stumbling sound followed by indistinguishable words. The door opened and closed. Then, there was silence for what seemed an eternity to Jonah. And then a whimpering. *Was mom crying?* Next, a crash could be heard. And another. Bottles hitting the wall? Jonah's heart sank. He crawled back to the bedroom, and no sooner had he clawed his way into his bed than he leaned over the side and threw up again on the floor. Morty lay completely motionless beside him. Jonah stumbled from under his sheets and tried to reopen his bedroom door, his hands coiled around the handle. The hallway was dark except for the light from the television. He drew his body as close to the kitchen as he could without being detected. Curled up in the hallway, small as he could be, the T.V. animated the kitchen with flickering light. His mother continued to pull bottles out of the pantry and throw them to the floor. The scene felt like it was happening on the T.V. rather than in real life. Both his grandma and his mother appeared in black and white. Grandma was in the corner, arms guarding her face against flying debris. His mother's actions appeared in a flurry and a fury. Unstoppable, as though something had finally been released from her innards, the broken bits of glass were her broken bits of life crumbling before them for both to see and genuinely acknowledge. When all the bottles were strewn in shards of glass across the kitchen floor, his mother collapsed into a chair and placed her head on the table. She appeared to be violently shaking.

Grandma approached her and gingerly placed her hand on her daughter's back. She didn't move it. She just kept it there and bent down to whisper something into her ear. He watched his grandma tenderly kiss her daughter on the head and carefully pick the broken bottles off the ground. Her slippers sloshed through the alcohol and shards of glass coating the linoleum flooring like she'd done this before. The whole house reeked of alcohol now. The scent reminded Jonah of his misdeeds, and he slipped back into his room and opened his window.

Jonah was confused. *What could cause a person to become so unhinged? Is that what vodka did to a person?* The woman who had created the scene he'd just witnessed was someone who terrified him. Although he'd seen his mother make bad decisions and stray from her role as his mother, he'd never seen the person in the kitchen that night. What could he do to fix it? It was probably the vodka, and he wished she'd stop, but even if she did, she might never be a mother to him again. She seemed broken. Jonah wondered whether he was destined for the same fate. Maybe if he never drank it again, he could avoid scenes like the one he'd witnessed. *Was his father like this, too?* He really only saw his father on Sunday. Every other day, he was at the pub. Even on Sundays, he worked until just after lunch. He slept until after Jonah went to school and came home long after he was asleep. He didn't really know his father. Jonah was getting the sense that he was an interloper in the complex lives of his parents. One was an alcoholic who had tried for years to pass herself off as a functioning human being, and the other was a dedicated businessman throwing himself into his work, undoubtedly, to avoid the home he couldn't stand. The feelings this thought produced made Jonah sad. *What if he wasn't there? What if he left? What if he died?* It was a scary thought, but he considered it. *What if he were to disappear and leave his parents to work things out for themselves?* Maybe they would be happier. His mother wasn't happy. He knew this. He wasn't happy either.

"You don't have to continue this way, Lucy." Grandma's voice was lighter. "You can make a conscious choice to leave the alcohol behind and redouble your focus on Jonah. He's a good kid. He deserves a mother."

"I know," Jonah's mom could be heard to say through tears. "I want him to be happy. I want both of them to be happy."

Jesus, Jonah thought, she's talking about him and Jack. *Jack is dead.* Why couldn't she get that through her head?

"It wasn't your fault, Lucy." Grandma approached the subject with great care. "Jack wasn't ready to be a part of this family. You can try again. You're young." Grandma was sweeping up the remainder of the glass. *Young?* His mother wasn't young, Jonah thought.

"I *can't*, Mom," His mother gulped air. "The doctor said," her shoulders trembled, and her head collapsed again to the tabletop.

"*Oh, honey,* I'm so sorry." Jonah heard the broomstick set against the wall. He watched from his open door to see his grandma wrap her daughter in a tight hug. So, he would be it for his parents, an only child with a legacy of death. Maybe he killed his brother in the womb. His mother had mentioned them roughhousing in there. Maybe that's what she believed? If so, how could she ever love him? But if she thought she had somehow indirectly killed his brother, how could she love herself?

If she felt like that... could he help her? They didn't hang out like they used to. Even over summer break, she left him with Morty, Grandma, or both. She was less conscious of him - less worried about him. *Was that the alcohol, or was that just how it went?*

Anxiety gripped him, and he fell back onto his bed, wrapped the covers over himself, and hyperventilated into his pillow as his body rebelled against him.

1973

A Victory of Conscience

After Jonah had endured a whole week of grounding, he was finally allowed to see Mort again. The mid-July sun was out, and the boys were ordered to stay in the yard as Jonah's mother lay down in a sun chair. She had been day-drinking and almost immediately fell into a deep sleep. Jonah then positioned the large patio umbrella over his mother with intense floral graphics and a rim of white fringe.

"This will keep her from waking up," Jonah whispered to Morty, a scheming grin on his slender face. "What do you want to do?"

Morty motioned at Jonah's mom and shook his head. "Yeah, but Jonah, she could wake up any time, and you'll be grounded again if we leave." His nervous nature betrayed him as he looked anxiously at the gate.

"Nah, she's been drinking all morning, Mort; she'll be out for hours," Jonah assured his friend, placed both hands on Mort's shoulders, and shook him playfully. The idea that he could sneak away without his mother's omnipotent gaze on him excited Jonah. Morty pushed Jonah's hands from him and turned to kick a soccer ball at the chain-link fence as if testing Jonah's mother's resolve. Nothing. *Free Bird* by Lynyrd Skynyrd came through the kitchen window and Jonah took the opportunity to mime the chorus to his friend, thrusting his thumbs at himself over his sleeping mother, *'I'm as free as a bird nooooow, and this bird you cannot chaaaange...'*

Mort laughed and waved away the nonsense. "Well, if we're going out, I'd like to go to the park and look for bugs," he said, his confidence growing. "Do you have anything we can put bugs into?"

Jonah retrieved a lidded container and handed it to Mort. "Will this do the trick?" Jonah was excited to move beyond his yard and from under his mother's overprotective veil. Mort nodded in answer to the question, and the boys moved outside the gated backyard, across the street, and into the park two blocks away.

Jonah admittedly felt anxious over the bold move but liberated as well. Mort seemed, well, like Mort, having been granted access to the outside world many times before. When Jonah had first heard this, he wondered if Mort's parents didn't love him enough to keep him inside and away from all the hazards the outside world threatened. At thirteen, he knew better.

Mort went immediately to work crawling on all fours around the edge of an elderberry bush whose berries were taking shape. Jonah joined Mort, mirroring how his thick little fingers raked the grass and soil, searching for new volunteers for his collection.

"What's this?" Jonah picked up a green, organic-looking nub of a creature. "I don't see any eyes or legs or anything," he observed. The eyeless, legless thing wiggled in Jonah's fingers, and he dropped it from fright. It was a most unusual bug if it was a bug at all.

"Oh, wow, Jonah, you found a cocoon!" Morty stated, nearly squealing. He picked the wriggling thing up and placed it carefully into the container. "There's more!" He exclaimed and gathered four others up. Jonah watched on in amazement as Morty explained the rarity of the find.

"These will turn into butterflies in about a week. They need to be hung up." Mort's expression assumed a severe nature as he reviewed the elderberry bush. "They must have fallen off this bush."

"So, we need to hang them?" Jonah thought this a terrible thing to do to anyone.

"Yeah, they need to dangle from something," Mort repeated, disregarding Jonah's apprehensions. "I gotta take these to my room and pin them up so they can come out butterflies."

"That's going to take a whole week? Then what?"

"Then, I have five new butterflies for my collection," Mort stated, focused on the cocoons in the Tupperware container.

"Okay," Jonah agreed, and they began the walk to Mort's place. Mort meticulously pinned the cocoons to his corkboard in his room, which smelled of model glue and had an entire wall dedicated to dead insects.

Mort's mom offered the kids a snack, and they accepted. Jonah began feeling guilty for betraying his mother by slipping out of the backyard. Still, this was the sort of adventure he'd always dreamed of.

"Your mother knows you're here, Jonah?" Mort's mom asked as she poured him a soda. She was a sweet woman with kind eyes who seemed a bit broken. Mort had clearly inherited his physical features from her side, whereas his father was much thinner.

"Yes, ma'am," Jonah answered in a practiced way. He had anticipated the question as Mort's mom knew how his mother was. He took a bite from the muffin baked fresh that morning and smiled warmly up at her.

After the snack, they made their way back to Jonah's at a leisurely pace while Jonah soaked up the freedom.

* * *

The following weekend, Jonah received a call from Mort, who insisted he come over as the butterflies were starting to emerge. Jonah begged his mother to walk him over so he could witness the metamorphosis. Happily, she agreed, putting down her drink and walking them the few blocks to Mort's.

"I'll come back for you in two hours, Jonah," His mother called from the sidewalk as Jonah approached the front door. He waved and nodded back at her and let himself into the house.

Mort greeted Jonah in his room, and they sat on the bed, watching the butterflies as they worked diligently to free themselves of the cocoons. It took a painfully long time, in Jonah's opinion, and once the first emerged, Mort immediately picked it up off the ground and allowed it to unfurl its wings on his fingers. Jonah was captivated by the process, linking it to his own struggle as he looked to a time when he would become a man and prepared to leave the cocoon of his mother's embrace. The butterfly's hard work had paid off and was commendable in Jonah's eyes. It was a beautiful bug, and Jonah respected the tiny creature for its determination.

"It's a Swallowtail!" Mort announced triumphantly as the wings expanded and fluttered. He roughly took both wings in his fingers and pulled them as far apart as possible without tearing them off. This act of aggression against the butterfly horrified Jonah. He watched in stunned silence as Mort pinned one wing and the other to his corkboard.

The bug writhed against the sudden and terrible confinement until Mort put a final pin through its head, ending its fight and its life. Jonah stood up to protest the cruel act and let Mort know it.

"Mort! *Why did you do that?!*" His voice cracked, and his brow furrowed.

On the defensive, Mort replied, "I *told* you I was going to," he looked hurt.

"I know, but I didn't think," Jonah felt confused and upset, "I guess I don't know what I thought, Mort. I didn't think you'd kill it after all that!" Jonah's voice rose, and he eyed the other butterflies experiencing the same struggle. Where there was new life a minute ago, there was no more. He couldn't get his head around the shocking violence. How did Mort feel so little over what he'd done? Did Jonah feel too much?

"You sound like a girl," Mort said, meaning to hurt Jonah. "This is how I collect bugs. They have to die." He explained with the cool manner of a boy who thought what he was doing was in the name of science.

"Don't kill the others," Jonah pleaded with his friend. "You only need one, right?"

"I guess," Mort agreed. "They're all the same."

"Then we can release them," Jonah said, trying to disguise that he was on the brink of tears, his body slipping between Mort and the cocoons.

"Sure, okay," Mort wanted only to please his friend.

As the others dropped from their cocoons, the boys gathered them and placed them in one of Mort's mother's Tupperware containers. They walked to the edge of Mort's front yard and let the butterfly wings dry on a large stone.

"We could feed them sugar water," Mort recommended. "It's like food to them." He returned to the house and remerged with a shallow water bowl. The boys let the trusting butterflies walk onto their fingers and gingerly placed them on the bowl's edge. Then, to Jonah's delight, their long tongues unrolled into the mixture of water and dissolved sugar. It was a moment he would never forget.

1973

Puberty

Secretly, Jonah had signed up for basketball tryouts at school. His mother would disapprove; *of course*, he could hurt himself. But despite the underlying fear of her finding out - and his glasses, Jonah bravely decided to go ahead with the gamble. So, he headed to the gymnasium on an afternoon where he'd told his mother he was going to Mort's to work on a model before dinner. It was the bravest thing he'd ever done. He was proud of himself. When he arrived, it looked as if the whole school had come out for auditions. Sweat glistened off the senior boys dressed in their team outfits, and squeaking sneakers echoed in the room, which doubled as the auditorium, as they ran up and down the court. It smelled of rubber and wood and something less appealing. If he made the team, his life would change for the better. He could feel it. But seeing everyone bouncing basketballs and throwing from the three-point line made him immediately nervous. Curious wetness began to pool inside his shirt. A smell followed the dampness, and Jonah made a point to discreetly sniff his armpits, confirming the smell's origin. Stunned, Jonah hustled into a blind sprint toward the change rooms. "Five minutes," one of the coaches hollered. Five minutes to get cleaned up and try out for the team.

Jonah unzipped his bag in the changing room and pulled out the purple shorts and shirt. School colors. White racing lines followed the seams as if guaranteeing every kid who wore them would be faster than the next. Jonah's athletic prowess was only imagined; this was his attempt to prove that he could be more. He dabbed at the wet marks forming under his arms and reeled away from the smell. This was discouraging. Never had his body made such a mess of his shirts. There were plenty of unpleasant scents in the locker room, but he trumped them all. Its body odor, he ascertained—another hurdle in the many hurdles he'd been facing with puberty. Just trying to keep his dick from pitching a tent in his pants every time someone or something rubbed up against him was difficult enough; this, along with his voice changing octaves every other word, would test his resolve.

Another sniff, and he wondered whether the other kids' BO smelled as bad. His timing couldn't be worse for something like this with a crowded gymnasium to return to, but at least it wasn't another boner. He didn't have anything to apply to his underarms. An antiperspirant would have helped, but he didn't have an antiperspirant.

In the gymnasium, the kids were lined up against the wall. Jonah was tenth in line to run the gambit. He watched the other nine go through the paces and studied their techniques. By this time, the kid next to him was waving a hand at his nose and grimacing at Jonah. This action caught on, and soon, he was dubbed the stinky kid at the front of the line. Jonah's audition went poorly afterward; his embarrassment over this new obstacle made him shaky. His attempt at a lay-up was well off the mark, his three-point attempt missed the backboard, and his dribbling produced a ricochet off his foot, which fired into the line of remaining kids waiting their turn. A chorus of laughter followed.

"Thank you... *Jonah.*" A coach said displeasedly; Jonah was sure he saw the man roll his eyes. Jonah made his escape. Humiliated, he returned to the locker room, where two kids who had gone before him commented on a smell. Jonah knew it was him and moved two rows over. After his display on the court, he knew he wouldn't make the team. If anything, he could expect further disapproving looks from his peers in the hallways and continued scorn where none was deserved. His mother was right; he shouldn't try things.

"Holy!" a kid said behind him in an amused tone. "It's *you* who stinks!" This kid was a year older in grade eight but nearly twice Jonah's size. His pimpled face and sneer were right up in Jonah's personal space. "Did you rub a dead skunk on yourself?"

Jonah shrank back at this. He wasn't good at confrontations and didn't have a witty bone in his body. All he could muster was "uh," then he jammed his clothes in his bag and moved to get past the senior who blocked him with his body. "Why the rush, *Stinky?* You need a shower." He looked up at the other boy, dramatically waving Jonah's odor away while he nodded with a sinister grin. Both boys then grabbed Jonah, one at the shoulders, while the other secured his ankles, and they held him under the cold water until Jonah managed to wriggle free. He fell hard onto the wet tile and slipped, getting to his feet, hugging his gym bag tightly. The elbow he landed on screamed in pain, but Jonah refused to cry. The boys laughed at his misfortune, as Jonah knew others would if he couldn't keep the odor under control. *Maybe he deserved this for being so bold.* He scurried out of the locker room, through the halls, and out the side door. It was cooler than he remembered, but the fact that he was soaked to the bone probably had something to do with that. The walk home was filled with regret. Had he listened to the voice in his head, he could have avoided the harassment and humiliation. The voice was beginning to nag at him, sounding like his mother. *It's just not worth trying.*

At home, he was found bawling into his hands by his Grandma Anne, who had been placed to watch him while his parents worked at the pub. She immediately sat on the edge of his bed to comfort him. "Oh, Jonah, what's happened, sweetheart? You smell like you've been rolling in a dumpster."

Jonah turned on his side to face her, a powerful frown pulling down the corners of his mouth. "I don't... know what's... happened, grandma," he confessed through sobs. "I got nervous... at school and just started to smell and... get wet." He sucked in through his nose. Grandma Anne placed a calming hand on his small shoulder.

"Oh, Jonah, you've never smelled like this," she wrinkled up her petite nose and stood. "I've never smelled anything like it."

"*Thanks,*" Jonah said, his voice thick with sarcasm. "I'm a *freak!*"

"Oh, you're not a freak, sweetie; you have an aromatic scent. We can take you to the doctor for that." Grandma assured him.

"Really?" Jonah felt suddenly hopeful, wiping tears from his red cheeks. "Can we go now? Can you take me right now?" As he sat up, the face cloths he'd secured under his arms fell to the bed.

"I'll call Dr. Monet right away, honey. Don't you worry now. We'll get you sorted." She left the room, and Jonah listened as she made the call. "Get into a new outfit, Jonah. We're going now."

* * *

Jonah sat on the tall table at the doctor's office, feet dangling, with the paper stretched across the vinyl cushion, making a crunching sound. Grandma sat in a wooden chair provided as the doctor reviewed Jonah's armpits.

"They're a bit red, alright," said Dr. Monet. His broad mustache moved comically as he spoke. "Obviously, sweating doesn't quite agree with you, Jonah," he smiled and winked at him. Jonah just smiled nervously back. "Puberty can be a difficult transformation," he turned to grandma to explain. "Jonah likely has Bromhidrosis. It's a condition where the skin coming in contact with sweat creates a much more pungent odor than average. It's not a death sentence," he turns back to Jonah. "Treatments include washing your underarms as often as needed. Shaving your underarms," the doctor reviews Jonah's armpits and comments on the shortcomings of hair there. "You'll want a couple of clean shirts to replace the soiled ones as necessary."

"Are you finding you sweat a lot in situations where you're not active?" Monet asked Jonah.

"I – uh – I don't know, I just – it just happened today." Jonah's embarrassment grew the more he thought about his day. He began to sweat just standing in line for no reason at all in the gym. He had begun to sweat just answering questions.

"Nervous perspiration happens." The doctor assured him. "Stressful situations can do it. Be mindful of what makes you sweat. Keep a journal, and maybe we can come up with a better solution."

"Is there no medication that can help?" Grandma asked her expression one of worry.

"Not at this time." Doctor Monet replied. He scratched at his balding head and chased the itch to his mustache. "It's really just a condition some people get and need to be conscious of. It may last only a year but could be with him all his life." He turned his attention back to Jonah. "You'll simply need to add a few steps into your daily routine. I'll write down a couple of brands of antiperspirant, which may help mask the odor." He handed Grandma the scribble and ordered Jonah to put his shirt back on.

Strange by The Doors plays in the background of the reception room, and Jonah couldn't help but place himself in the song's lyrics. *Shit, I am strange.* Then that was that: a cruel sentence he would carry for the rest of his life. Why him? He didn't make friends as it was, so he would retreat further into himself, do less and less to avoid people and continue on a path of isolation.

1976

It's a Blur

"Jonah," he could make out his best friend's voice even through the haze of last night's bender. "Jonah, man, we gotta skitty," Morty's tone took on a sense of urgency Jonah hadn't heard in all the years he'd known him. It was unnerving. He opened his eyes, which watered immediately from the brilliant sunrise. His hand rose unconsciously to shield him from the raging star. "Seriously, Jonah, get up." Mort was pulling at Jonah's other arm. *Where were they?*

"Where are we?" Jonah asked in a daze, slow to get to his feet even with the leverage Morty offered.

"Never mind *that* just let's find your shoes and get the fuck outta here." Morty wandered off to look for Jonah's footwear. *Why wasn't he wearing shoes?*

Jonah could make out *The Boys Are Back in Town* by Thin Lizzy as it played quietly from a second-story window above him. With his eyes adjusting to the light, Jonah was able to review his surroundings. They were in a yard. An in-ground pool is the centerpiece to more bodies littered around it on lounges and beach towels. He had not been so lucky as to have landed on a lounger. His back ached from the lumpy lawn. His mouth produced no saliva, and he smacked his tongue against his pallet. He was wearing a bathing suit. Not his. He had a sweater on and dry blood around his nose.

"Holy *shit*, Jonah, can you pick up the pace, please? Harriet's parents are due home this morning!" Harriet, Jonah thought, disoriented; it's Harriet's house -

the girl from school. The one Morty had been permitted to finger a week earlier. *Were they boyfriend and girlfriend now?*

"What – why are we here?" Jonah managed, running fingers through his mop of brown hair tussled and sideways.

"*Jesus*, Jonah, you don't remember shit, do you?" Morty let out a much-needed sigh and explained in a hurry. "Harriet ran into us at the corner store last night and invited us to her house. I thought I was going to get to third base. There was a party going on?" He whispered, urging Jonah to recall the event. "No? *Nothing?*" He waved Jonah away. "You need to relax on the drugs."

"What did I do?"

"What *didn't* you do?" Morty asked back, astounded at his friend's lack of self-preservation. "Just about everything you could smoke, drink, or snort!"

"Off the hook," Jonah replied with a sardonic smirk. Drugs and alcohol had been welcome additions to his high school career. He rode on Mort's coattails to get invites to parties as Mort's personality seemed desirable to some of the elite. They tolerated Jonah for Morty's company.

"What's cool about it? You don't *remember* anything."

Maybe that was the point, thought Jonah. After the abuse he'd experienced in high school the last three years, he was looking for the right high. Drugs: cocaine, he assumed. Weed? Booze was an obvious choice, following in his mother's footsteps. But cocaine... that made him forget everything.

"Listen, when you called out the entire basketball team, you became a live wire, flailing your arms all over the place. Man, you're lucky they were good about it. They thought you were out to lunch, *tripping.*"

"So, let's blow this taco stand?"

"If you'd like to survive the day, then yes." The intensity of Morty's gaze compelled a sense of urgency in Jonah.

Jonah remembered nothing but understood why, in a drug-induced state, he would verbally attack the basketball team. The humiliating tryouts of three years ago were one thing, but the continued abuse over his owning a pair of Converse Pro Leathers had him wishing he'd never considered going out for the team.

As Jonah resisted another tug at his arm by his hefty friend, he focused on the pool and the body floating in it. *Facedown.* That couldn't be. People can't float like that without – "*Jesus*, Mort, is that -"

"Fuck, *yes*, Jonah! It's Harriet." Morty released Jonah's arm, allowing it to fall to his side. "It's what I'm saying, man. We need to go!"

"Leave?" Jonah's voice sounded distant, even to him. "Is she *dead*, Mort?"

"She's not alive," Mort replied frankly, his hands massaging his round cheeks. He wore his favorite outfit: an IBM t-shirt stretched over his robust frame, jeans, and sneakers sans socks.

"And you know this *how?*

"*Jonah*, she's fucking floating face down in the pool. What more do you need?" Mort's voice cracked.

"How did it happen?"

"Last I saw her was when she went to bed." Mort waved off the explanation. "We said good night, and I found you snorting a line of coke as long as your forearm."

"That's a lot of coke," Jonah stated, rubbing his nose and inspecting his filthy glasses. He was shaky, and the realization their hostess might have drowned in her pool was distressing. But more so was Mort's indifference that she might be dead. It reminded him of the ease with which Mort ended the lives of insects, offering them up as sacrifices to his corkboard.

"So, can we *leave*, please? Your mom's car is parked on the street."

Morty was clearly not himself, and Jonah began to wonder what the rush was really about. Arms crossed and pointing slowly at the young woman's lifeless body moving to the whim of the pool's jets, Jonah's face began to tingle. He was still very drunk and a bit high. This had been going on now for two years. High school was a nightmare, and for every free moment he had, he dedicated himself to drinking and, more recently, smoking and snorting whatever he could scrape together. It was his coping mechanism. His parents had no real idea, and any support he'd once experienced there had gone. He still got good grades, but he was a raging alcoholic at sixteen.

"Jonah! *Seriously.* This is not our problem."

"You were with her last night, Morty; how can you say that?" The haze from the night before began to clear as Mort's continued denial sank in.

"For, like, twenty minutes, man. Listen, I don't want to be here when everyone else wakes up." His whispers began intruding on the sleeping masses as Jonah watched them stir.

"But Mort, everybody knows you were with her last night." Jonah focused very hard on remembering anything, and that was the one thing he seemed to recall. "The cops'll question you."

"Maybe, but if we're not here when they get here, *that* won't happen." Morty's gaze was fixed on Harriet. Jonah was convinced Mort was still drunk. He was acting bananas.

"You'll look like you did it, Mort, is what I'm saying. You *need* to be here." Jonah explained through bloodshot eyes and a fuzzy face. "This is *important*, man."

"Fuck," Morty fell into a deck chair and surrendered to the idea. "Well, what do I do?" Tears came next. He became a blubbering mess, holding his face in his large hands. The reality of what was happening had finally sunk in.

Jonah found his pack of Lucky's in the grass and lit a cigarette. He took a deep drag from it and let the smoke exhaust through his nostrils the way his mother would. "Man, you need to call the cops."

"*Me?*" Mort's face left his hand, and a trail of snot followed. He wiped his hands on his shorts. "Why me?"

"You found her. No one else is up. Gotta do the right thing, man."

"Should we pull her out and try CPR?"

"How long's she been like that?"

"I don't know. I saw her, like, five minutes ago."

Jonah blew more smoke as he laid eyes on the poor girl again. "Yeah, let's pull her out, and you need to try CPR."

"I don't even remember how," Mort confessed. "How, what do you do first?"

"Fuck I don't know, Mort," Jonah said and coughed. "But we need you to look like you tried." Anxiety entered Jonah's chest, and the remainder of his buzz evaporated. Sobriety crept in.

"Okay, I'll do it." Morty wrung his hands as he took his first tentative step toward the pool. His heart raced, and he was sure he'd felt a murmur. His father had heart murmurs. They had resulted in a heart attack a year ago. Mort felt like a heart attack might be a better option than pulling Harriet's body from the pool.

"Be gentle with her," Jonah whispered, still unsure whether what was transpiring was, in fact, a real event. Morty waved off the obvious statement, his expression one of nausea.

When Morty was on the third step and up to his waist in the cool water, he slowly waded to where Harriet was floating and reached out to take her hand.

Then Harriet sprang out of the water and stood on her own two feet. Morty screamed in his feminine way, and Jonah gasped. Harriet wasn't dead! Instead, she was wearing a mask and snorkel. Her long, abundant red hair had obscured both as it spread along the water's surface.

Harriet was sound as a pound but stunned to have been met by a screaming Morty, who had lost all color in his face and nearly fainted. "What? What is it, Mort?" Harriet shouted back at the big man, her slender fingers pulling on his tight, wet T-shirt to steady him.

"I thought – I thought you were," Mort hugged the girl, and to Jonah's delight, she hugged his friend back.

"Thought you were dead," Jonah shouted at her, winked, and lit another cigarette. It wasn't real, after all.

All the hollering disturbed the other guest's uncomfortable slumbers, and Jonah noticed a look coming from one of the jocks. It was a weary glare with an undercurrent of loathing. Jonah located his shoes and snapped them up, hurrying to the door. "Mort, peace out, home fry!" He called as Morty and Harriet remained wrapped in one another's embrace.

1977

The Black Tar

Where is the joy in my addiction? Where once addiction satisfied a need, it now only worked to satisfy itself. The street was filled with shadows. Creeping shadows. Frightful shadows that shifted behind corners into alleyways and scampered up brick walls and fire escapes. Did he see things that weren't there? It wouldn't be the first time. He needed to satisfy his addiction. Drinking from a bottle Jonah had pilfered from his father's pub satiated one need but not the other. The other had begun to scream demands, which drew him out of the relative safety of his parent's home and into the streets.

A group of men huddled around a lit garbage can between a pizza place and dry cleaners. *Crackle, crackle, crackle.* Wet snow remained two feet outside the can's diameter. The men's feet danced beside the bin's base, warming toes in ratty shoes. They shared a pipe between them. Jonah licked his lips and, driven by addiction, approached the circle with far less caution than he ought to have observed.

"I have whiskey," Jonah told them. A man missing his bottom teeth smirked and pulled a great plume of smoke into his mouth. His eyes rolled back a moment as the drug took effect. Jonah's addiction was raging now. *Take the pipe, run!*

"I can trade you," Jonah explained to the solemn assembly of street dwellers. "I-I need what you have."

A filthy man extended a filthy hand to receive the bottle, and Jonah reluctantly parted with it in the hopes he would be offered the pipe. The man drank from the bottle, tipping it up while it rested on his bottom lip. *Glug, glug, glug.* By this time, the stink from the makeshift dwelling caught Jonah sharply in the face as a warm breeze shifted the exhaust of the building they were squatting next to, carrying the wretched smell away from the men and to Jonah. He gagged and took a step back, slamming into someone on the sidewalk. He lost his balance, stepped on the person's foot, and fell elbow-first onto the cement.

He let out a cry and grasped his elbow in fear he'd broken it. *Can elbows break? What bone is that? More than one.* The pipe was being offered to him by the toothless one. Nodding at him. Smoke or breath, animated in the cold, escaped the thin man's nostrils. The pain radiating from his elbow forgotten, Jonah reached out to accept the smoldering pipe.

"Ya don't want that, ya," said a voice whose hand took Jonah's wrist and pulled him from the temptation. "That's the Black Tar, boyo. That'd be yer end, *that.*" Jonah turned his attention fleetingly away from the prize, and to the man with an accent, he couldn't place. "Are ya so far gone ya want the *Black Tar* now?"

"Black Tar," Jonah muttered the phrase back, confused whether that meant hash or what. "I can handle it." He told the older man whose interest seemed out of place. This foreigner was a bum by all appearances. Likely hooked on the juice and running lines up his nose of every variety.

The man cackled and blew his nose onto the sidewalk with his free hand, narrowly missing Jonah's leg. "Have ya no sense, boyo? It's *Opium*, a death sentence. Do ya have a death sentence in ya?" He kept a firm grip on Jonah's wrist. He was wiry under his many sweaters, Jonah could tell, but he was strong. He pulled a small baggie from his many-pocketed trench coat and placed it roughly into Jonah's hand. "*This* will git ya what yer looking fer. Don't touch the Black Tar."

The man dragged Jonah with him to an alley a block from the Black Tar-smoking Street people to his gang of outlaws. Under the older man's watchful eye, he shuffled Jonah toward a large trash bin and ordered him to sit. At this point, Jonah was afraid for his life. His anxiety had hit a glass ceiling, and he'd begun to feel dizzy. *Why would he bring me here to kill me if he'd warned me away from the Black Tar?*

"Look at what I gave ya," The man demanded, motioning at Jonah's closed fist. "I'll light it up fer ya. You take a good long inhale and get yer self home." A pipe is handed over, and a match is lit. "Well, *put it in,*" the man nodded demandingly, his voice raised an octave, and Jonah pulled the weed from the bag and stuffed the pipe's bowl. "Put it to yer mouth then," Jonah obeyed. The man put the flame into the chamber and ordered Jonah to *suck*. He did.

It's just weed, Jonah thought as the taste filled his mouth. But it's good weed. His head started spinning, his vision blurred, and a lighter-than-air feeling made standing difficult.

The man cackled again. "Ya enjoy that." His laughter sparked the same from his trio, who watched on, which carried Jonah away on a wave of vibrations. He slid down the bin slowly, his legs no longer capable of keeping him upright, landing him on the cracked, stained, and squalid alleyway.

His gaze landed on the wet cement. Cracks dug deep into the structure, and he found himself falling through them. Canyons towered above him. Darkness settled around him. Sounds became notes, and soon, an orchestra echoed in the cavernous canyons below the feet of the men making merry so far above him. *Were they singing? Could a group of blurry-eyed drifters put their thoughts to a song like that so beautifully?* Jonah moved through the fissure, keeping one eye attached to the world above, which he ought to be a part of. The canyon forked at several junctions, and Jonah stopped at each to consider his options. None seemed more pressing than the other, so he stayed true to the original path. Why veer off and find himself in peril at the mercy of an ant or a spider? No, keep with the path ahead of you. Stay with what you know. Life doesn't reward the bold; it cripples them and says: *I told you so.* To his relief, the canyon walls began to shrink, releasing Jonah from his revere and filling him with the necessary anxiety required to snap out of his - what, two, three hours lost to exploring the fractures in the alley?

As the effects of the drug lessened, Jonah turned his head to find the man seated next to him with one of Jonah's cigarettes in his mouth. "Ya don't mind, do ya, boyo? Tit for Tat and all that?" Jonah's head shook slowly. He felt happy but knew his expression didn't carry that message. The man pulled another cigarette and placed it between Jonah's lips. He lit both with Jonah's Zippo, encouraging him to suck on the filter.

Jonah spent most of the night with these men. Sensing a kinship, he listened to their stories and asked if he could return another night. They welcomed him back several times before the city began their crackdown. Jonah was caught up in a melee between the police and the *riffraff* several weeks later. His parents were called to pick him up at the station.

"Oh, *Jonah*," his mother said in her defeated way. Always the victim regardless of the situation, Jonah thought. Still, he hated disappointing her. She was a good person who didn't deserve a son like him.

"Is it because of me?" She wouldn't let it go as they sat in a closed, windowless room waiting on social services.

"Mom, it's just - ah, I don't have an answer for that, Mom." Jonah struggled with placing blame on his mother. *Was it her fault or her faulty genes? Bit of both, perhaps, but why put that on her?*

She had one hand on his while the other held a cigarette like it was her lifeline. Was it wrong that the alcohol on her breath made him crave a drink?

"Your father would be here, but the pub, you know," she explained on behalf of his absent father. Frankly, Jonah was glad he wasn't directly involved. The disappointment on his face would have enraged Jonah.

"Hello, sorry for the wait," a short, round man named Kevin announced as he threw the door open, startling Jonah and his mother.

"*Jesus Christ,*" Jonah shouted, in turn, startling Kevin. Kevin apologized for his dramatic entry.

"It's these doors in here," Kevin explains of the station, "I never know which one weighs a thousand pounds and which weighs ten." He chuckles to himself. Jonah and his mother stare at each other. "Honestly, you wouldn't believe the difference." He sat down with a forced smile and a heavy sigh across from them.

"Jonah," Kevin opens a file folder. "This isn't your first offense, I see," his eyes dance behind his glasses as they read his rap sheet. "Drunk and disorderly twice. In possession of marijuana once," he peers over his glasses, "good you had so little; a trafficking charge would stay with you a lot longer." He closes the folder and leans in to speak candidly.

"As a minor, you've been getting away with a lot. The system feels it's being abused and recommends that you go into rehabilitation. Your file has been reviewed, and a judge has been placed to preside over your case."

"A *judge?* He's only 17," his mother said, lighting another cigarette. "What are they thinking; they can try a child as an adult now?"

"No, ma'am, but as an underage person with obvious signs of addiction, the system is considering *forced* rehabilitation. They don't want Jonah entering adulthood as a drain on society and a danger to himself or others."

"A danger -" His mom squeezed down on Jonah's wrist. "He's in no danger,"

"If the judge decides he's a danger to himself or others, he will be placed in rehab and will have to complete it as long as he's a minor."

"What's rehab?" Jonah feels vulnerable, even with his mother's grip on his wrist, maybe because of it.

"It's where people showing signs of addiction are taught to manage their addictions and go on to live good, productive lives. You want to be productive, don't you, Jonah?"

"Like, *AA*?"

"Exactly. But more intense. You don't leave the facility until you've completed your rehabilitation."

"I-I don't want to do that. That's wrong, man, that's like, taking my freedom -" Jonah is stopped mid-speech by Kevin.

"You should hope the judge puts you in rehab *now*, while it's out of your control, because when you're an adult, and you're picked up on charges like these," he taps the folder, "the freedom you so cherish will disappear for *years* rather than months.

"Oh, *Jonah*, I think this might just be the thing for you," his mother says, loosening her grip on his wrist. "You could be so much more." Her doe eyes catch him in their sad gaze, and he's transported back to childhood, safe in her golden fingers.

"We'll talk at home, Mom," Jonah assured her.

"Oh, no, no, you're being held overnight until the verdict comes in, Jonah. Flight risk. You understand, ma'am," he addressed Jonah's mother directly. She nodded, and tears fell quickly from his mother's eyes. Jonah is stunned. He'd never spent a night in jail. His father would be embarrassed.

1977

Rehab, Relapse, Rehab

"Jonah, I'm James," the court-appointed counselor greeted Jonah in a cavernous room, which echoed his salutation. Folding chairs formed a circle where James Forcible stood to welcome his newest member. "Please, take a seat."

This was a new experience for Jonah, who was forced into rehabilitation. He didn't like the look of all the chairs. It made him immediately anxious. AA posters adorned the white walls. "Are we expecting someone else?" Jonah asked timidly, hands pushed deep into his jean's pockets. He pulled out his lighter and Lucky's and lit a cigarette.

"Not today. This is set up for an evening session with more experienced members. You won't be involved in group sessions for the first week." James surveyed Jonah's features, trying to get a read on the troubled youth. Breaking his stare, James motioned to a chair for Jonah to sit. He decided to stand.

"Sit or stand. I want you to feel comfortable. Most choose to sit." James sat and crossed one leg over the other; his bell bottoms relaxed over his slight ankles. A clipboard sat on his lap. He quickly skimmed the typed form he'd read earlier.

"I can't feel comfortable in a place like this," Jonah admitted, studying the sterile, white walls, tiled ceiling, and parquet flooring.

"Why's that?"

"I don't want to be here, *James*." Walls up, Jonah made it clear to the tall, thin counselor that he had no interest in staying. James looked like any one of the hippies Jonah would buy from; bell-bottom jeans and a button-up, wide-collared, untucked shit. His hair was longer than Jonah's but tied in a ponytail.

"I get that, Jonah, but circumstances beyond your control brought you here. How old are you?" James knew full well how old Jonah was. That information was on his clipboard. But he wanted to bring Jonah out of his shell and get him to answer straightforward questions.

"What does it matter?"

"Why so defensive?" James asked, head tilting slightly toward his shoulder. His teeth were uneven.

"This place feels like a punishment."

"We've no intention of punishing you, Jonah. You've punished yourself long enough. This is the treatment."

"It feels like punishment."

"That's because anything outside your norm will feel like punishment. But your norm has been a self-inflicted sentence. Why you've felt the need to punish yourself is part of the treatment."

"I don't know... I don't know that I can do this." Jonah's head shook, his shoulder-length hair brushing the long collar of his shirt.

"If you can be truthful, you can do this. If you're truthful, we can help you."

"I don't want to be here," Jonah said flippantly.

"That much is apparent, but you're a minor and have been sentenced by a judge to cooperate. So, you can let it feel like a punishment, get nothing from it, and we'll see you in another three months, or you can take charge of your life, give it a chance, stop wasting your time, and try to be the man you're meant to be."

"That sounds like you think there's some greater purpose to my life."

"That's true for everyone, Jonah," James said candidly.

"What makes you say that?"

"Experience, Jonah."

"You don't know me."

"I'd like to get to know you. I've seen many like you pass through these halls. Most of them found purpose. Some didn't. I couldn't help some, but those I have helped appreciate their second chance. This is *my* purpose. I help those who want help. Those who don't... well, let's say, 'I accept the things I cannot change.'"

"You think you can change me?" Jonah laughed off the claim.

"It doesn't matter what I think, Jonah. What you think ultimately decides whether you find purpose or waste what gift you've been given to live in the bottom of a bottle, or a needle, or a baggie, or whatever your flavor of addiction is."

"So, it's up to me."

"The judge made it clear being here isn't up to you, but what you do with your time here is absolutely up to you. If you don't get a pass from me, you'll be doing it all over again until you're clean."

"So, *no* choice then."

"Give it time, Jonah. You should want to make yourself proud. Living as an addict offers only pain. Do it for you; do it for your family."

Jonah laughed a throaty laugh. "My mother is a *flaming* alcoholic, and my father a workaholic, and – I'm pretty sure, both are adulterers - if that's a word. So, if I'm going to participate, it's not for either of them."

"Good. It shouldn't be. It should only be for you."

"Then why did you mention them?"

"Different people have different triggers. Yours is family. When did you discover your mother is an alcoholic?"

"Uh, ten, I think. I was ten. I didn't know what it meant, but that's when I started to notice all the bottles. At thirteen, I took my first drink."

"Why?"

"To see what all the fuss was about." Jonah sat and dabbed his ash into the pedestal ashtray.

"Did you get sick from it?"

"Oh yeah," he chuckled at the memory.

"How long before you tried it again?"

"Not long," Jonah shook his head, staring at the cigarette burning between his fingers. "Probably a couple of weeks later. Didn't get sick that time."

"No? Did that make you feel anything?"

"Good, I guess?" He shook his head.

"By fourteen, how often were you drinking?"

"Every day. Smoking too. No one at home knew because they weren't there, or Mom was so drunk she passed out on the couch. Grandma died when I was about to turn fourteen."

"That must have been devastating for you." James tapped his pencil on the paragraph within the court papers stating the grandma's role in Jonah's life.

"She was more a mother to me than my own mother from eleven on. She was a rock. She knew when I'd done something wrong. She cared I'd done something wrong enough to dish out punishments. I'm not saying she was mean – just strict. Probably a good thing, considering."

"You lost someone significant at a young age during a confusing time." James summed up.

"Like I said." Jonah ran the fingers of his right hand through the greasy length of his brown hair.

"Did your grandmother's death give you permission to drink more?"

"Is that how it works? I permit myself?"

"Sometimes. The thing is, Jonah, if you give yourself permission to drink, you can permit yourself to stop."

"I don't want to stop." He took a long drag from the cigarette.

"You want to live with purpose, don't you?"

"I don't know what that is."

"It's a reason to get up in the morning. A reason to participate in life rather than shut it out."

"Is that what you think I'm doing?" Jonah shifted his meager weight in the uncomfortable chair.

"Isn't it?"

"Fuck, I don't know." He stubbed the butt out in the ashtray.

"I do. *Everyone* on earth has a purpose."

"What purpose does a starving kid in Africa serve?" Jonah was proud of himself for asking.

James reacted quickly to the question as though he'd answered it a thousand times. "They serve as a moral reminder to those who have enough to eat and enough to share."

"So, the bloated skeleton on TV exists to help someone here, in the first world, to what, open their wallets?"

"And their *hearts*, Jonah."

"So, someone like me is feeding your purpose." Jonah understood.

"You could say that."

"So, if I decide not to participate, where is your purpose?"

"In those brave enough to get clean. Those willing to do the work I prescribe. Those who can visualize a life beyond their addiction."

"Rosy," Jonah said of the vision mockingly.

"It can be, Jonah. Be grateful you've been given a second chance. Many are not, and so must experience it again and again."

"Like, what, reincarnation?" Jonah had read a blurb on the dogma whereupon dying, a soul reanimated in another. *Can't imagine doing this again.*

"Yes. If you can't overcome the lesson you were meant to learn, you're destined to repeat it. Whether in this life or the next."

"That's what you believe? I thought this was going to be all about God."

"The work includes God, but it's about whatever resonates with you. God, Buddha, Unicorns, whatever. But finding that something is a big step. If it's your grandmother, use her. Draw your strength from her memory."

"Seems fair, I guess." Jonah crossed his arms.

"Then give me a chance to help you, Jonah. You're worth it, even if you can't see that right now. Your grandmother did. I do."

"You don't even know me."

"I do know you, Jonah. You're *me*. Six years ago."

Jonah's first week of rehabilitation was arduous as he battled against the unrelenting agony of withdrawal. First, the anxiety over his last drink and snort. He should have had another when he'd had the chance. Whisky was a poor choice. Then nausea. That stayed with him the whole week. Confusion over where he was and why clouded his ability to comprehend anything James said from his bedside. Hallucinations were oddly welcome, offering a reprieve from the angst due to an unusual heart rate. Feeling endlessly agitated wasn't unexpected or even a foreign sensation, but it ramped up a hundred-fold. Cold sweats released his unfavorable scent, and nurses changed bedding around the clock. Fevers, itchiness, that impossibly sinister sensation of something ineffable crawling just under your skin. Knowing it would all disappear with a drink was maddening. That there was nowhere he could procure a drink on the grounds and no one willing to bring him one regardless of his relentless vows of sobriety seemed ruthless, considering he couldn't drag himself out from under the covers. It was a week he'd have happily died. But he lived.

Medication - another addiction to look forward to with none of the fun side effects. This is what became of Jonah as the months trudged on. Rehab had become an ever-numbing experience. Though encouraged in group, feelings were challenging to bring to the surface. Jonah felt little to nothing most of the time. He was too young to be diagnosed with much more than an addictive personality but placed on enough medication to subdue his urges. He still smoked cigarettes but had no genuine interest in alcohol or other drugs. He didn't make friends in rehab any easier than on the outside. His condition continued to keep him distanced from others.

When he went home to Mom and Dad, he remained on the meds for a few more months and tried to concentrate at school but slipped into bouts of depression due to the sedation and difficulty focusing on any given subject. Jonah blamed the medications and so began to play with dosages himself. He also realized he could sell his powerful meds and, in return, purchase street drugs to continue his experimentation with alternative treatments. Alcohol didn't really factor in, as he would feel sick while still on the pharmaceuticals if he took a drink. This gave him more permission to try other drugs until he sold all of his prescriptions for cheaper drugs that offered the desired effect.

As his grades continued to slip, and the guidance counselor continued to alert Jonah's parents of his ongoing difficulties, Jonah was removed from school. He found himself back in rehab just three months after his release. He would turn eighteen inside those walls.

"I want out," he complained to James five weeks into his twelve-week rehabilitation.

"Do you really think that's the right move?" James, who'd cut his hair much shorter, leaned back in his chair, seated behind his blue, metal desk. *Solsbury Hill* by Peter Gabriel spun on James' turntable behind him.

"I'm eighteen today. I can leave if I want," Jonah was excited to take his life back, and no one would talk him out of it.

"So, you're an *adult* now," James leaned into his desk and flipped a folder open to reveal Jonah's information. James was clearly unhappy with Jonah's decision and wanted to fight him on it. "That means more than signing yourself in and out of rehab, Jonah," James studied Jonah's expression carefully. "It means the next time you're found drunk or high and the police arrest you, you won't have the protection of the courts. You'll go to jail."

"I'm *clean*, aren't I?" Jonah stood and paced the small office. "What more can you offer me? My class already graduated. I'm so far behind in school I'll have to take summer school if I don't want to do another whole fucking year. I can't waste my time in this place." Jonah's fingers snapped nervously at his sides.

"I appreciate your interest in school, Jonah, but I wouldn't release you now if you were seventeen. I'm asking you to stay and finish this out properly. AA is a process. If you don't continue the work, you will relapse, and I don't believe you will continue the work if you leave now."

"Well, I'm *not* seventeen, and I'm not *you*. I told you that the first time I met you. I'm telling you again. I don't need this anymore."

"Do I need to remind you of the stats against someone leaving rehab early? Or at all?" James had an arsenal of statistics showing relapse and suicide rates for people like him. He's seen them. He knew them by heart. It didn't matter to Jonah. He didn't have to stay, so he wouldn't.

Jonah shook his head and continued to pace. Why was he still there? Why didn't he gather up his shit and leave? *Surely, you don't care what James has to say. James doesn't care. He gets paid to do this.* Jonah's mind raged.

"What about your parents?" James used the wild card on him. *What about them? They would be furious with him, at least his father would be. He was paying for this, and there would be no refund for the seven weeks Jonah wasn't there. The parent card was a good one to play. They may throw him out of the house for leaving the program prematurely. He may become homeless.*

Jonah toppled his chair with a swipe of his hand, and it crashed to the ground. James didn't flinch. He was used to this kind of behavior. He knew how to make Jonah stay. He knew so much about Jonah.

Jonah sighed heavily and squatted on the floor with his hands interlinked over his head. He belted out a high-pitched cry, which lasted several seconds and fell to his back, crying in frustration over his choices.

A security person opened the office door and noticed Jonah on the floor, on his back, covering his face and groaning. The man looked at James, who signaled it was okay and to leave. Once the door was shut, James rounded his desk and crouched next to Jonah's curled form.

"You're only experiencing this frustration because you don't want to disappoint your parents or yourself," James explained softly with a hand falling on Jonah's shoulder. "You're not your addiction, Jonah. You deserve a better life. You deserve to be better. We can get you there. We've made adjustments to your treatment. The odds improve the second time around, *believe* me. You *will* find lasting recovery. School can wait. You need to work on yourself first."

Jonah knew the look he'd find in his father's eyes if he bailed on treatment. He knew the depression his mother would fall into, knowing her son had failed as she had. As much as he hated the program, he loved his mother more. He did want to be better. *Who would choose this?* Jonah nodded and lowered his hands from his face.

"I'll stay."

1979

The Invisible Man

Finishing High school without his only friend, Morty, forced Jonah to sink deeper into himself. After rehab, he'd returned to school to make up for his lost and missing credits. Mort had graduated and was in college to become an engineer. Jonah spoke to his friend on the phone every Friday and got an earful about college life. It sounded like a lot of fun if one were geared toward that kind of fun. Jonah wasn't. Not really. Drinking alone was more his speed. Parties just meant more harassment and embarrassment at the hands of those fortunate enough not to suffer his conditions.

During his final round of high school, Jonah discovered comic books. After rehab, it was suggested he find a hobby he enjoyed to distract from his addictions. The Invisible Man quickly became a favorite - from the Marvel Classics collection. It was a single issue telling Griffin's story, a scientist who made himself invisible and enjoyed random acts of violence. Jonah thought it was the perfect existence to be invisible to everyone. No more finger-pointing and humiliating judgment for the enjoyment of others. He could move from place to place, unseen and unapproachable.

Merely existing was a prison he couldn't seem to navigate. The addictions, the Bromhidrosis, his fear of making friends, his fear of living, and the feelings of inadequacy all contributed to what felt like living in a bubble. In contrast, others carried on with their lives. *Would the bubble ever burst? If so, what would follow?*

Weeks later, he found an H.G. Wells hardcover novel of The Invisible Man in a used bookstore and bought it for a song. It smelled of age and someone else's bookshelf, but it brought him joy to be united with the original author's work.

Jonah found his mother and father seated in the living room at home. It was rare to see them in the house simultaneously, let alone sharing a room. His mother's hands were folded around a glass, and his father's folded on his lap. Both looked despondent. Both had their heads bowed as if in prayer. The afternoon had given way to evening, and the yellow hue of the streetlights pushed into the small living space through the front picture window. The light created deep shadows that fell across both parents, further expanding the mood that seemed to permeate the room. Jonah's heart sank, and his addiction muttered something.

"What's up, guys?" Jonah attempted some levity. "Is the pub running itself?" He stood in the foyer, removing his shoes, as the anxiety crept into his chest. His father looked up slowly and patted the seat next to him on the couch.

Jonah removed his jacket and dropped it on the floor beside the door. He moved tentatively to the free chair and sat, placing his new book on his lap. *Make me invisible to this*, he pleaded to an uncaring universe.

"Son, you're not so young anymore," his father began stoically. "You understand your mother and my relationship. You know your mother shares your addictive personality." He took a deep breath while Jonah looked past his father to his mother. She wore a frown that etched itself into her lovely yet lined face. Jonah felt a pang of sadness for what was to come.

"The long and short of it is that we're separating, Jonah." He said, nodding once and standing as if that were all there was to say on the matter. Jonah put it together quickly: his mother was an alcoholic, and his father couldn't stand it another minute. His mother whimpered and took a drink from her glass as if in surrender.

"I've already moved my things to the pub," Jonah's father said as he surveyed the room. "A friend is taking me in for the foreseeable future, and your mother will no longer be helping out at the pub."

"So, you're getting a divorce?" Jonah knew this day was on the horizon for the last eight years or so, but it still stung. Whether he witnessed it or not, he was used to his parents being together. He needed stability. His mother alone couldn't offer him that. He feared he would spiral back into addiction - the voice of which was already starting to nag at him.

"It would seem that way, Jonah. But this doesn't affect you," his father insisted. "You've done well with your addiction *and* school. Please don't allow this event between your mother and me to play any role in your relapsing. You've all the tools you need to stay clean. You're better than your addiction." He laid a fatherly hand on Jonah's shoulder and squeezed. Then he let him go and moved past him to the front door. "Do pick up your coat, Jonah. There's a hanger right here." Then the door opened, and his father left him with his broken mother. Jonah's ears pricked up when *Goodbye Stranger* by Supertramp rumbled down his street in an El Camino with the stereo blaring – His father was like a stranger to him. *Then, I guess, this is goodbye.*

It wasn't lost on Jonah that his father hadn't made any attempt to make plans with him once he vacated the family home. Jonah never felt much for his father because he'd never received anything from him. Not a hug, not a kind word, nothing, really. Jonah shrugged and changed perspectives to his mother.

"I-I'm sorry, Jonah. I wasn't strong enough for you," His mother said, breaking down and placing her drink on the coffee table. "You're from a broken home now." Jonah instinctively joined his mother on the couch and put his arm around her. She turned into him and cried into his chest. He was sweating profusely and could smell himself wafting up through his mother's sobs. What a pair they made, he thought. Was he any stronger than her? She'd never even tried rehab. He'd been twice already. *And you'll be, again,* announced addiction.

1980

Five Years Gone

Severn never forgot that night. Or the fact that no one came looking for her. Another runaway, she'd be called. Whatever they might have called her, she never discovered. She was immediately sequestered in a basement or warehouse somewhere. There were no windows, live T.V., or radios. There was nothing but the words of a man she knew only as Dominus. Dominus was deeply invested in human trafficking and the sex trade. He would tell her she was safe and should be grateful for his protection as if she hadn't been better off in her *real life.*

The dim lights overhead flickered a moment and then brightened up the common room, triggering heart palpitations in all its prisoners. Light exposed the stained walls and cracked cement floors. But more than that, it exposed Severn to the daily reminder that she hadn't dreamed it all.

She awoke with a start. She couldn't remember a time when she hadn't. The damp facility, which had become her prison the last five years, always smelled of mildew, perfume, body odor, and sex. It was a curious lesson learning that sex had a scent all its own. The place was saturated with it.

"Up," Dominus called out, kicking the girls and boys who lingered. Severn had to peel the vinyl mattress from her arm as she worked to free herself from the thin, damp polyester sheet to avoid a boot to the stomach.

Dominus is how he'd introduced himself to each new victim. He was of African descent with cruel features and large eyes. Thin but strong. A slap from him collapsed the sturdiest of girls and boys. She'd experienced it more than once, his coarse and calloused palms stinging against her soft flesh.

A victim of human trafficking, Severn had learned to fall in line when ordered and saunter off to one of the private rooms to greet her *John*. It was much more challenging when she was just thirteen and fourteen - confused and terrified out of her wits. Many lessons were learned in those tentative years. *Lessons a child should never learn.*

At fifteen, she'd become pregnant from one of the pedophiles. This was not a free pass out of Hell and into a hospital. It more closely resembled a death sentence. What good was a pregnant child to a pedophile? None, it turned out, so she suffered through something more revolting and excruciating than rape; it was rape at the hands of a butcher. She hadn't shown for weeks and didn't understand the sensations she was experiencing. Cutting the three-month-old child from her womb took a toll both physically and emotionally on Severn. It scarred her internally and made sex more painful than before. She wondered what she must have done in her short life to deserve such an abysmal present.

"You're lucky, Blondie," Dominus told her, removing his fedora. "You get to dress up tonight." He threw what appeared to be a Halloween costume at her. She nodded and turned to undress. "What do you say, Blondie? That's a brand-new fucking outfit."

"Thank you," She managed.

"Thank you, *what?*" Dominus demanded.

"Thank you, Dominus." She finished, her shoulders raised and back bent in fear. She shuddered, and Dominus left.

"Pink Room. Ten minutes." He ordered, stopped a moment, and went silent. His fingers snapped, and he turned to face her once more with an ugly sneer on his gaunt face. "Hear that song on the stereo?" Severn focused and listened as a woman sang. She'd heard it before. Most of what Dominus brought in played repeatedly overhead. "She's called *Blondie,* too. Just remember, I gave you that name first." He turned, puffed up his chest, and sauntered away, singing to himself, *"Call me, duh, duh, duh, nah, nah, nah, call me, call me any, anytime..."*

Severn sank to her knees and knelt on her thin mattress. She cried for just two minutes, careful not to appear like she had. The *Johns* didn't appreciate that, at least, most of them. Another girl helped her up and sat her down to apply Severn's makeup. She was the oldest and had been there the longest.

"The *Pink* Room... that's the nicest of the bunch." She told her in a whisper as she brushed Severn's long blonde hair. A sigh followed. "It never gets better; you've been here long enough to know that." Severn nodded and blew her nose. "One day, we'll see the sun again, and these assholes will be the ones getting sodomized in their cells." She said it like she believed it. This was *Darling*. At least, that was the name they'd given her. Her real name was Amélie. She was strong, experienced, helpful, and kind.

The sodomy comment made Severn flinch. She never knew what a John would 'request.' She had her regulars, but new men made up the lion's share of her experiences. The outfit Dominus supplied was called *Sexy Pirate*. The cellophane crinkled in her hands. That could easily take her into rough sex territory, which included unspeakable acts. Another tear escaped, and Darling caught it with a tissue.

"It never gets easier either, Severn. If it does, it means you've given up. Means you've given in. Don't give them the satisfaction of losing your soul to this place." Severn's lips felt the light touch of a black lipstick being applied. "Just let them have your body. It's not forever."

But it seemed like forever to Severn. She'd been doing it for five years. She lived in a state of fear and humiliation, longing, and pain. Each session seemed to drag on as the John explored her body as though it were his own. Fingers, cocks, fists, and tools she had no name for had found their way inside of her; once, a man pulled a molar out of her mouth. The range of sick pleasures humanity had dreamed up was indeed the realm of the Devil. Severn always referred to her Sunday school lessons when she couldn't sleep. Those she still remembered. They were of small comfort.

"There, you look *beautiful*," Darling said in her native French accent, but Severn knew her looks were what put her here. To be called beautiful no longer gave her that sense of warmth and pride. The men who violated her called her beautiful too, but they did it hungrily like she was something to devour and shit out the following day. She was a pretty little girl with aspirations of her own once. Now, her only ambitions were to survive the tumultuous life of a prostitute and be reunited with her mother.

Standing on unsteady legs, Severn thanked Amélie for her kindness, slipped the ridiculous costume over her head and pulled up the fishnet stockings, slid into her pair of high heels, and walked down the hall to the Pink Room, where any number of atrocities would be committed against her young body. Still, she straightened up and wagged her hips as she'd been taught.

* * *

After her *'date,'* as they were called, Severn showered and scrubbed her body as forcefully as she could with what they had. In the shower, Amélie also stepped in to rinse; it was one of the few pleasures they enjoyed. Amélie looked especially pretty even as the makeup ran down her flawless face.

"How long?' Severn asked her. Amélie looked at her and smiled a sad smile. "Too long," she said back. Severn backed off the question and shook her head. "Sorry, I - I just wonder how long is enough.'

"A minute is enough, a *second*, but you know that." Darling's accent sounded abrasive as she spit the words out. Then her face became serene, and her voice soft. "There is no end to how long we'll be here, Severn. I'm twenty-four, I think. You're what? Nineteen?" Severn nodded and corrected her, "Eighteen."

"I came here fifteen years ago," Amélie said, "I was *nine.*" She rinsed the shampoo out of her hair and squeezed the end of her ponytail. "*Fucking* nine years old, but I'm a survivor. You will be, too. They can't keep this place a secret forever. One day, someone will come."

"Do you believe that?" Severn's expression betrayed the hope in her heart.

"If I didn't, I'd have tried harder to leave."

1984

Funerals. Jonah, 24

Jonah had overcome addiction more than once. From his first court-ordered action to attend a three-month rehabilitation clinic at seventeen to the two self-imposed rehab sessions, which lasted a month each, he knew he could bounce back. Therefore, he was able to talk himself into drinking binges somewhat regularly when the mood struck him.

At twenty-four, he'd have more reason than ever to fall back into that comfortable state of sloth. This is what he told himself. Still, there was substantial reasoning beyond simple selfishness this time. His mother was dead.

It happened while he was at college, trying again to make his parents proud by seeking higher education so he could lead a productive life. This was his second attempt. His father hadn't demanded much of him save rehab and common sense, but education was at the top of his list. A hard-working member of society, his father had died young one year earlier. Jonah hadn't found himself mourning his father as others might theirs. He was okay because he never really knew the man outside the pub. His mother had cried when she'd told him over the phone and cried at the funeral. Jonah was a pallbearer, tossed some dirt in the open grave, and never gave his father's passing another thought.

He received the call about his mother after completing his final exam. For all intents and purposes, he should graduate. The call came from an aunt he'd only ever met at his father's funeral, his mother's older sister. She lived a plane ride away but had been distant from his family in more ways than that. She'd had a falling out with Grandma Anne before Jonah had been born. The call was cold and sterile; like her, Jonah remembered.

When his aunt relayed the message, Jonah had dropped to his knees in the campus counselor's office. "I received a call from your city mortician," she began. "My sister's dead. Your mother is dead." Then, a pause followed while Jonah processed the information. "Did you hear me? Your mother is -"

"Yes..." Jonah whispered, his head spinning with the news. His stomach caught up, and he felt nauseous. "When?" He asked absently.

"Yesterday... apparently. She was found by an employee behind the bar at the pub. You can imagine how she died." Her tone was practiced and hollow—void of emotion. Jonah could guess how his mother went out. He'd always known how she would die. His addiction wasn't of his own design. It was a family inheritance. He couldn't control it any more than his mother or grandfather could. It was his family curse. "I suggest you go home and deal with the lawyers and have your mother buried in the family plot with mother and father. Why she insisted Luca end up there too is beyond me."

His whole family was gone. Buried in a single plot where he, too, would one day rest. "Are you coming?" He asked out of fear of managing all the details himself.

"I'll be staying at the same hotel I did for your father's funeral. I'll be there tomorrow at 8 am. I'll call you after breakfast." She was already thinking of breakfast. Jonah didn't feel he would ever eat again. His mother had alcoholism, but she was his rock, too. The void she would leave in his life would be immeasurable; no one to come home to... no one who cared.

He packed his gear and chartered a ticket with the Greyhound to take him to an empty house. He wanted a drink the entire way but refused to muddy this memory before the work was done. He owed her that much.

So, she drank herself to death. After his dad died from an apparent heart attack, his mom had really checked out. She couldn't run the pub and had hired an old friend to make a go of it. All she ever did was sit at the bar with the regulars, tipping a glass to her deceased ex-husband. Even by Jonah's standards, it was a grim existence, but the drinks were free.

He moved through the small house with intention, bypassing all the memories it threatened in favor of getting the work done. Jonah had called the morgue holding his mother's body and dealt with the details of a funeral, coffin, and all the rest. He spoke to the family's lawyer and had him come to the house to sign documents and offer condolences. Then, somewhat reluctantly, Jonah visited the pub where both parents had perished.

It was evening, and the place was closed. It was rarely closed before 2 am. It was a strange sight, feeding the surreal sensation Jonah had experienced all day. A sign on the door told customers that the Fox & Ferret would be closed indefinitely due to a family emergency. Jonah placed his key into the lock and let himself in, locking the door once inside. The smell was always the same: fried foods and beer. He turned on a single light over the bar and helped himself to a drink.

Next, as he stared into the veil of darkness encompassing the rest of the pub, his mother's face appeared as a vision, the version of her he knew best. She was young and beautiful. He would have been ten, still enamored over the golden fingers and fascinated over her pouty lips, which she used to kiss away his fears. A memory took hold, and Jonah shook his head to wish it - along with the heavy sensation in his chest, away. He was emotional enough over her death; he didn't need tender memories assaulting his senses. Still, the memory was relentless. Her voice was unwavering in the back of his head, telling him how much she loved and needed him. This invariably left Jonah feeling safe and focused. His mother needed him. His mother loved him. He was doing his job simply by existing. Simpler times, he thought. Purpose was so easy to come by. His mother would then lightly trace his small face with her fingertips, ending at the tip of his petite nose, and express what a handsome little man he was. Nothing ever felt as good as his mother's touch. Nothing could rival the security he felt at ten years old, lying in bed with his mother's full attention upon him. And now that was gone forever.

With a guttural sigh, he placed both hands on the bar, steeled himself against the memory, and eyed the fresh pint of a favorite lager. Without too much deliberation, Jonah snapped up the pint and lifted it in a *'cheer,'* "To you, Mom! You never did know when to quit." Realizing the irony of the moment, he pushed down the whole pint with a practiced hand—eighteen months of sobriety down the shitter.

The moment the alcohol slipped past his tongue; he knew it was going to be a late night. He poured another, added two, three, four shots of whiskey to the pint, and turned on the sound system. He rifled through several cassette tapes and landed on one of his mother's mixes. It was teeming with more memories. *When Dove's Cry,* by Prince. *I Can Dream About You,* by Dan Hartman. *Fuck. Off.* The more he drank, the more he wept over the loss of the only woman who'd ever loved him.

To date, he'd had two girlfriends. Neither had loved him and one, he was convinced, had barely liked him. But that was his Modus Operandi: Women who would entertain a man with clinical body odor and demonstrate a specific talent for sobriety. If they were drinkers, he would drink. That wouldn't work. Neither had lasted longer than six months. But this wasn't going to be about that. This was about his mother, the woman who was devastated by his twin's death and assumed an overprotective role to ensure Jonah survived. She was the mother whose coping mechanism was booze—the wife who'd lost her husband's interest to alcoholism. The mother who had begged her son not to follow in her footsteps yet couldn't lead by example, and the kind-hearted woman Jonah felt had gone too soon at just forty-four.

As the night drew on, Jonah became increasingly emotional. The alcohol wrenched free all of his hurt and years lost to his abuses rather than time spent with his mother. *I Want to Break Free,* by Queen, set off a murderous rage. Glasses were thrown across the pub, mirrors smashed, and tables turned over—an appropriate response to his loss.

This devastating event would go unnoticed by everyone. Still, he would further cement the idea that there was nothing for him here. He had no one. His whole family had disappeared. It had begun with Jack. Jack, who hadn't even existed to anyone but his mother, the twin whose memory he'd fought his whole young life to rise above. Jack, the boy whose shadow so completely corrupted his family - mother drinking him away while his father kept himself too busy to remember the loss. Jack, who turned their mother into an alcoholic, turned his father away from his family, and whose loss molded Jonah into the man he was. He cursed Jack's name and spit a line of tequila onto the plank, wooden floor as though spitting at the faceless brother he'd never known.

"Fuck you, Jack!" He'd spoken the phrase to himself more than once—Jack, who'd stolen his mother and father and his life without so much as uttering a word. Jonah wondered, as he had thousands of times before, how different his family life would have been had Jack survived birth. How different would his own life have been?

Why did you leave me like this, Mom? How could you leave me like this?

1986

Leaving on a Jet Plane

Severn had imagined herself escaping Dominus' hold more times than she could count. Everything about her life was utterly terrifying, save one small offering. There was a story that had gone around for years before Severn had been indoctrinated into this Hell. It told of a young girl who had found freedom after only a few months under Dominus' thumb.

Charlotte was her name - *her real name*, and it made it all the more real to see it engraved on the shared wall. Charlotte Simpson. The story went that she'd dug a hole in the wall of one of the private rooms, which led to another interior and then to the outside world. The information had been offered by Charlotte herself to one of the other girls servicing the pedophiles. Charlotte was thirteen at the time of the telling, the same age Severn had been when she'd disappeared from her life. Charlotte's story became a legend after she'd left for good. The girl who'd received the information died of asphyxiation days later. Still, she'd told enough of the others about Charlotte that the story became a legend and anyone who'd heard it had hoped to find the secret passage in one of the private rooms.

None had, and so the legend became all the more compelling. Of course, Severn remembered the game *'Broken Telephone'* and wondered whether the story had retained its original message. *Was the hole to freedom not in a private room? Was it in one of the other dilapidated rooms she'd seen within the labyrinth-like facility?* There were twenty-two private rooms. She'd only serviced Johns in a portion of them. A new generation of girls and boys would challenge one another to locate the hole once they'd heard the story and relay the location.

The trouble was the longer you were there, the less energy you had for the game. The more beatings you received and the more drugs you were fed, the less interest you had in much of anything. Maybe that's why Charlotte got out. She was in and out within two months, so the story goes. Not so long that she was utterly broken, and just long enough to perhaps dig that hole while a John slept off his vile euphoria, or while she waited for them to enter, or both. When not working, the children were sequestered in the common room.

It was a nice story, but if Charlotte had escaped, why hadn't she warned the police about the place? This piece of the story had always bothered Severn, like a sliver too deep to reach, seen, and felt but unattainable. It frustrated her. It was an unfinished fairy tale. Still, she kept the story alive by retelling it to the new kids. She offered them the same hope she'd once been given, that there was always a chance that the hole would reveal itself one day and they would find their way home.

After eleven years, Severn had given up on the secret hole but not on the hope of escape. To lose that would be to give up on everything. No, Charlotte was most certainly caught and killed and buried in some unmarked grave under the building's floor. Severn imagined the scene: concrete pulled up, a hole dug, and fresh concrete poured over her broken body.

The John Denver song, *Leaving on a Jet Plane*, would occasionally play over the sound system and put Severn into a kind of trance. She remembered the song from before her world was turned upside down and inside out. She imagined herself taking that flight, looking down at the city, waving at her mother. Mother enthusiastically waved back from their property in the affluent neighborhood. There was always a breeze in her hair as she imagined the scene. Sometimes, her father would join her mother at her side. If it was to be a fantasy, why not complete it?

To actually contemplate escape was something else altogether. Angry-looking men with rifles continuously surveyed the halls and small crevices within the facility, occasionally taking a girl for themselves when business was slow, and Dominus wasn't in. They were animals. Primal creatures without feelings save the hint of a reaction revealed in orgasm. To entertain escape, she'd have to be willing to kill or be killed. The thought had crossed her mind as the men's engorged penises recklessly thrust into her. In those brief moments, she could see herself slashing a throat and arming herself with his gun and shooting her way out. But where would she acquire a knife? Which way was out? That was another mystery. She wouldn't get far, nor did she know how to fire a gun. So, escape plans disappeared along with the hope of ever seeing her mother again or returning to a normal life.

Escape was a fantasy every bit as much as taking that flight and seeing her father again. Hopelessness was her reality. Still, she wouldn't place that hopelessness on the new kids. She would tell Charlotte's story and encourage hope in others. It's what was done for her. Each would discover the lie in their own time.

Severn sat in the common room with one of the new little boys stolen from his life to land in this place. He was of South American descent, spoke no English, and cried without end. His eyes were swollen from the tears. He'd come in the day before with a girl about his age, Severn guessed around nine. They didn't seem related, but they were from the same area: olive skin, dark black hair. She was holding up much better than him. Severn rocked the boy upon her crossed legs as a movie played on the T.V. above.

She desperately wanted to soothe the child and was grateful he was receptive to her attempts. Many were not. She whispered calming phrases into his small ear, often biblical quotes she could still recall from her Sunday classes. He mumbled the same thing repeatedly through halting breaths: *mama, mama, mama.* It was a devastating plea to the consciences of those ruthless fucks who could rob a mother of her child and commit them to this Hell. But Severn knew those capable of such atrocities were without conscience. Devils were wriggling and slithering inside those men - Godless animals whose dark eyes confirmed they acted without the benefit of a soul. Their cruelty knew no bounds, and they came in every color, shape, and size.

She brushed her fingers through the boy's hair, fearing for him and his future. He would be broken within the week and put to work on the eighth day. She wondered if it were more humane to smother him in the night when he lay exhausted from all the crying. There was no doubt, but then they'd go out and steal another child from another loving mother and ruin more lives in the act.

She hugged him tightly and kissed the nape of his neck. A film of dirt coated his body. His shuddering lessened after an hour, and Severn felt he would soon sleep. She rolled them both over onto their sides on her mattress, and she let him settle into a comfortable position with her, never fully letting him go. She continued to soothe him with her whispered hymns and passages until they both fell asleep. At the same time, Snow White played above them, the dwarfs whistling their way to work.

1988

Thirteen Years Gone

Severn had accepted her lot in life, was cast into a role no child should experience, and was sold repeatedly for the pleasures of wealthy men. Dark pleasures their wives wouldn't go for, escorts wouldn't put up with, and mistresses denied them. All their dark fantasies lived here, and if they were privileged enough, they knew how to get here.

Severn suffered the whims of pedophiles her first few years locked in captivity and sympathized with the new children brought in month after month. Televisions in the common room were mounted to the walls with bars in front of them. There were dozens of movies to choose from, and Severn had watched them multiple times- most of which catered to children. That such a place considered a child's sensitivities seemed almost beyond comprehension. Still, when you lived it, it made more sense than Severn wished it would.

She remembered being excited for her time away from the private rooms to lose herself in an onscreen fairy tale. Some frightened her, though; even with all her painful and confusing experiences, evil witches and cruel stepmothers terrified her.

At twenty-five, Severn was given to an older clientele who weren't there for the children. She was young enough, pretty enough, and experienced enough to offer the more seasoned men a guaranteed orgasm. Some still wanted her dressed up in a prom dress from circa whatever year they attended their high school prom, but most were just there to get their rocks off and get out.

She broke down as she stood in front of the discolored, full-length mirror in the common room, a faded yellow 1978 formal cross-strap with calf-length slip dress on. Dominus had told her that the man who brought the dress wanted to fantasize over his daughter's best friend, whom he'd pined for the last ten years. That was nothing new. Some of the outfits that were bought specifically to live out a John's fantasy remained in Severn's wardrobe. But this one stung deeper than most.

1978 would have been her graduation year from high school. Whenever something like this happened, she would recount the many milestones she'd missed. Her first date, first kiss – John's don't count. A boyfriend – Johns don't count, even the regulars; how could they? Football games in the open air. Losing her virginity to someone she loved. Falling in love. Driving a car. Her prom. Her wedding. A proper pregnancy. A child who wouldn't be ripped from her womb six months too soon but born, loved, and cared for.

Severn turned slightly to watch herself in the mirror, imagining the camera's flashing and a corsage slipped onto her wrist by her date. She'd done something similar when asked to dress as a bride once. She was interrupted by Dominus, who stood at the threshold of the common room.

"Done admiring yourself?" He spoke in a halting way, nothing flowery about it. He never used more words than he needed to convey his will. "How 'bout we let your John admire you?" He fixed his fedora and waved her to him, never considering how dressing up might have affected her psyche. *Don't Worry, be Happy* by Bobby McFerrin played over the sound system, and Dominus snapped his fingers as he led her out of the common room. He'd mentioned the song earlier that week, stating *'number one song of '88.'* The wretch was a music lover. This served Severn in understanding what year it was when he brought in brand new music. He was happy to answer a question like that.

He escorted Severn down the hallway, blacklight blurring her into the role of the best friend for a man who took his fantasy as far as he could without raping a *real* girl in the world. Good for him. Maybe Severn was helping the women of the world, working through men's dark desires to overpower women. As long as they did it here, she would be their sacrifice. Her body would save countless others. Her abuse would ensure other's freedoms. There was purpose in that.

1993

The Shrink and the Shooter

Jonah sat in a plush leather chair, waiting for Dr. Sturgis to appear from her office and invite him to join her. The waiting room was tranquil enough. Something gentle played at a low volume overhead. The place smelled of lavender. He only knew this because it's how he remembered his grandmother smelling and had since had the experience of a yoga retreat at a lavender farm.

"Jonah," the tall, slender Dr. Sturgis addressed him in her calming tone from the threshold of her office. "Would you join me?" Her approach was always easy. Like saucers in her pretty head, her eyes offered a sense of calm. Jonah knew he would be well cared for in her sanctum and looked forward to their hour together every two weeks.

This working relationship began with the realization that Jonah's company covered this sort of vanity counseling. Once he'd experienced it, though, he discovered it was much more than a reassuring pat on the back but rather a look inside himself, his past, and its effect on his present.

Jonah nodded at the doctor with a whisper of a smile as he pushed off the leather chair. Dr. Sturgis was dressed in her thatched pencil skirt, heels, and a blouse he'd never seen her in before. She was a well-put-together woman. He wondered what it must be like to be her. She turned to enter the room, and Jonah took a moment to notice the dark seam on the backs of her nylons. His gaze followed the seam until it disappeared under the skirt. Jonah shifted the growing bulge in his trousers before he sat down.

Positioned as doctor and patient in Sturgis' minimalist decorated office, Jonah worked to camouflage his excitement with a throw pillow strategically placed on his lap. He shifted a moment uncomfortably and willed his erection to go flaccid. It took longer than he'd have liked. The doctor had looked especially attractive - her dark hair pulled tight into a high ponytail. Her long neck included a bedazzled, fitted necklace, and her lips seemed unusually pouty. *How can someone have it all like Dr. Sturgis, and he so little?*

"Comfortable, Jonah?" The doctor asked as she reached for her pad of paper and a stylus with her right hand's delicate fingers adorned with three metallic rings. Jonah nodded and pressed down on the pillow, which had the opposite effect on his growing erection. His psychiatrist was his go-to image to undress and– in a consensual fantasy – engage in sexual acts when he felt randy.

"How have you been feeling over these last two weeks?" Now, she'd placed her reading glasses on, enhancing her beauty as she peered over them. The end of the stylus entered her mouth. Next, the rounded point of her pink tongue moved along the smooth metal. None of this happened in slow motion; in fact, every little move she made would likely go unnoticed by most, but in Jonah's mind, it was an orgy of sensual gestures. He looked forward to these sessions more than anything. The woman was a goddess. But she was also no-nonsense. A professional. She helped him realize things he hadn't considered. He respected her, just not enough not to imagine himself with her.

"I tried acupuncture the other day," Jonah told her, his attention more on the pillow than on her. He was blushing; he could feel the heat in his cheeks. "It was... different."

"How so? Was there a specific reason you tried acupuncture?" She liked to get right to the meat of it. This made for very effective sessions.

"I guess I just wanted to try something else," Jonah answered in his trademark, withdrawn tone. An itch attacked his temple, and he raised a hand to scratch it. The doctor waited for him to volunteer more. "You know I've been trying things, alternative things to fix myself."

"Yes," Dr. Sturgis replied, reviewing her notes, rhyming off his attempts, "Tapping, Reiki, yoga, meditation, past-life regression therapy, hypnosis, and now acupuncture." Jonah felt a little embarrassed having the list read back to him like that. "Self-discovery isn't anything to be ashamed of, Jonah. It's productive. It's akin to letting your child take dance, horseback riding, art classes, drama, and music so they are exposed to as many opportunities as possible in the hopes that one might stick. And since we're in the infancy of your treatments, I like that you're doing this. It shows dedication to yourself."

"I'm just not interested in pills." He explained. The discomfort under his pillow had lessened. She supported his journey to right himself in a drug-free way. It was progressive. He'd already suffered a tumultuous relationship with drugs in his teens and again in his early twenties. "Honestly, I don't know what the acupuncture did for me. I had a sore shoulder, and it seemed to fix that. The needles in my ears, though," he placed a finger in his left ear and felt around for the holes, "They're supposed to help with addiction. The cigarettes. But I've burned through a pack since then." He was disappointed. He was always disappointed when a new technique proved unhelpful with his smoking.

"We've discussed the cigarettes, Jonah. They make you feel closer to your mother. I don't necessarily want you going off them all together just yet. Not until we complete the workup of your relationship. If you can manage how many you smoke in a day, that's enough for right now." She'd leaned in closer to him in offering this reminder. Jonah looked up to meet her gaze and felt immediately calmer. Long lashes fell slowly, moistening her expressive eyes. She was it for him. Perfect. If she wanted him to keep smoking, he would. He'd do anything she asked.

"How's the self-talk?" She tested, leaning back and crossing her legs.

"*Self-talk?* I don't talk to myself." He replied, shaking his head earnestly. Did she think he was crazy?

"We *all* talk to ourselves, Jonah."

"Everyone's *crazy* then?" he shook his head at this.

"Well, that's a topic for another day," she said, the corners of her mouth turned up as though remembering a joke to reveal straight, white, immaculate teeth.

Undeterred, Jonah reaffirmed, "*Crazy* people talk to themselves."

"Crazy is a relative term. So, tell me, what do you say to yourself when you're alone?"

Jonah didn't need to think long on this. "Not very nice things, I guess." His expression dissolved into a frown.

"Why?"

"Because... I'm not happy with myself?" The doctor noticed he'd formed the statement like a question. "Is that something you want *me* to answer?"

"Uh - yes?" He said indecisively, his armpits dripping like a faucet in his undershirt. After trying every antiperspirant on the planet, he'd realized that none were up to the job of preventing or even containing his rare affliction with body odor. Dr. Sturgis was always so good not to react.

"No, Jonah. That's a question only *you* can answer. You ask the question and answer it. There are no unanswered questions in internal dialogue." This was a new concept for Jonah. Sure, he had whole conversations with himself at home, at work, walking down the street. It was as if every moment was filled with questions, and the answers were often the same.

"Okay, then, yes – I mean - I'm not happy."

"So, what do you tell yourself?"

"I don't know how to answer that."

"I'll give you a hypothetical, and you fill in the blanks." She nodded at Jonah with her intelligent eyes. He nodded back. "You're home alone. You consider going to a movie alone. How does your inner dialogue react to that?"

Jonah shifted on the couch. "I wouldn't go to a movie alone." He said quietly.

"Why not?"

"It's embarrassing. People would think I'm a loser."

"Are you a loser?" The doctor's question startled Jonah.

"That's a *nice* question," he replied, hurt and hugging the pillow.

"You ask it of yourself all the time, don't you?"

"Why do you say that?"

"Because you just expressed it to me." She wrote something down in her notebook.

Jonah's thin face wore a confused expression. "*I* didn't say I was a loser. I said **others** would think I was a loser." Saying the word **loser** over and over had begun to irritate him.

"Yes. But you thought that of yourself **before** giving others a chance to think it." She watched as Jonah's expression fell. "Because *you* said it at all," Dr. Sturgis continued, "tells me exactly what your inner dialogue is. It's self-deprecating. It keeps you at home. It keeps you from being someone and seeing yourself as someone who matters. It's a crisis of confidence. It says you don't feel you deserve to be loved and appreciated. You ask yourself if you could go to a movie alone and answer yourself in negative self-talk. What else do you tell yourself?"

Jonah felt found out. "I - I don't have a lot of good things to say to myself."

"Why? Would you be friends with that guy if he wasn't you?"

"No?" That made perfect sense.

"What's keeping you from telling yourself you're someone who could attend a movie alone?"

Jonah considered that briefly and felt despondent over his answer. "Me?"

"Right. *You*, Jonah. You have that power. Stop giving your power away to hypotheticals. I want you to do something for yourself tonight."

"Go to a movie?" Jonah wondered aloud.

"Face a fear. If going to the movies *alone* will accomplish that, I want you to do it. Use your visualization methods. Consider the work you've accomplished with cognitive behavioral therapies. Set a short-term goal and accomplish it. You'll feel better for it."

"Okay," Jonah felt empowerment creep in.

"Good. *Own it*, Jonah." Sturgis's expression adopted the thoughtful gaze Jonah had become accustomed to when leading up to a sobering question. "Tell me, do you experience thoughts of self-harm? Suicide?"
"S*ure*, don't we all?"
"No." Her head shook.
Sturgis answered so quickly Jonah felt embarrassed for having admitted it without a pause. "Hmm." He considered this a moment, then pushed himself back into the couch, wanting to disappear in its plush leather cushions. "Okay, so, it's not a *normal* thing like self-talk?"
"It's not. It's more a warning sign."
"Of things to come?"
"Have you ever self-harmed - physically?"
The question seemed tailored to his past experiences. "With drugs, I guess. Sure. I mean, that's a *form* of hurting myself, right? It's not like I'm *cutting*, or banging my head against a wall, or burning myself with cigarettes."
"Good. *Yes*, drug use is a form of self-harm. Drug abuse can destroy you from the inside out, but when *you* used, were you doing it out of compassion or maliciously?"
"Can someone abuse drugs compassionately?" Jonah couldn't contain a sardonic smile.
"If they feel they're improving their quality of life by quieting their self-talk, then *yes*."

"Okay, that sounds like me. It was like a vacation away from being me, from living in my shoes."

"Okay, so you're not one to outwardly hurt yourself."

"I don't think so. Drugs were more of a coping mechanism. Like you said, Compassionate." He reflected on his drinking habit and decided that, too, was done with empathy.

"So suicidal thoughts exist, but you've never attempted to take your life? Be honest."

"Right, they come and go. Part and parcel with the self-talk. Sometimes, it wonders why I bother. Offering helpful examples on how I could end it." He senses a lump forming in his throat. This was painful to recount. It seemed pathetic. He sniffled and took a facial tissue from the side table. He blew his nose and pocketed the tissue. "I, uh, haven't followed through on any of the *suggestions.*"

"Good, that's very good, Jonah."

* * *

That evening, Jonah sat at the end of his double bed in his two-bedroom apartment and considered Dr. Sturgis' challenge. *Or was it an order?* Regardless, it was solidly outside his comfort zone, but he knew that was the point. He'd invite his roommate but thought better of it. Jonah sighed and inhaled deeply, using the technique his meditation teacher had taught him: slowly in through the nose, out through the mouth. But he had no patience for it. It's not as though he was filled with anxiety over being in a public place. It's the reaction he expects from others when their opinions intrude upon his personal space. "Other people's opinions of you are none of your business," he said to himself, another coping mechanism he didn't buy into.

"I'm doing it." He said aloud, standing as straight as his years of slouching would allow. "For Dr. Sturgis." *Please don't do it for her. Do it for yourself or don't do it at all,* his inner voice told him. Then his mother's voice pipped in; *it's a pointless exercise that will make you uncomfortable. Why do you want that?*

"Shut up!" He ordered his ego through clenched teeth. He hadn't considered it a separate entity until the doctor had mentioned the self-talk. It made sense. Still, egos are in place to protect you, aren't they? Maybe listening to it now isn't a bad idea. "Goddamn it, get out of my head!" He commanded, threw his jacket on, and marched out the door before he could persuade himself to stay in.

The public transit in his small city ran every fifteen minutes, not a block from his residence. There, he boarded the bus. He'd never gotten his driver's license.

Too dangerous, he'd decided. His mother's voice telling him: *Don't even think about it.* So, his world continued to get smaller. At the theatre, he sighed heavily, watching the families and couples moving through the ticket line. He felt slightly nauseous. *How will they see me?* He knew the answer: *as a loser.* Facing his fear of their judging eyes, he pushed through the exercise, got a ticket to a movie he was waiting to come out on VHS, picked up popcorn and a drink, and found a seat. It was a twenty-seven-dollar investment in his mental health, he explained. The chair was comfortable. It had been years since he'd been to a movie. As the lights went down, someone started shouting - was it a name they were shouting? *Was it his?*

Bang, bang, bang, the sound was deafening. Jonah squeezed his drink; the soda spilled onto his lap at the sudden, alarming noise. *Was this part of the movie?* It hadn't even begun. The lights came back on, and the theatre cleared out like it was on fire. Jonah remained in his seat so as not to be trampled by the startled mob. Someone stepped over his head and fell into the row before him. It was chaos! Confusion, shouting, and bodies flailing around him sent his adrenaline soaring and his fight-or-flight response to full effect. That's when he saw it. Two men bent over in their seats in the front row. Above them stood a manic-looking figure wielding a pistol at the screaming crowd who were desperately trying to evade the gunman. When the shooter had let them clear out, he shouted expletives at the two seemingly dead men and then turned his attention to Jonah. Jonah swallowed hard; his hand had gripped his popcorn so tightly his fingers had pierced the bag. His drink was all over his lap. He was embarrassed to stand but frozen in place. The dark face of the shooter grimaced at Jonah. His face was long and thin - his eyes bulging. This is it, he thought. *Go ahead. Point that at me. Finish me. I don't really exist.*

The shooter seemed to read his mind and raised the pistol. Jonah smiled a nervous smile, still fixed in his seat. His heart raced as never before. Heat enveloped his neck and face in anticipation of the shot to come. A film of cold sweat enveloped him. He was no stranger to sweat, but for every pour to open at once. Was it some bizarre defense mechanism? As if a thin layer of sweat could deflect a bullet? Jonah was rigid with fear. Was there something more profound than fear? He'd been afraid before, but this was something different. This emotion touched every molecule. Was he having an out-of-body experience? This was it, the climax of his story. Murdered in a movie theatre on the very night he stepped outside his comfort zone. Somehow fitting, he thought. Then the man lowered the gun, called Jonah a *little bitch*, and left the theatre through the emergency doors.

Why didn't he fire his gun? What mental fallout would follow this event? Should he leave the theatre as everyone else had? If he doesn't, will he be considered for the two men's shooting deaths eleven rows removed from him? Jonah looked down at his pants. It will appear as though he'd pissed himself in fear. Maybe he had, and that scent was now mixing with his cola. Something smelled off. *Was it the gunpowder? Did bullets employ gunpowder anymore?* One of the men in the front row coughed a wet cough. This startled Jonah into action. He wanted to drop his popcorn bag, but his hands wouldn't relax. He was standing. The cola or whatever dripped down his inner thigh.

He didn't know First Aid. What good would he be in this situation? Where are the police or the theatre rent-a-cops? There was more coughing from the victim, and Jonah moved tentatively down the deep steps on shaky legs, popcorn trailing.

"Help," a voice said in a quiet gurgle from the unmoving man. He was still slumped over. "I've been shot," as if there were any question of it. Jonah nearly laughed at that despite himself. The stress was beginning to play on his mind.

"W-where were you shot?" Jonah squeaked out in a whisper, surprising himself.

"At... the movies." The man said plainly but with a sense of urgency. Again, Jonah had to stifle a laugh. *Did he really say that? He must be in shock. That happened to people. He'd read about it.* He bit down on his lips. He stood before the man with both hands pressed against his stomach. Blood oozed through his fingers. It was a dizzying sight. A quick look to the dying man's right and Jonah could see inside the other victim's head. It was more than just blood. The exit wound was massive. The man's head must have fallen forward after the blast. Impossible to think anyone seated behind him would have escaped the organic shrapnel. *What would skull fragments do to a person?* Brain slipped out of its casing and slithered down his shoulders. Though Jonah had never imagined himself in this position, staring at a fresh corpse, the image was as captivating as it was horrifying. He felt bile rise in his throat and proceeded to throw up at the feet of the deceased and dying.

"Step aside!" called a voice from a commanding presence behind Jonah. Jonah's eyes were filled with tears as he emptied his stomach onto the theatre floor. He was weakened from the episode and staggered to his left, grabbing a chair back to steady himself. Paramedics had arrived with a complement of police officers, one of whom took Jonah by the arms and threw him roughly to the ground.

"On your knees!" The man shouted, his face right up against Jonah's ear, twisting an arm behind his back. The smell of the officer's dinner didn't play well with his nausea.

"We have eyes on a suspect, Danny," another officer said. "It's not this one." Jonah hoped she was talking about him. "Let him up." She demanded.

Next, Jonah was pulled to his feet, facing a stern-looking woman. He wiped the vomit from his chin with the sleeve of his shirt. She studied his expression and softened her approach.

"Why did you stay behind?"

Jonah just shook his head slowly. Words were not forthcoming. "I - I couldn't," he tried, eyes wide and watering, throat burning, and mouth agape. Paramedics pronounced both men deceased.

"It's okay," the officer reassured him with a hand on his shoulder. "Did you get a look at the shooter?" Jonah nodded. "Good. We're going to need you to help us identify him." Jonah nodded again. He longed to return home, to bury his head under cool sheets and shut out the cruel world.

1992

Seventeen Years

Within a week of landing in this place, she was broken in by Dominus, who had stolen more than just her innocence. She felt hollow after that. Empty. She remembered leaving her body during the violent act. The indifference Dominus had shown in deflowering her was truly criminal. She'd struggled against his advances at first, sealed into a dimly lit room with only a high metal table, something you'd find at a Vet's. Dominus pacified her with a disabling punch to her sternum, and she reeled over in shock and pain, having never before been struck. He kept her bent over them and robbed her viciously of her virginity. He'd taken everything from her that day and was told in no uncertain terms that she would let other men do the same.

She was a child, terrified when she awoke to this place. It smelled of smoke and sick. Girls were allowed only one meal daily to keep them thin and weak. No fight meant no issues with the *Johns*; some liked to hit. More than one of the younger girls had died within a few weeks of being there. Rumor, a twelve-year-old from Singapore with the sweetest eyes, Severn remembered, had her pretty little face collapsed during a dominate/submissive rage session. As if a child of ten could have been anything but submissive to a 200 lb man.

Severn, who'd been renamed to keep her identity ambiguous, had wept openly when the first twenty or thirty Johns occupied her young body with violent thrusts - spittle flying out of their frothing mouths. She remembered thinking them possessed. She feared for her life each time. Some liked to tie her up. Some liked to beat her as if she had any strength to deny them their wicked addiction to children. Soon, the fear of death disappeared. *Why fear death when life is so painful?*

1992, she'd guessed, and she was a thirty-year-old woman. It had been some years since Severn was there for the pedophiles' pleasure. New girls and boys were brought in from all over the world. The older girls would comfort them in the common sleeping area. They would do each other's hair and makeup to pass the time. The black light in the rooms made them look even younger than they were. Severn felt helpless to save them, so she consoled them as best she could. But there really was no consolation over the life they'd been forced into. Perpetual night, the rattle of ducts overhead, an endless run of music to occupy their attention, their bodies and minds no longer their own. It would always feel surreal. It would always feel like a nightmare where the monsters were genuine.

Drugs were another thing they'd done to her. Severn was a full-blown addict and itched for her morphine shot daily. It usually came after a meal. What time that was, she could only guess. The itch, however, was like clockwork. It also started her workday. She was a sex worker, like it or not, and it **was** work. The only satisfaction she gained in 24 hours was from the morphine, sleep, and time alone. The rest was brutal and soul-crushing. Though her body numbed to the activities, her heart still bore the full weight of what had happened to her - what was still happening to her.

She wore expensive-looking lingerie under torn track pants with no top and sandals worn through the heels. The pants came off when she went to work. A camping mat and sleeping bag were her only possessions. Cigarettes were available as a reward, along with alcohol. She managed to steer clear of the alcohol.

Thirty years old and a sex worker since the age of thirteen - it's beyond tragic. Even while in a morphine-induced euphoria, reality still slipped in, like the rats who navigated the toilets from the sewer to terrorize them daily. Severn rarely cried anymore unless she experienced an especially painful *John*; they liked it when she cried.

Severn lay down to sleep to the usual sounds of muted whimpering and self-exploration by the newer arrivals. She had seniority. She was the oldest and so claimed the corner of the room. Here, where the old plaster gave way to broken lath and cement bricks at the base of what she imagined to be an outside wall, she ran her fingers over the etchings. Each girl and boy who had come through had chiseled their name here. It was non-negotiable. Severn and those who came before her insisted on it. It was a record of their having lived. If ever they were to escape, Severn thought it might ease the minds of those who'd lost someone to this place. At the very least, it was their shared headstone.

Severn traced out Darling's real name amongst the etchings. Darling had been murdered two years earlier for cutting her last John from the taint to the navel. He'd bleed out loudly. Severn remembered the night as the John's cries of agony reached the common room. Darling was never seen or heard from again. Severn missed her friend. All they had was each other.

With three tattoos gracing her thighs and lower back at Dominus's request, Severn certainly looked the part. Died black hair cut short against her pale flesh, piercings in her nose and eyebrows, navel, and seven on each ear also lent to her new goth look. The genre had gained interest from the younger Johns, most of whom were professionals. Severn's Johns sometimes lay with her after, as if they were doing her a favor, and revealed snippets of their lives. They led the exciting lives of the wealthy elite who could come and go at their pleasure. Admittedly, she enjoyed hearing about the world beyond her prison. She even became animated at times when asking about advancements in technology.

Once, she asked a John to visit her mother's house and leave a note explaining that she was alive. This got back to Dominus, and she was branded for it. Not another tattoo but branded with a hot iron. It took weeks for it to stop hurting. In Dominus's defense, she was given the option of being branded or losing a nipple. She scolded herself for thinking any humanity resided in those who paid for the sexual pleasure of children. *Why would someone committing an atrocity like that do anything that might later implicate him?* She thought she could appeal to his morality, where none existed. Her fault was in her naivety.

Severn often found herself reliving moments from her youth. Her father came to mind mainly because her memories after that had more to do with her mother's addiction than anything else. But if she could travel back to the night when she was abducted and never leave the house, whatever life threw at her would have been like an endless trip to a favorite theme park compared to where she'd ended up. Severn quickly became embittered toward her lot in life after her fear and sadness subsided. Hope had died, and anger had kept her alive, but complacency dulled her senses, and routine became her undoing. Escape was never an option. In fact, she wondered what Dominus might do to her if she attempted it. It would probably be the end for her. Might that be a better alternative to this? She'd considered it, but there was no guarantee she would be murdered. They may blind her or cut her tongue out. They were a sadistic bunch. Though they'd tried to brainwash her, it never took. She still hated every one of them, even through the haze of euphoria when on her morphine.

Dominus did have a soft side, though, offering the girls a choice of how they wanted to be punished, putting the onus on them, but he was the only one. The others, the guards, forced themselves on all the girls and some of the boys whenever it pleased them. They were careful not to spoil the merchandise but weren't gentle about it. Not surprisingly, they weren't hiring conscientious people. Severn and the others were just cattle to them.

1993

Tattoos

Jonah would get a tattoo to commemorate the shooting, he decided. He wondered what and whether he should see Dr. Sturgis soon rather than wait the two weeks for his scheduled appointment. Would she apologize for pushing him in a direction that made him uncomfortable? Would she hug him in a sterile doctor/patient way when she realized what had transpired, or would she feel so responsible over his recent trauma she'd throw herself at him? *It could happen.* Either way, that scenario went into the spank bank.

After the ordeal at the police station, which included a police sketch artist, a reference library of hundreds of criminal mugshots, a positive ID on the shooter, and a terrible cup of coffee, Jonah was beyond ready for bed. A cruiser dropped him at his home a few minutes before midnight. The ascent to his third-floor apartment felt closer to climbing thirty flights before he arrived at his door. Inside, he brushed his teeth and dressed for bed.

Did that really happen? Of course, it did. As he lay in bed, Jonah stared up at the ceiling. There, a watermark stared back down at him. He often thought it looked like the classic portrait of white Jesus and should he take a picture, cut the drywall out, and auction it online for thousands. *Nonsense.* What really just happened? He was an eyewitness to a double homicide. Two men blatantly shot to death in a movie theatre. *Would he next be diagnosed with PTSD from this experience?* Sturgis wouldn't believe he'd been there for that. Her image materialized in his mind's eye, all five foot, five inches of her slight frame, and he reached into his boxers to fully appreciate the vision.

Not long after, he fell into a deep, fuzzy sleep, but the urgent need to pee at 3:33 am brought on a lengthy wakeful spell. He anxiously replayed the scene at the movies in his mind. The man whimpering 'help' with his head still resting on his chest. Jonah realized he'd never actually seen either man's face. He couldn't focus. He hadn't bothered to kneel and look at them. He was definitely in shock. *Why did he stay? Why did he approach the scene? Why, why, why?* The memories kept coming. He felt nauseous again, sat up in his bed, and forced a belch. Better. He wouldn't sleep again. He knew that. At 5 am, he showered, 2 hours ahead of his usual time. The police had told him to expect a call to attend a line-up when they apprehended the shooter. He wasn't looking forward to that. He had become quite distressed over the fact that the shooter had seen him. *What connections might he have in the criminal underworld? Could he find Jonah and end him before he was given a chance to identify the tall, thin, hat-touting black man roughly forty-five years of age? Would it matter?*

"Shut up," he told himself, over-filling his palm with shampoo. *Who would it matter to?* It was a fair question, but he didn't feel like giving himself the third degree. *You'll never do it yourself, so why not this guy?* "Fuck off!" he shouted at the voice in his head. This wouldn't be his ego. An ego protects you. It protected him from the deaths of both parents. It protected him from the pain and loneliness he felt thereafter. It assumed his mother's voice long before she'd died. This was something else that had always been there too, as long as he could remember - the negative 'self-talk' as the doctor put it. Never had it said anything remotely positive. His ego wasn't exactly optimistic either, but it seemed to have his best interests in mind. Neither voice built him up; one told him to be careful, while the other told him he wasn't worth the effort of trying.

Remarkably, Jonah had survived his parents' loss, put himself through school, and come out the other end with a job. The 'remarkably' remark was the negative self-talk. It had always encouraged defeat. *Why? Why would anyone's psyche include such a discouraging voice?* His mother's voice was one thing; he didn't think he could ever shake it, and a part of him didn't want to. This other voice, though, served no purpose but to discourage.

There are pills for that, he knew, but after all the unconventional drug use of his twenties to quiet the voice, he was frightened of pills. He had an addictive personality. He was an alcoholic. A functioning alcoholic, they called it. Dr. Sturgis didn't know this yet. He hadn't shared this information with her and never showed up to her office under the influence. Just thinking about it made him crave a drink. Not surprisingly, vodka was his go-to with an orange juice in the morning that got him through to lunch, where he'd pair six ounces with a diet cola. The following hour and a small sandwich with a bag of chips let him ease back into the workday. Not to say he hadn't missed days because of his addictions – he had. He'd missed an entire week once yet convinced his boss he'd booked it for vacation time. That was a bender he barely remembered. Since those early days, he'd been able to manage his intake better during weekdays.

At the office where he'd worked for four years, he stashed the worn, leather shoulder bag containing his lunch and a new bottle of vodka under his desk. No one suspected anything. He'd made a point to stay out of the lunchroom and away from the water cooler. He was the office loner, and that's the only way he felt he could actually do his job. He didn't attend Christmas parties or birthday cake cuttings. He was rarely invited out for a drink by his co-workers and discouraged their advances as best he could. He wasn't interested in taking the chance of making a friend. That was his mother. He would disappoint them. That was his self-talk. They both worked against him, but he was accustomed to it. Besides, with the impossible feat of disguising his unfortunate body odor, he felt it best to avoid everyone.

Jackson & Weiss was the firm he worked for since graduating from community college. He'd gotten a late start on account of the rehab attempts. Jackson & Weiss was a collections agency that exclusively collected debts for businesses. They occasionally bought delinquent debts for medical loans but mainly focused on commercial debt. Jonah's role· kept him busy with hardship settlements where the lawyers had decided a business couldn't repay. It was neither dull nor rewarding; it simply was, like the rest of his life.

Jonah picked up the phone and called Dr. Sturgis's office. No openings. "Can you tell her something for me?" He asked the receptionist. "Tell her I was at the theatre last night, the one with the shooting."

"You're kidding!" The perky young woman replied. "I caught that on the news last night. What was it? Two men gunned down?"

"Yes," Jonah wasn't ready to discuss the details, certainly not with Kim, the receptionist, but he wanted to instill the urgency he felt in her. "I was actually in the theatre as it happened."

"Wow, okay, I understand why you're calling for an earlier appointment. I'll check with the Doctor and let you know. I'm sure she will want to see you before two weeks."

"Thank you, that's all I'm... I'd like to see her as soon as possible." He freed his fingers, anxiously wrapped in the landline's cord, and left it at that.

Jonah called his local tattoo parlor and arranged a time to see them next. What design would a shooting envision? *A gun. A corpse. A near miss after the pistol was pointed at him. Spilled cola? That was personal.* Maybe he should add to the increasing vocabulary on his left forearm. What word would describe something like that? He typed near miss into this thesaurus, and 'lucky escape' caught his eye. Wasn't anything lucky about it. If the man had decided to end a third life that night, he could have. More a decision on the shooter's part than anything. What's that called? Serendipity? Destiny. Fate. Fortune. *Do you really count yourself fortunate to be sitting at this desk again, living this life?* Jonah shook off the intrusion and tried to focus on the task at hand. Perhaps *chance* is a better word. A chance encounter where fate and destiny can mean good or bad, chance is just that.

Later that evening and having consumed 18 fluid ounces of vodka for the day, he stepped into Squid Ink, his local, to get his latest tattoo. The tattoo artist, Sid, who he considered a friend, was heavily pierced and would be hard-pressed to find a square inch of flesh on his body left to ink save his face, which Jonah felt he ought to leave alone. When his head was shaved bald, more tattoos appeared. They say it's addictive; get one, you'll get another, and another. That proved true for Jonah. He had twelve already, but he had an addictive personality.

"You ever gonna tell me what all these words mean?" Sid asked as he prepped the arm with alcohol wipes. "You slowly forming a sentence?" He laughed at himself. Jonah smiled up at Sid's dark eyes. He liked Sid because he imagined the man to be misunderstood. That, and he never once mentioned Jonah's unpleasant scent, and he sweat a lot during the process.

"They wouldn't mean anything to anyone else," Jonah began in a whisper. "Each represents an event."

"*Chance*, I like it," Sid said of Jonah's latest tattoo. "You a gambler?"

"Not a gambler." *Not in this lifetime!*

"Adrenaline junkie then? You jump'n outta planes and shit? Takin chances."

Jonah smiled and jerked backward in a mock laugh. "No, no, that would not end well for me." *Or would it?*

"You're not tell'n." Sid offered a toothy grin as he placed the vibrating needle against Jonah's soft flesh. "I get it, John." He doesn't even know his name. Jonah didn't care.

"Chance can happen to anyone at any time."

Sid whistled. "You sound like a poet." The artist's expression transformed as the gun buzzed to life. "I like the font you picked for this one, John. You got an eye for this."

Jonah tried to relax and leaned his head back on the repurposed dentist chair. The needle didn't cut so much as burn. That always surprised him.

2020

December. Darnell

Seated at his modest desk in a brownstone located less than five city blocks from where he grew up, Darnell sits up a little straighter as he reads the email in front of him. His charities had made him a famous voice for the subjugated and abused within his city's borders, and this email confirmed that sentiment.

He was asked to speak at an upcoming event to share his experience growing up in an abusive home. It was an honor to impart his trials to others and offer them solutions to their own hurdles. His business was built on the idea that anyone could be gifted a second chance at life, regardless the environment of their upbringing. He used himself as an example of that time and again, always well received for being so translucent.

A second email set his jaw to flex as memories of his young life intruded upon his present. An act of kindness that set up the rest of his life in service to others was laid bare before him. A woman he had once helped, along with many others, has contacted him. The name *Severn* alone has his heart skip a beat. It is not a common name and one he has never forgotten after first hearing it. Tears teeter on his lower eyelids as the name commands. When he'd learned of her harrowing experience, he couldn't turn a blind eye to her need. It had been years for the many who had been enslaved in this very city. Twenty-seven years later, one of the victims is contacting him - an extraordinary victim.

Dear Mr. Darnell Lincoln,

It has been many years since you gave me a chance to live my best life through your generous monetary donation and services arranged through private counselors. I never had the opportunity to express my gratitude as I was experiencing difficulties remembering those lost years. My mother had kept me blind to the trauma, and only recently realized what a profound effect you had on my life from that moment forward.

I'd love to meet you and explain what I've discovered and hoped you might reply to this email with an appropriate time and place.

Sincerely,

Severn

Darnell leans back into his comfortable chair with a hand stroking his strong chin and then covering his mouth. The dark fingers of his free hand rest against the stark white finish of his desk. The cool, smooth texture slides under his palm. This is the one who'd forgotten, he remembered, his heart now racing. She'd completely blocked the experience. Darnell was all of seventeen when it had happened. The local news covered the story for weeks. It had gone national soon after. It fed his purpose and made him the man he is today. Darnell wrote Severn back immediately.

Dear Severn,

I'm thrilled to hear from you and equally thrilled to learn you have accepted your past. I will certainly make myself available to meet with you.

I want to suggest tomorrow, at 3 pm, at my office if that works for you. My address is in my signature below.

Thank you for reaching out.

Darnell

A smile grows across his handsome face, the white of his teeth a charming contrast to the color of his skin. He scratches at the tight curls covering his scalp, caught in the memories leading up to the event, which changed everything for him. The event that empowered him to help thousands of others realize a better life. He would approach her as he had the others, full disclosure. It's the only way he felt he could move forward with them. He was connected to the event that ruined Severn's young life.

Severn replied affirmatively to his suggested time. Tomorrow he would meet a recipient of his generosity all those years ago - and hopefully, make a new friend.

1993

Inner City

Life had never been more challenging for Darnell. Not only was he one of the underprivileged black kids in an impoverished part of the city, but he'd also lost his mother to a fatal shooting a year earlier, had a father who barely spoke to him, and had recently been expelled from school. He wasn't a good kid. His father had told him that. He'd been telling him that long before he'd turned sixteen. The two of them lived in a busted up old turn of the century house in the middle of shit town. The neighbor's homes weren't any better—no pride of ownership in this neck of the woods. Survival was enough. That the rain didn't fall on their heads as they slept was a victory. That they had a working television and cable placed Darnell's family head and shoulders above most. Occasionally Darnell's father would have friends over to watch the basketball. His dad's temper had gone unchecked after his mom died. He'd always been verbally violent toward Darnell, that much was known to everyone, but it had evolved into physical violence after his mother's death. Still, his father brought home wads of cash almost daily. He did something through the night to earn all that cash. What, though, Darnell had never asked.

"You been to school today?" His father asked as he woke for dinner. "School might make a man of you yet."

Darnell hesitated. His father hadn't made it past grade eight, so how pissed could he get over this? "Been expelled," Darnell said, handing over a sheet of paper. His father ignored the paper, pulled a frozen dinner out of the freezer, and placed it in the microwave.

"Expelled," the tall, thin man repeated, rubbing sleep from his large eyes, his back to Darnell. "That means you're going back next week?"

"Not *suspended*, dad. *Expelled.* I'm done for the year." Darnell's shoulders were slouched, and his face filled with hot regret for mentioning this. At sixteen, he wasn't a small kid. He was not as tall as his father but slightly thicker. He'd well-rounded and muscled shoulders and a strong back. Maybe he would get a job in construction? *Insane in the Brain* by Cypress Hill was caught up in Darnell's head after listening to it for the first time the day before. He enjoyed its aggressive, yet playful sound, and couldn't shake it.

In the dated and dilapidated kitchen, the microwave left its place on the laminated countertop. It hurtled toward Darnell in a shock of violence. It crashed into his chest, knocking the wind from his lungs. He was sure several ribs had broken, perhaps even his sternum. His father followed closely behind, swinging haymakers at his breathless son. He shouted and slammed fists at Darnell's surprised and terrified expression. Pain screamed from each successful fist that landed on his face, kidneys, stomach, and neck. Darnell's arms flew limply in an attempt to defend against the unannounced assault.

The beating only ceased when his father grew tired. Darnell lay broken, turtled on the kitchen floor. This wasn't the first time he'd received a beating like this. He'd only just recovered from two black eyes his father had given him. The fight he'd started at school, which led to his expulsion, left his knuckles bruised but his face intact. He knew he bullied kids. It was a pattern, right? *Do unto others that which is done to you.*

Darnell could taste blood.

His father leaned against the square kitchen table, breathing heavily. It was hard work laying down a beating like he had. Sweat dripped from his creased, high forehead. The fridge opened next, and Darnell heard the clinking of bottles. His old man would drown his thirst with beer. Then he'd get even more agitated. Darnell knew he had to get up and get himself to the hospital. Everything ached.

His father studied him as he struggled to stand. "Guess it's up to me to make a man of you then." He growled at his son. A fist full of bills came out of his front pocket, and he handed Darnell a few. "Go get some more beers and a carton of Lucky's." Darnell reluctantly removed a protective hand from his ribs to take the offering.

"Don't be late." His father called after him. Their eyes never met.

Darnell walked to the hospital, where the receptionists knew him. He dropped the money on the counter and asked if he could see someone. He looked like he'd been hit by a car, so that's what he told them. As he waited for a doctor or nurse to see him, he evaluated his life.

He missed his mother terribly. His father hadn't been good to her either but never had Darnell seen him lay a hand on her. She was the queen bee. Darnell missed how she would defend him against his father's cruel streak. He missed everything about her. He would have had a chance if the shooter's bullet had found his father rather than his mother that fateful night. His father's negative energy was all-encompassing. It drove Darnell to be the bully he was at school. The thing is, he enjoyed school for all it offered. But, once his mother had died and all he was left with was a father who hated everything, Darnell included, life wasn't about anything anymore. There was no light to come home to. No one to impress. It was a hollow existence, and if the rage was all he could act on, then he would play it out on his peers.

After being seen and sent home with pain meds - which he sold on the corner to replace the money he'd spent on the doctors - Darnell picked up his father's beer and cigarettes. He handed them off to the asshole who was sunken into his reclaimed La-Z-Boy, watching a daytime opera on his T.V. Pausing a moment to analyze his father, he ruminated how he'd been little more than a sperm donor to Darnell. *Nothing fatherly about him.* Lying down in his bed was a chore. They'd confirmed one cracked rib and wrapped his torso at the hospital, cleaned his cuts, and asked if he wanted to speak to a counselor. He declined again. What good would it do him?

In the early morning, Darnell got up to piss, and as he opened his door, he found his father kneeling in the small hallway pulling up the floorboards. The drunkard hadn't heard him and had his back to Darnell. *What was he doing?* Then it hit him; this is what he did with his cash. His heart raced, and excitement gripped him. He wondered how much money might be hidden away under the floor. He slowly slipped back into his room, turning the doorknob, careful not to make a sound.

Money could free him of his nightmare. But he feared his father and his connections. They were all bad to the bone. They would find him wherever he went. *But wasn't it worth a shot?* That depended on how much money we were talking about.

1993

The Culling

When Severn turned thirty-one, she wondered if she'd die like Jesus died for her sins. He was crucified in his early thirties, she remembered. She wondered if he'd died for Dominus's sins, too. *What about the others who worked in this building? Did he include them in his sacrifice? And the Johns, enabling people like Dominus, without whom sex trafficking wouldn't be an industry – were they forgiven? If so, then nothing was sacred. Nothing was off-limits, not children, torture, sodomy, rape, or murder.* She'd seen it all – experienced it all. Could God truly forgive all of that?

She struggled to understand why they kept her. She'd become more an assistant to the aging Dominus than a sex worker once she'd turned thirty, availing herself at his pleasure and given charge over all new recruits. She likened herself to the House Mother.

"Make them feel special." He'd tell her in his trademark whisper. His tongue would run over his lips to soften them after every sentence, darting here and there like a lizard's. "Make them understand it's in their best interest to cooperate." Dominus's dark skin looked weathered, as if he were the one servicing strangers daily. Severn never questioned him on anything. His comically large eyes went days without blinking; she was sure of it. His teeth were adorned in gold - what he called a grill when speaking to the guards. He wore a fedora and a neatly ironed white t-shirt almost exclusively. He sported slim-fitting jeans and, maybe, snakeskin shoes. They were some kind of reptile. His demeanor was slithery, like a snake, and his aura frighteningly cruel. The short, thinning afro upon his spotted head resembled a black cloud he was meant to suffer the rest of his miserable life. He was quick to punish disobedience and enjoyed using his belt on the children to make his point.

Severn had thirty-two people to convince they were in a better place, give or take two or three. If some didn't kill themselves after the first week, they could easily be killed in a session. Some died of untreated STDs. Why bring in medicine? It was cheaper to pick up another kid. They lost about eight to ten people a year. When Severn reflected on her time, the math averaged nearly two hundred – two hundred missing children. Two hundred gone forever to this violent dungeon. She considered them the lucky ones, though. They'd spent a short time in Hell before ascending into Heaven. But suicide was a sin in itself, so Severn hadn't truly considered it. Once, she begged a John to choke her out. To make sure he didn't let go until she was gone. He left in a huff, unable to finish. She had been beaten severely for the request when it had reached Dominus.

The years in Sunday school and her confirmation at thirteen offered her some sense of peace in her damp, dark world. Nothing is forever but your soul. This life would end, and she would be granted a place at God's side and experience eternal happiness. They'd taken everything else from her, but they'd never taken her soul.

"Blondie," Dominus called out to Severn, using the name he'd given her years earlier. He sounded in a rush. Something was happening. Suddenly, loud clapping sounds were heard from above. Footfalls on the ceiling. Thumps and crashes. Dominus approached Severn with a fierce look in his bulging eyes. There was a knife in his hand. Long and jagged. His hat had left his head, and the thin, black curls that sat upon it glistened with sweat. He swung the knife wildly. Severn backed away instinctively.

"Take it," he demanded, shoving the knife's handle at her. She willingly took it; thankful he hadn't thrust it blade first into her abdomen. "*Do* the rest." His arm flew from his side, waving at the children and adults in her care. "They all need do'n. *Now!*" He barked.

Severn jumped at his order and turned to look at the terrified faces under the black light. The eyes staring back ranged in age from six to twenty-three. Severn opened her mouth to ask what Dominus meant, but he'd rushed out of the room, slammed the door, and proceeded down the hall, clearing the Johns. Shots rang out one after another.

Where did Dominus want her to take all these people? Surely, he didn't mean she was to *kill* them. But upon reflection of who Dominus was, the way he'd said what he'd said, and the knife in her hand, she thought herself silly for questioning his meaning. She faced the huddled group, one hand gripping the handle while the other ran a slender finger down its blade accompanied by an absent stare. She jumped again, having cut herself. She gazed at the blood as it slid down into her palm, then looked back up at the huddled mass, pleading with her not to hurt them.

"No, oh, no, I - I won't, I wouldn't," she began to explain when Dominus returned with a pistol.

"*Blondie,* what did I tell you?!" He was furious, but a hint of fear also crept into his voice. Whatever was happening above them had him scared. He raised his gun at Severn, who had decided she would take whatever punishment Dominus would dole out for refusing him. She would not kill anyone. "You'll be the first, Blondie." He threatened; a guttural groan followed, not realizing that Severn had made peace with herself over her decision. Nothing he could threaten would make her stand down. A click came from the pistol when Dominus pulled animatedly at the trigger. Again and again, the gun clicked angrily at her. The group was heard gasping along to the sound. Severn's heart stopped with each click, expecting a bullet to burst forth. When it was apparent there were no bullets left, Severn mourned for those in the session rooms he'd gunned down, straightening herself and brandishing the knife as menacingly as possible.

"Come," Severn told the group, waving them forward with her free hand. She'd bent into a crouched position. Dominus shouted for her to hand him the knife. "No," she told him flatly.

Dominus stepped forward, using a technique that had worked hundreds of times. He pumped his chest out, rolled his shoulders back, and barked at her to drop the knife. Severn shuddered but kept her ground. The group saw the strength in her and picked up whatever they could to defend themselves against Dominus.

He took a step back. This was unprecedented, Severn thought. Euphoric energy had attached itself to her. She took a step forward. Dominus took another step back. Chills rang through her body, exciting her flesh and the long hairs on her arms. Another step forward. Still, sounds of distress came from above. Rattling and kicking and screaming. But in the room, Severn had spent nearly twenty years, a stillness occupied her mind. Her hand stopped shaking. Her focus had narrowed to one task. She felt nothing outside of herself and thought nothing outside her goal. Years of anger, humiliation, cruelty, rage, pain, sadness, and fatigue found a singular purpose. The muscles in her arm twitched. She was due for her morphine soon, she knew, but she had to keep it together long enough to see this thing through.

"I'll beat *all* yer asses for this defiance!" Dominus shouted callously, the gun still in his hand, pointing madly at the group. His head turned to see what, if anything, was behind him, then turned entirely and went for the door. It slammed in his face. *"KILL HIM!"* a small but powerful voice demanded through the door. It was one of the girls from the session rooms. It was Lacy. It was later determined that she'd crawled to the common room with a gunshot wound to her abdomen. Severn had spotted her behind Dominus and knew exactly how this would go down without a word between them.

Dominus kicked and punched against the locked door. When he returned his attention to the group, Severn thrust the blade into his guts, nicking a vertebra. The pain was exquisite. Dominus dropped to his knees. His bulging eyes swelled comically, and Severn heard someone behind her laugh. His jaw went slack. *Was he trying to say something?* Severn hadn't released the knife, and his calloused hands wrapped around hers to remove it. She struggled against his efforts, but he was much stronger.

"Help me!" She shouted to the others. Soon many hands pushed on the butt of the knife, driving it further into the slim man's abdomen. The monster they'd all needed to conquer. Dominus screamed out in agony as the knife pushed in every direction, hollowing out a significant hole in his stomach. When blood and guts poured out of the wound, Severn and the others backed off. Dominus's hands held the intestines and bladder. An artery had been severed in the attack, and they watched as the blood spit a little slower from the gaping wound. The smaller children cried at the sight while the older, more seasoned shouted at the monster, trying desperately to heave the length of his intestine back into place.

Severn laughed at the spectacle, severely in shock over the scene. She couldn't feel her hands even with all the gore upon them. Either whatever was happening above them would save them, or they would be murdered for this act against Dominus. Either way, she knew it was over. This would be their last day here. There was a comfort in knowing however it panned out. Suddenly, Severn's senses returned, and *Mr. Vain* by Culture Beat materialized, playing at a low volume over the cheers and tears. Dominus had told her it was a popular song of '93. *1993.* She'd arrived in 1975.

"Open the door!" A little boy begged of Lucy, but the way Lucy had looked at Severn before closing the door told Severn she was dead. "*Please*, Tommy, please, be quiet. Be still." Severn said. "Help me move Dominus from the door." Two women in their teens assisted in dragging the still-moaning Dominus from their exit. Blood had pooled at the threshold, and one of the girls slipped in it. Dominus reeled in agony as her foot caught him squarely in the groin.

"He's not dead," Tommy said, standing over the wretch. Then he looked up pleadingly at Severn. "Please *don't* let him live." Severn knelt and pulled Tommy into her, hugging him close. "Murder is a sin."

"Oh, fuck it, I'll do it," said a girl of twenty with pigtails, blush on her cheeks, and a lollipop in her mouth, snapping up the blade. She bent over Dominus, stepping on both arms and spat in his eye. She followed that up by ordering his pants removed. Once completed, she took his manhood in her hand and slowly sawed it off with his scrotum intact while others sat on his legs. She held it up for the group to see and then forced it into Dominus's open, screaming mouth. The very tool that maliciously robbed each of them of their virginity, their pride, and their lives reduced to a sick joke. Dominus died after the procedure, but not before blinking hard at his penis and scrotum squeezed between his victim's hands and being gagged by their girth in his mouth.

Voices on the other side of the door came quickly after that. Many were terrified over who it might be. Severn calmed the younger ones with a prayer from her youth while the older ones quietly raged against what might come through the door. They swore if it was more of the same, they would give their lives to their end. Sixteen stood crouched and ready to pounce when it opened. A voice called through the door.

"How many of you are in there?" It was an authoritative, masculine voice, not unlike what they were used to. "It's the Police. You're safe. I'm going to unlock and open the door. Please stand clear."

True to his word, the door latch could be heard snapping open, and the door soon followed. A man in uniform with his hand at his gun still strapped to his hip reviewed the carnage from the threshold. He stepped over the pool of blood while his free hand motioned that everything would be okay.

Severn couldn't hear the man for the ringing in her ears. *Had this happened? Were they free?* Confusion began to set in, and she absently scratched an invisible itch on her upper arm. "I've been missing for eighteen years," she managed through a gasp of relief. The officer looked sympathetically at her and the others.

"I'm so sorry," he offered. "Please follow me upstairs. How many are you?" Severn had never been upstairs. None of them had. Knowing that there was an upstairs was freeing in itself. There was a world beyond the Hell they'd endured. But they'd endured it for this moment. A smile inched its way up Severn's thin face. Tears spilled down her gaunt cheeks. She began to shake violently. More officers poured into the common room, placing blankets over everyone. Severn was grateful for this. From that moment on, she would be grateful for everything.

1993

Freedom

Darnell sat cross-legged on his narrow hallway floor, eyeing where he'd watched his father peel up floorboards and place a stack of cash. He was reluctant to slide the flathead screwdriver into the knot and pry the boards up. His father had only left an hour ago. To count it, Darnell told himself. Dad would be gone all night if history was any indication.

Darnell stood up, shook out his aching legs, rolled his neck, and completed three short jumps to release his anxiety over this betrayal. His father would kill him if he knew, of that Darnell had no doubt. Still, not knowing how much was resting under his house was maddening. Darnell searched the house and double-locked the front and side doors. Returning to the hallway, he resumed his intense gaze at the floor. *Fuck it.*

He knelt and jammed the screwdriver into the opening, wrenching one board up after another until the hole in the floor was a foot square. He thumbed the knob on his flashlight and peered into the dark space. A rubber sack lay on the naked soil next to a plumbing pipe, zipper wide open. A cool breeze escaped the hole and caught Darnell in the face. It smelled of dirt and destiny. Excitedly, he reached into the bag and pulled up handfuls of cash neatly formed into what he would count as five-thousand-dollar stacks. His heart soared. Is it real? He asked himself. *How could it be real?* But if his father was hiding it under the house, how could it be anything but?

Hours later and Darnell was surrounded by fifty-seven rolls of equal value. He was looking at $285k. It was more money than the whole street was worth, not that any of its residents owned any of their homes. This was life-changing, life-altering. This much money could help him disappear from under his father's thumb. The man didn't care if Darnell lived or died. This stash was his father's ticket to a better life, but he didn't deserve a better life. Whatever he'd done and was still doing to accumulate this kind of cash could only be illegal. That realization carried with it some powerful new reasons to bust out of his current situation.

A *bang, bang, bang,* pulled Darnell from his deliberation and back into the real world. It was a world of shitty people and shittier living conditions. His anxiety over the interruption flung him into action, quickly shoveling the stacks of money back into the hole. He hadn't done a good job of replacing the loot into the sack, and if this were his father at the door, he was about to be found out. Next, he replaced the flooring to secure the secret. Darnell looked for the bat they kept in the kitchen. The same bat that had fractured Darnell's forearm during one of his father's beat downs. Once both hands were gripping the bat, he called out to the locked door. "Who's there?" He hollered in his deepest tempo.

"Is that Darnell Lincoln?" A voice penetrated the door and rang in Darnell's ears. The accent sounded a lot like one of his father's friends.

"Yeah, it's Darnell. Who's asking?" His grip on the bat tightened.

"Darnell, it's the Police. We have a search warrant for your residence." The man replied hastily. Darnell went to the front window and drew the heavy blinds back to reveal the red and blue lights.

"Slide it under the door," Darnell demanded. "And your badge." Luckily there was a three-inch gap between the bottom of the door and the concrete. His Rottweiler's final act before his father's temper put it down.

Sure enough, the warrant and the badge emerged, and Darnell studied them closely. They could be fakes for all he knew, but they looked legit enough that he unlocked the door and pulled it open until the chain lock caught. Three officers stood, waiting for an invitation. It was midnight, but the street was alive, gathering around the two cruisers.

"What's this about?" Darnell asked innocently while his heart raced. Had someone reported the child abuse?

"It's about your father, Darnell. He's," the officer stopped himself and started again. "Your father is deceased."

Darnell was in shock over the announcement, a smile reluctantly growing up the right side of his face. This would have been good news on any day, but today, this was a blessing after counting all that money. "*Dead*, you say?"

"Yes, son, I'm sorry, but he was killed earlier this evening." The officer explained. "Could you let us in, please?"

"What - why a search warrant if he's dead?" Darnell was concerned about the money. They could find it if they looked hard enough.

"The work your father was involved in wasn't exactly on the up and up, son. We need to search the home for evidence." The officer said in a calm and orderly manner. "The things he's done are... well, you'll learn all about it soon enough. He was a bad man, your father."

"You don't have to sell me on that," Darnell agreed, squinting as the lights from the cruisers caught him in the eye.

Darnell felt trapped knowing about all the money in his floorboards and the police ready to tear the place apart. If he didn't cooperate, he would be detained as an accomplice. Still, if he did cooperate, he might lose his only opportunity to flee with the cash. Everything had happened so quickly. He released his grip on the bat and laid it on the kitchen counter, opening the front door.

"Thank you for cooperating," the officer said as he and the others moved into his home to look around. Darnell handed the cop his badge back. "How old are you?" The officer asked.

"Just turned seventeen," Darnell replied, his head lowering. "Guess I'm headed into the system, huh?"

"You'll have a social worker to bounce those questions off." The officer laid a hand on Darnell's shoulder. "For what it's worth, I'm sorry for your loss." Darnell shook his head and thanked the man while the others began their search. Darnell made a pot of coffee and kept an eye on the hallway. It wasn't obvious, and Darnell had no idea how involved their search would be. Maybe just filing cabinets and cupboards and closets and mattresses would be searched.

An hour later, the social worker showed up with several other police. The social worker wore a kind but worn expression. Darnel worried that she would want to take him with her right away. He had things to collect from his room and the floorboards. After tonight, his house would be under police scrutiny with caution tape blocking the door and maybe an undercover positioned outside. At least, that's what T.V. would have him believe. If he couldn't secure the money soon, he may never have another chance.

News of this father's death had impressed a sense of freedom on him which warmed his chest and face, but the search had stymied that. Still, his father was dead, and the money now his. He wondered briefly how much his father was planning to save before he ran off. The social worker was talking at him, but he wasn't really listening.

"When will they be done here?" Darnell asked the heavy-set woman, considering his options. "Will I be able to return home?"

"Darnell, we're going to make sure you have everything you need," she began in a regional accent Darnell didn't recognize. "You just let me know what, and I'll work to get it for you."

"I'm seventeen," he mentioned absently. "I - will there be a funeral? What happens to my dad?"

"We can discuss all of this at our offices, Darnell. Right now, I need you to pack a bag and be ready to come with me in a half-hour."

Darnell's head was spinning. How could he grab the cash and escape while all these people were turning the place upside down? *Why did he ask about a funeral?* Buying time, he'd guessed. He nodded blankly at the social worker, whose name he hadn't processed, and stood up. He walked slowly to his room, catching the police in his peripheral. He stepped over the floorboards concealing his future, and a loud squeak reached one officer's ears.

The large, mustached man turned to see Darnell stop and cringe. He berated himself as he stood there and then bent to one knee to retie the laces of his left shoe. He worried that the officer might investigate the squeak further. Sweat built up on his puckered forehead as he continued with the charade, fumbling with his laces. The officer approached Darnell and bent down to meet him.

"Darnell, right?" The big man said. Darnell nodded; a sinking feeling entered his stomach. "You ever go with your dad to work?"

"I slept while he was at work," Darnell assured the man. "When I was at school, he slept. We met for dinner, and that's about it."

"You didn't know what he did for a living?"

"No." Darnell tried not to hyperventilate.

"He had a cash-only business." The officer said. "No bank account. No nothing like that."

"All I know is he bought the groceries and had friends over sometimes. They watched T.V. and played cards." Darnell kept his answers as short as possible.

"You think he might have stashed his winnings around here somewhere?"

"Does this look like a house with money?" Darnell asked with a sarcastic laugh. "I've never known money, officer. I've never *seen* money. I doubt my father had any either."

"His business associates say otherwise."

"None of my business."

"It is if you know anything." The officer commanded Darnell's attention with his greedily, staring eyes.

"I don't." Darnell rose confidently and moved on to his room. "I gotta pack. Going into the system now, you know."

The officer glared at Darnell as he entered his bedroom. He looked down at the floor and sighed. Then he swatted a painting of a horse off the wall.

Darnell feared the officer was hoping to find the money for himself. A man like that wouldn't leave it alone. He'd come back. Darnell had to free that money and himself, but how?

Then he remembered how the house was set above ground on cinder blocks. Under the floorboards was earth. When he'd reached to pull up the money, it was at least a foot and a half down. If he could find an outside entrance, he could crawl under the house and retrieve the money. The reality of this heist had begun to tickle Darnell's chest with excitement.

Darnell closed his bedroom door, looked at his window, and then looked out the window to see if there was any activity outside. The back of the house had a crumbling woodshed, three 15-inch car tires, a dozen rims, and the Rottweiler buried in the center of the postage-stamp-sized yard. It was a warm July night, and the sun was far from setting. Light permeated the back despite the towering low-income housing apartments directly behind it. Still, no one was out there. He quickly packed a backpack and pushed open his window. The screen was long gone. He slipped out and crouched next to the one level house.

Darnell moved along the base of the house, pushing at the siding which concealed the opening along the perimeter. When one section bent for him, he pulled it outward. The metal siding remained turned up when he let go. *Jesus*, this was happening, he thought. He removed his backpack and slithered under the house on his stomach.

With only a lighter to illuminate his way, Darnell pulled himself on his forearms. He pushed with his feet through the hard dirt and decades of junk collected under the house. He found a plumbing pipe and followed it, remembering the pipe next to the treasure. Another pipe crossed his path, and he decided to follow it next. Then he hit pay dirt. Several rolls of money were loosely scattered around the bag. Darnell feared he was taking far too long and scooped large sums of the money in a sweeping motion with both arms to his chest. Then he shoved them into the bag. His neck strained to keep his head up, and a muscle spasmed in his lower back, seizing. He reached back to massage the uncooperative muscle, his head pressed to the ground. Dust fell through the cracks above him and nearly forced a sneeze. People were beginning to gather in the small hallway. Voices were heard but not understood. Darnell decided to shuffle back the way he'd come regardless of the pain in his back.

He extinguished the lighter. His leg caught on something, and it tore his pants, leaving a gash along his calf. *Fuck.* That could slow him down. His heart was pounding like a tribal drum. His body soaked in sweat and grime. How would he explain his sudden and filthy appearance to the social worker and the police? He couldn't. He would have to flee now.

1994

The Return

Severn woke from a medically induced coma a week after she'd been rescued from captivity. She and the others had been shipped to the General Hospital to undergo extensive tests, be hydrated, and be allowed to heal. During this time, each victim underwent a general psych analysis to curb some of the negative effects their captivity and abuse would have on their personalities. The other concern was how their fragile states would take to being released back into the general population.

This was where Severn went off the deep end. The moment her mother walked into her hospital room, sporting a much shorter hairstyle than she remembered, greying at the temples and no makeup to hide the premature wrinkles in her fifty-three-year-old face, Severn became mute. Something snapped in her. She watched her mother slowly approach with boney hands reaching out cautiously, as though Severn were a wild animal not to be spooked. The woman wore the saddest smile she'd ever seen, and then Severn watched as the older version of her mother broke down in tears.

"I'm so sorry, Severn," her mother cried on Severn's shoulder, stroking her hair with one hand and gripping her daughter fiercely with the other. "It's all my fault. My fault..." She continued as if this were something she'd been waiting years to say. The skin of her mother's face was soft and thin, Severn noticed. She pushed herself off her frail daughter a moment later. Cold hands wrapped around Severn's face. "My baby... my baby's come back to me." Her mother sat up straight on the edge of the bed.

"You'll come home with me when this is done. I'm *better* now, Severn... been better a long time." Her mother nodded as if she were convincing Severn she was telling the truth. "Your room is just as you left it. Nothing's changed. I knew you'd come back to me..." Her voice was racing and her eyes darting this way and that.

"Ma'am," an orderly addressed her mother. "We need to just finish up here with your daughter's psych evaluation, and you can sign her out. It'll just be a moment."

Severn's mom nodded again and smiled brightly at her daughter, taking a seat in a guest chair. A man with a clipboard entered the room next and asked Severn if she'd like to recount her experiences of the last 18 years. Severn only shook her head, confused why anyone would want to know about the last 18 years. *What had happened in that time? I'm missing time.* Her mother was there and going to take her home. She was in a hospital - that much was obvious. She'd hurt herself, she guessed. Mom was there to bring her home. Nothing else made any sense.

The man asked if she would write out what she remembered, and Severn shook her head again, no. The man looked perplexed. "If you feel this is too soon, I understand, Severn, in your own time. But I may need to keep you here a few days for observation." Severn's gaze caught her mother and begged her to intervene.

"No," her mother said, standing. "She's coming home *tonight* with me." The man quickly assessed the situation and nodded in agreeance. Severn could breathe again. "Get dressed, baby, we're leaving." Her mother ordered her, pointing to the bag she'd brought from home. When Severn opened it, she found the bag was filled with her mother's clothes. She slid off the hospital bed and went into the bathroom to change but left the door ajar. She seemed to have an aversion to closed doors. The thought made her uncomfortable; anxious.

Severn's mother took her hand and hurried her through the halls, signed her daughter out at the front desk, thanked everyone, and they exited the hospital. In the car, Severn felt cloudy. Her head seemed to float like a balloon tethered to a ribbon. Something odd had happened to her.

"You don't have to remember if you don't want to, baby." Her mother explained, though what she was referring to, Severn couldn't connect. "You're home now. That's all that matters. Life can begin again like it did for me. Your life is your own again." The bony right hand of her mother's landed on Severn's hand and squeezed. It was frigid. "I'll never let you out of my sight again. Not *ever.*"

"Mom? What did I miss?" Severn asked in an uneasy tone, utterly confused over the events of the day.

"Never mind what you missed, baby. You're home now. That's enough." Her mother answered. It wasn't an answer at all, but Severn didn't think she would get a real answer out of her mother.

"You changed your hair," Severn mentioned absently. "You look more... distinguished." A tight smile appeared on her face, and her mother lifted a hand to experience it. The gentle touch felt foreign on her face. "Am I... *okay*, mom?" She wondered.

"Why yes, baby, you're fine. You're with your mother, and I *love* you, and we'll be home soon. Are you hungry? We could order something in." The motion in the car made Severn feel a bit off. *I'll Stand by You* by The Pretenders played softly on the car radio, the beat mimicked the sound of the road under Severn's feet. The lights from oncoming cars gave her a slight case of vertigo. Mild claustrophobia accompanied the drive.

"That would be nice." Severn's voice hadn't raised an octave; it was still soft and distant. "Pizza?"

"Whatever your heart desires, Severn, pizza was always one of your favorites." The boney hand sought out Severn's face again and closed around the back of her neck, massaging her taut muscles. Severn relished her mother's touch. Their relationship had been so toxic for so long; this was reassuring.

"What changed for you, mom?" Severn asked innocently.

"*You* changed for me, baby, *you.*" Her mother looked at her a long moment, careful not to lose sight of the road. "I've missed you for so long, Severn..." her eyes released rivers of tears as they stopped at a stop sign a block from the house. She put the car in park and turned fully to her daughter. "Have you... missed me?"

"Oh, yes, mom, yes, I *have.*" They hugged a long time, crying into each other's embrace. Severn cried for the alcoholic, the emotionally unavailable mother she'd had in her young life. She cried tears of joy over her mother's miraculous recovery and promise that she was better. If she was meant to have missed her mother for the past 18 years, then she was stumped. Whatever she'd suffered - a bump on the head - to have forgotten so much of her life, would surely reveal itself the following day. The way her mother spoke of the lost time, though, led her to believe maybe it wasn't worth remembering.

Severn and her mother were met at their drive by a small contingent of representatives from different media groups. They were milling about the front lawn, some with heavy cameras mounted to their shoulders and others with pen and paper and recording devices. The camera turned to their car the moment it drove up the cobblestone driveway. Severn felt anxiety well up inside her at the site. She accepted her mother's light jacket, gently placed over her head. "Stay put," her mother told her softly, taking on the role of Mumma Bear, moving to intervene the journalists. Severn rolled her window down enough to hear her mother's desperate pleas while peering through the jacket. "My daughter has been through a traumatic experience she does not remember. She'll be of no use to you. There's no *story* here." Her mother took hold of the camera as it approached Severn and roughly pulled it down. The cameraman swore, his expensive camera very nearly shattered into pieces on the driveway, and then fled, discouraged to his van. "Leave my daughter out of it!" She pushed a microphone away from her face and nearly shoved the woman reporter into the hawthorn bush. The appalling spectacle went on a few minutes more before the vultures thought better of their position and accepted their eviction.

It was a troubling scene that had left Severn shaky and with more questions than answers. But she was proud of her mother, so roused by the mysterious events that had led the news people to their door. She had come a long way. She had become the mother Severn needed.

1995

Lost Time

Severn had enjoyed the company of her mother for what seemed like the first time in her life. A sober mother was an attentive mother.

Friends she had known since childhood began to surface, and in the past year, she had reconnected with Maribel. At first, Mary couldn't help but stare at Severn most uncomfortably at the most inappropriate times. She wore a constant expression of empathy. She might have thought she was conveying compassion, but in reality, it only made Severn anxious. *What did she know? Should I just ask and get it over with?*

"No one who loves you would want you to suffer a second time," her mother assured her. She remembered her friendship with Mary. It was one of pure innocence, one which transcended time and space. Knowing her twenty years after her disappearance was no different save their age and the secret which separated them. Otherwise, they were very compatible.

Mary had a husband and a small child. Severn had met them both and experienced an unnerving dinner where questions and conversation spanned everything but those missing years. It became a game for Severn to ask about the eighties just to see the looks on the faces of those who knew she'd missed them.

Severn often theorized over her lost years. *Was it an alien abduction?* It was all the rage at the movies and on T.V. Real-looking people were coming out and telling their stories. Maybe she had a story to tell. Maybe she fell down a well and spent twenty years living off algae while befriending rats whose collective

Michael Poeltl

backs she eventually rode up the slick, rock walls to freedom. Perhaps she'd been a willing participant in a cult who had brainwashed her and been stormed by the police. The possibilities were endless, but none seemed to trigger a memory.

Severn had asked her mother countless times over the past year to give her a hint or act it out in charades, but her mother refused to play along, saying, "some things are better left unsaid." This left Severn with an anxious edge, always wondering. She'd visited the library to review their microfiche and trace her disappearance back to 1975. There must have been news of the event, but her mother had gotten there first and asked the Librarian to remove any mention of it. This she learned years later.

The internet was on the rise about this time, too, and Severn asked her mother to update their home with the required technology so she could write electronic letters to friends. Her mother called it a fad and that she wouldn't spend money on something that would be gone tomorrow. Still, the internet had some exciting possibilities. The library had computer consoles and the internet. *Mother couldn't block the whole internet.*

Then one night, a conversation with Mary as they sat on Severn's childhood bed changed everything. After an evening at the movies, Mary joined Severn for dessert at her mother's home. When they'd finished their cheesecake Severn turned to Mary and asked pleadingly, "What happened to me?"

Mary looked disappointed that she'd asked again and shook her head. "Severn, it's not my place to say -"

"You're my *best friend*, Mary," Severn urged her. "We used to tell each other everything."

Mary sank into a thoughtful gaze at her friend. "You know, I thought you just blew us off that night. Or that your mom had come home drunk, and you had to look after her again or something. We were *pissed*." Mary explains. Would she give it all up now? "Then when I called the next day, your mom answered and went to get you. Then she told me you weren't there. I knew something was wrong."

"Did you go to the police?" Severn was hanging on her every word and hugging a decorative pillow tightly into her slender frame.

"Your mom seemed indifferent about it at the time. Probably hungover, you remember your mom." Severn nodded, absorbed by the story, hopeful Mary would spill the beans. "I told her we were to meet the night before, but you never turned up. That caught her attention, and she started asking questions. I got scared."

"Then, mom went to the police?"

"Yes, with my parents and me. We all went, and I gave my statement, and they wanted to give you another eight or ten hours to show up before anyone panicked. I *hated* that idea. Your mom, I think, took some comfort in the thought you would return."

"But I didn't return."

"No, well, *yes*, here you are, thank God! But it took eighteen years."

"Right, eighteen years I'll never get back."

"*Exactly*. Eighteen years you don't want to get back."

"I do want them back, Mary. I want to *know*." Severn surprised herself saying it aloud.

Mary shook her head, and a tear escaped down her round face. "You don't want that, Severn. It's what everyone has been saying. You *don't* want that." She sounded frightened as she said it. Mary wiped her eyes and opened her arms, inviting Severn in for a hug. Severn accepted, and the two women embraced for a long time, Severn comforting Mary's convulsive sobs. *What the hell had happened to me?*

I'll Be There for You by The Rembrandts came on the television and Severn's mom called up to alert her. It was a Sit Com that taught Severn how to exist in a world she'd been absent from so many years. The social cues and humour helped her adapt to her new reality.

Seeing how scared for her Mary was gave Severn pause. Maybe she didn't want to know. She did, but maybe it was better she didn't. It had been her goal the entire year to know.

"Please don't look anymore," Mary pleaded with her. "Sometimes, we aren't meant to know. You've blocked the experience for a reason. Let it go. Embrace life. You're not defined by your past, but if you discover it... I'm afraid you'll let it."

Mary took Severn's hands in hers and squeezed. They looked into each other's eyes, and Severn saw the warning in Mary's. It was not to be taken lightly.

"*Promise* me," Mary begged. "Just be grateful you've been returned to us; we are. Live your life and go to school and become the person you were meant to be."

Severn acquiesced and promised her friend she would live.

1994

A New Beginning

The beginning of a new year should be celebrated and embraced as an opportunity for change. For Jonah, it was another sign from the great whatever that he was not worth the paper his rejection letter was printed on. Another one, Jonah, just stared at the words. A form letter not unlike the others. They all stated the same thing; his vision did not align with their own, and at this time, they could not commit. *But good luck.*

It never got old. It always stung. He had forced himself to feel positive this time. He'd really tried. Positivity wasn't his strong suit. Sure, when he was a kid, he remembered that sense of wonder over things like his mother's golden fingers and only saw the bright side of his captivity. But that tower fell with the rest of youths' lies like Mothers, Fathers, Santa, the Tooth Fairy, the Easter Bunny, and love. *All lies.*

It all made him want a drink so badly, but it had been six months since his last. Another attempt at sobriety spawned by another near-death scenario attempting to purchase street drugs might help him make something of himself. *Or not,* rang in Self-talk. Fuck off, Jonah told himself.

He slid the letter in a drawer with the others. There they could console one another on a common theme. He refused to talk about it to anyone. He'd often imagined how he'd celebrate once an acceptance letter came through. He'd tell Mort and attend readings and signings and become a celebrated author of great renown. After all, he'd written what he knew. That's what they tell you; write what you know. So that's what he did. He wrote about addiction and self-abuse and how a life can just slip into the darkness, never to be recovered. How some people can't live in this world - weren't suited to it. He wrote about his epiphany, which confirmed that he didn't know how to live without the addictions, so he made a conscious choice to keep the cigarettes while he flushed his system of the cocaine and pills and alcohol. Dr. Sturgis only asked him to journal his experiences, to write down his past in an attempt to understand it, how it affected his life and how he'd overcome his obstacles. She didn't expect him to write a book. She told him to be realistic about publishing. Not to allow rejection to pull him back down.

But the more he wrote about his experiences, the more he wanted to share. He wanted the time he'd invested to mean something rather than just go up in smoke, watching from his place in a derelict park or alley as others burned out like ash rising from a roaring dumpster fire. They'd slipped free of the burning and drifted into the cold abyss. But somehow, he'd made it out alive. Perhaps if he'd died in his own story, someone would read it. *Maybe I need to see an editor.* But that costs, and what if they wanted him to rewrite his own story? He hated doing anything more than once. Reliving it again and again through proofreading had become less and less medicinal. Besides, at thirty, he was probably finished. Isn't that what they say? People peak before their thirties in whatever they might find success at. The great whatever has spoken. *The book was probably shit anyway.*

Jonah looked around his shared apartment. Morty, his best friend since grade five, could be heard puttering around the kitchen. It was his favorite room in any house. Their kitchen was small and smelled of fried foods.

"Jonah," the big man called in his unnaturally deep voice. "Do we not have any pasta left?"

Jonah snapped out of his sadness a moment long enough to answer, "No, you *ate* it." The reply was sharply delivered as Jonah had hoped to make a pot the day before. The weather caught his attention next, and he squinted against the bright white sun. *Too bright.*

"Shit," Mort could be heard to say. "I guess I need to hit the corner store. You want anything?"

"I'll come with you." Jonah rose and pulled his jacket from its place, hanging on his bedroom door. He slipped into unlaced Doc Martins and joined his friend. "Do we need a list?" His voice was a whisper, but Morty could always decipher Jonah's mumbles.

"Let's just hit every aisle." As Morty winked, his round face closed around the winking eye like a fat seal. At thirty-one, Morty was obese. Approaching

128

morbidly so. He knew it. He'd always known it. Apparently, it was an underactive thyroid and no drive to eat right or exercise—a pity. The only looks he ever got were of disgust. He was used to it, but why should someone have to get used to something like that? *Why get used to rejection letters? Because that's your reality. The sooner you accept it, the sooner you can move on.* Jonah thanks his mother's voice for the usual optimism to any gamble he might take on and lights a smoke. The two men exit their apartment and join the growing crowd of morning commuters.

Mort had lost his umpteenth job as an engineer. Apparently, he sucked at it. Jonah had stopped asking what had happened, rather admitting that when someone continuously lost their job, it was pretty clear it was the person and not the job. Now they shared their mornings together until Jonah went to work at the firm he'd managed to trick into hiring him out of college. Fake it till you make it. He hated going there and hated being around so many people, but a budding author observed. That's what all the books told him: you have to experience shit to write about it. So, he kept his 11 am to 8 pm job to pay the rent and watched his peers as they joked, flirted, and shouted at one another from one cubicle to another.

Turned out he was pretty handy with numbers for no good reason he could understand. He had a knack for his work. It wasn't interesting. It wasn't boring. It was simply there. It paid okay, and he could expect one day to be promoted, but that wasn't a goal he prized. To be published is how he wanted to become someone. *Maybe you should have gone to college for journalism?* Hindsight. *Fuck off.* It's too late. Jonah tossed his butt to the sidewalk and entered the mini mart they'd supported the past year.

"Half-Moons?" Morty raised an eyebrow at Jonah with a box of pre-packaged pseudo-baked goods in one beefy hand. "You're right," he said comically, "Two are better than one!" He laughed his throaty laugh and dropped the junk food into the tiny cart. More followed as the two men walked the aisles.

A group of teens admired the pipes under glass at the back counter where drug paraphernalia was sold. Jonah remembered all too well, pulling great gulps of smoke into his lungs from similar models. His twenties were more experimental than his teens and are why he'd taken so long to graduate college.

Jonah caught the teens at the counter as they stared, astounded as Morty wheeled their mini-grocery cart to the next aisle. "*Jesus*," one of them could be heard to say, clearly targeting Mort's weakness. "Maybe lay off the fucking pastries," he said loud enough to have the rest of the patrons looking and snickering.

Jonah's adrenaline soared, and he lifted a middle finger to the group, who feigned innocence and chuckled at his friend's unfortunate disability. "Fuck them, Mort." He said as he'd stated many times in their past. His best and only friend had suffered the same assholes his whole life. Mort, such a sweet guy, and such a fucking target for ignorant pricks, Jonah thought. He could walk over there and explain his friend's thyroid issues and make them understand the difficult path it had placed Mort on, but he knew he couldn't bring himself to confront them. Not in a group. It just wasn't who he was, and so they would get a pass, continuing to live in ignorance of other's battles, inflicting unnecessary pain on complete strangers.

"It's fine," Mort replied, but Jonah knew it wasn't. How much longer could his gentle nature take the endless abuse of others? Life wasn't fair. Jonah's own life documented that statement. This made him sensitive to other's plights, careful not to point out a weakness. He'd never build himself up by breaking someone else down like that. Morty was the same. They were brothers bound by a shared history and social shortcomings.

"We have everything we need," Mort said a few minutes later, his voice increasingly nasal as the comment from the minors continued to eat at his soul. Jonah knew it would be a long night for Morty, reliving the cruel comment, and laid a gentle hand on his friend's warm shoulder and squeezed, offering encouragement.

"If you think so, Mort," Jonah agreed, himself feeling a lump form in his throat over the damage to his friend's morale.

Goddamn, those little shits. Jonah's face flushed with anger, and he simply couldn't ignore the cruelty any longer. He told Mort to wait outside the mini mart as he'd forgotten something. Back inside, *Sabotage* by The Beasty Boys exploded overhead and became Jonah's fight song, stirring up the necessary adrenaline to see the thing through. He found the teen that had the nerve to call out Mort's weakness in short order. The prick was eyeing up condoms, *alone*. Jonah did the only thing he could think of, measured his distance behind the kid, and swung his leg, connecting foot to groin, forcing the fucker to the floor. Then Jonah, salivating, grabbed the kid's scruffy hair and leaned in to whisper, "I fucking hope your kids are born without arms. I hope you lose your nose in an industrial accident. I hope you have the chance to experience the kind of misguided cruelty you put on my friend today. I hope you live in fear of being in public because of it."

Jonah pushed the kid's face into the shelving, backed off, and stared a moment at the bent over prick who thought he'd gotten away with his heartless comment. He felt good about this confrontation. He felt accomplished. His face was hot, and he restrained himself from kicking the teen in the back of the head. Still raging, he turned and left the store, wiping away tears of anger.

Rejoining his friend, Jonah lit a cigarette to cope with the ire he felt over the incident. Mort broke open a box of the Half-Moons for a similar reason. They walked in silence as both reflected on the scene. Jonah knew Mort would be busy wishing he'd taken a left rather than a right at the aisle. He would play out scenarios for the rest of the day and self-soothe by eating.

At home, they unloaded what little they'd bought and joined each other on the sofa to play WWF RAW on their Saga 32X. Losing himself in video games had become a replacement for drinking. He'd been clean for six months and was taking it day by day. He was proud of himself but knew a drink or a snort were just a reaction away. That Mort wasn't a drinker gave him strength as the two men were mostly inseparable.

"So... you *good*, Mort?" Jonah asked, the question playing on his mind. Mort had hurt himself before over cruel comments directed at his weight, and Jonah sensed he was hurting from this recent attack.

"I'm fine, Jonah. Don't worry about me, man," Mort insisted, no inflection in his voice. His posture was slumped, and his eyes focused on the game.

"For *real*, Mort?" Jonah felt he had to ask, his shift would start soon, and his friend would be left alone for the next ten hours. "Just remember you're all I've got. Without you... I'm completely alone." The two men looked at one another from their places on the couch. Mort even paused the game mid-body slam. "Seriously," Jonah reiterated.

"So, what you're saying is.... I'm the *love* of your life," Mort reverted to comedy, as he often would when approaching a serious subject. A manufactured smile gripped his massive face, and though Jonah knew this was just another coping mechanism, he laughed out loud. Mort could always make him laugh. He stood and slapped his friend on the shoulder.

"Stop using the Undertaker," Jonah pleaded, referring to the video game, "he's mine." A wink and a smile, and his friend looked better for it.

At 10:30 am, Jonah left the apartment to work his 11 - 8 shift managing the clients who couldn't meet their obligations. It was another nine hours lost to the void for a paycheck that kept him treading water. He wondered how his life might have been different if he hadn't pissed his inheritance away after his mother had died. So many days and nights lost to his addictions. Whole weeks had gone without a trace. Morty was the only one who could pull him out of his grief. He was grateful for his friend but wondered, too, if he'd been left to his own devices, whether he would have died like his mother and grandfather. *Maybe you should have.*

The pub itself sold immediately for a fair price, explained the real estate agent. He didn't want the memories. Jonah left the family home as well. It was rented, and so no money came from it. In the end and after all the fees and family debt, he had a bank account showing $130k, the net worth of his father's hard work, which he then burned through in two short years. Two more rehab attempts, rent, drugs, alcohol, three tries to complete college, and several 'loans' given to acquaintances he never saw again. It was a regrettable time, but it's how Jonah coped. He hoped never to go back to that place in his life but always felt the pull of negativity drawing him there.

He could call Dr. Sturgis and explain how he felt and get some feedback, but he'd save that for his next session.

Work was work, and it went the way he'd planned. No real socializing, no shared dinner break, and his cigarette breaks found him taking a stroll down the busy street before returning. At 8 pm, he boarded the bus and avoided eye-contact with everyone but the woman who seemed to mirror his route at this time. Though she did not exit the bus at his stop, he imagined she didn't live far. Of course, he kept his distance to avoid her nose wrinkling up at the smell of him. Jonah's embarrassment over his body odor continued to keep him disconnected to others. Not unlike his drinking when he drank - paired with his natural disinterest in joining a conversation or sparking one up. It kept him single. It kept him alone. That's why Morty was so important to him. *Who else would have you?* Yup.

Jonah admired the woman's long, dark hair and her Grunge style t-shirt over a long-sleeved, beaded necklace and pierced nose. She was petite yet; her expression suggested a confidence that ignored her size. She carried herself proudly and wore Doc Martins, like him. Outside of Dr. Sturgis, this was the only woman in real life who gave him all the feels. He knew his alter boy glances were childish but how could he offer her anything more? Then she looked up, and he was found out. It wasn't the first time. He blinked his gaze away and shifted his attention to the ground. He felt so stupid, never having the balls to just hold that gaze and see what came of it. Maybe tomorrow? *Not if you know what's good for you.*

Jonah's stop arrived, and he timidly got off with a couple of others. When he started up the street to his apartment, there came a whistle from behind him. He turned to look and then chastised himself for the act. No one would be whistling like that at him, and now he'd placed himself in their sights. But it wasn't a construction worker making a lame attempt at a joke at his expense. It was the girl on the bus. She'd gotten off at his stop. Jonah turned again to take her in.

"Want to buy me a drink?" She asked, shouting over the sound of the bus moving away. She was every bit the confident woman he'd envisioned. A smile erupted on her pretty face, and Jonah's heart soared. *A drink, though...* he knew what that would mean. He couldn't take her up on it. Even being in a bar was death for him. Jesus, why had he fucked his life up so badly that a simple gesture like a drink could kill him? *Because you're an idiot.* Yup. Jonah lifted a hand and waved.

"I don't drink." He explained, the words reaching his lips before he could stop them. His heart sank.

"I didn't ask if I could buy *you* a drink," she replied sarcastically. "But I understand if you can't." She looked a little crestfallen, and Jonah was in utterly unknown territory. He didn't traditionally have this effect on women. He took a step closer, careful not to frighten her away.

"It's just that, it's late, I... I want to buy you a drink, I do, I -"

"Don't overthink it. I thought you might like to get to know me - rather than just staring at each other." Her smile never faded. She was generally interested.

"I'm Jonah," he said with a dry mouth, the two still several feet apart. He worried his BO would catch her any moment, and she'd turn to flee. He'd had a long day already. His armpits were soaked just participating in the conversation with the woman he'd been admiring from afar.

"June," she offered her name next. At least Jonah assumed it was her name and that she wasn't spitting out random months of the year. Unless she suffered from that disease that made a person shout out random words... turrets? "I've considered approaching you on the bus," she continued, "but I'm not a fan of having an audience watch you turn me down. If you'd like to get a coffee, I'm free right now."

"A coffee," Jonah hadn't expected her to make conciliations for him. Was this girl for real? "Uh, *sure*, I'd love that." She took a couple steps closer, and he instinctively backed off. "I - I've had a long day though and would rather get out of these clothes and into something fresh if that's alright with you?"

She shrugged. "Sure. You live near here, I guess?"

"Yes, just up the street. Did you want to wait for me or..."

"Can I use your bathroom?" She asked brazenly, but Jonah couldn't bring her up to his apartment. It was a mess, probably smacked of him and Morty's combined scents, and that wouldn't impress anyone.

"My roommate is there and been playing video games all day so maybe just meet me up the road at the '50's Cafe, you can't miss it. They've clean bathrooms. I'll take a decaf if you're ordering, and I'll get the bill." Jonah surprised himself with all the words coming out of him, hoping his explanation wasn't off-putting.

"That works." She was very agreeable. "See you in ten?" Jonah nodded and ran the rest of the way, up the stairs and into his apartment.

Upon entering the apartment, he found Morty still seated comfortably in the crevice he'd worked into his side of the couch, playing a first-person shooter game.

"Hey, there's some of those pot pies in the oven if you're hungry," Mort shouted at him. "I went out and got this new game. You need to try this."

"I'm just meeting someone at the cafe in ten, Mort. I gotta change." Jonah relayed, moving into his bedroom. "The girl from the bus," he called out optimistically.

Mort paused his game and stood with great effort. "No, shit!" He walked off a dead leg, shaking it out as he waddled his girth about the Livingroom. "How the fuck did this happen?"

"The only way it could have happened, Mort," Jonah explained, tearing off his shirt and towel drying his armpits.

"She talked to *you*," Mort guessed it. Jonah nodded with a genuine smile.

"It's fucked, I know, but she's waiting for me up the street where we're having coffee."

"Nothing else, though, right?" Mort warned.

"Just coffee, Mort. I'm not fucking this up." Jonah assured his friend and himself. "Do you still have that cologne?"

"Never used it," Mort shuffled off to retrieve the bottle. Jonah accepted it with thanks.

"You know, it wouldn't offend me if you did," Jonah said jokingly. Mort punched him in the shoulder, too good-natured to put the comment back on Jonah.

"Just don't drown yourself in it," was Mort's advice. The two men panned through Jonah's closet and found a reasonably unwrinkled sweater that would complement June's own style. A pair of jeans, fashionably torn at the knee, a big, buckled belt, and his Doc's and Jonah was ready. His hair fell mid-length and still retained its natural brown while his wire-framed glasses fit the Grunge genre that June seemed partial.

"Thanks, Morty. I'll be ready to play RAW with you when I get back. Save me the Undertaker!" Jonah took a step and then paused. Mort noticed his apprehension.

"You're good, Jonah. You *got* this." His friend assured him. "She approached you, man. All you gotta do is show up." Jonah decided he was right. Still, the butterflies wouldn't stop fluttering against his chest.

Jonah had a cigarette on the way to meet June, unsure how she would react to smoking. His heart was happy, but his head was frantic. His mother's voice resurfaced, warning him against any action that might see him hurt. He did his best to shoo the voice away and confidently entered the diner. At least, as confidently as he was capable.

Sweeping the diner, Jonah studied the layout and surveyed the red and white leather booths seeing no sign of June. *Well, that figures,* his self-talk said. The tickle in Jonah's chest became heavy and toxic, only rebounding once June entered his line of sight. He could breathe again. He watched as she sat in a booth by the windows. She picked up her coffee and sipped. Jonah made his way to her and sat.

"Hello, Jonah," June said with an impish smile. "I *have* to tell you; I'd imagined your name a few times. Jonah wasn't one of them. But I like it for you."

She was a chatty one, but probably a good pairing for Jonah's mostly non-verbal lifestyle as she could get him talking. "Hello, June," he lifted his cup and drank nervously. "What names did you come up with?" It seemed a harmless question.

"Oh, I don't know, *Matt* was one. *Mike*, because, like, literally, everyone is named Mike. Playing the odds there." She smiled brightly. "Um, *Bruce?* Something about your hair said Bruce to me one night. Oh, and *Kurt* this time you were wearing something Kurt Cobain would have. Before, you know," she formed a gun with her hand and put it against her head. That was still pretty fresh. Kurt's suicide happened in April - just two months ago.

"Kurt, I like *that*," Jonah admitted, wondering whether she'd ever considered him a *Jack*.

"So, you have a job, I'm guessing," she began. "Or are you visiting your sick grandmother every day?"

"Oh, my grandparents are all dead," Jonah answered. *This is why you don't talk to people;* his self-talk reminded him. "I mean, no, uh, no, I do have a job, *yes.*" The sweats were starting.

June looked at him with kind eyes, tilting her head. "Oh, please don't be nervous, Jonah. I feel very comfortable with you. That's why I'm being a shit." Her hand reached out and landed on his as she giggled to herself.

This act set the waterworks into full steam, and his new undershirt began to collect perspiration. Would he never be able to carry himself like a normal human being? *Nope.*

"I – uh..." Just tell her everything and save yourself the embarrassment later, his ego urged. "I work at a collections agency uptown. Both my parents have passed. I'm a recovering addict and live with my childhood friend." He couldn't bring himself to tell her about the rest.

June's eyes grew wide. "An over-sharer!" She laughed heartily at this. "I'm kidding. Thank you for telling me all of that."

Jonah felt lighter for her reaction to his hurried description. "I'm also thirty-four," he added.

"I'm thirty-one," June replied. "I know, I know, I don't look a day over thirty," she joked and flung her long, dark hair over one shoulder. Jonah laughed while admiring her elongated, sculpted neck.

"So, are you visiting a sick grandmother or what?" He asked, feeling more at ease.

"Yes, actually..." Her face fell, and then she looked up to assess his reaction. *"Kidding,"* she admitted with that same impish smirk. "I'm a bit of a bitch aren't I?" She laughed at herself again. Jonah liked this girl. She was fun. "I work too. I'm an exotic dancer."

Jonah laughed at this; sure she was kidding again. She did not laugh along with him this time. He waited for her to admit she was joking, but his smile faded before she continued.

"I *know*, it's not what you'd expected," her hands propped up her small chest underneath the layers of clothing. Her breasts most certainly weren't fake. Jonah immediately regretted his reaction.

"I - it's not that, you're *beautiful*. Of course, you could be a *stripper* - uh - exotic dancer, I just, I thought you were kidding again," Jonah was babbling. He could smell himself as sweat continued its assault on his undershirt.

"Oh, Jonah, you need to know how to *read* me," she said again with those kind eyes. "I am a stripper, but that's not *who* I am."

"No," Jonah agreed, "we're not our jobs."

"No?" June wondered. "What would *you* rather be?"

"Me? A writer, I guess; an author." Jonah told her without hesitation. "What about you?"

"Me... Hmm, A comedian?"

"You've got the material," Jonah said with a grin, picked up a napkin and wiped his forehead as discreetly as possible. "While we're being honest, I have this condition..."

"Oh, the *mystery* round, I'm intrigued." She leaned in, and Jonah was certain she'd caught a whiff of his unique scent, but she continued to smile through it. "You have a tail. You're a *serial* killer. No, a superhero..."

"Yeah, hah, none of those things," Jonah felt odd bringing this up on what could be considered their first date. Likely their last when he tells her the truth. "I have a condition... ah... it makes me perspire a lot more than a normal person. It has a scent to it that can be...well, pretty intense."

"Yeah?" She said without backing off, leaning full into him over the table on her forearms.

"Yeah," Jonah repeated, dumbstruck at her lack of a reaction to the obvious pong.

"Is it happening right now?" She asked, her intelligent eyes continued to command his gaze.

"Uh, yeah, it is." Jonah looked at the server as she poured them each another decaf.

"Then I don't smell it." She said, leaned back, and picked up her cup. The waitress made a face at her only Jonah noticed saying, *are you shitting me?* "If anything, you smell good to me. That's science, though. In fact, your scent is one of the things I was attracted to on the bus. That and I've never seen you at the club, so I knew you hadn't recognized me and were creeping on me. You were just a guy who thought I was pretty enough to steal glances at."

Jonah's entire body relaxed. This was impossibly good news; a woman, a beautiful woman who wasn't repelled by his scent. He was at a loss for words. This was an unprecedented response. *It's because she's damaged goods,* his self-talk warned. Fuck self-talk. Jonah's smile grew until it hurt. He felt emotional.

Don't cry. He reached out to her vacant hand and squeezed. Maybe there is someone for everyone.

"How do you feel about my profession?" She wondered, taking a more solemn tone.

"I'm still processing your complete disregard for my B.O.," Jonah admitted.

"Okay, let's not call it *that.*" She made a face and laughed to herself. "Seriously though, not a lot of men can deal with what I do unless they're on the receiving end of a private dance and not the one I'm coming home to."

"I've honestly no experience to back up anything I say. If you wanted to one day come home with me... all I could ever be is grateful."

"That's very generous of you to say, Jonah." June's other hand fell on his, and it was electric. Jonah often questioned how things happen, tracing them back to their event horizon. This time he was going to simply let it be. If something came of this chance happening, he would allow it the freedom to advance independently. June made him feel like maybe he did deserve someone. *Closer* by Nine Inch Nails played behind the noisy kitchen clatter two booths over. *Could there be a more awkward song playing on a first date?* Jonah closed his eyes and drained his cup.

His coffee emptied; Jonah wondered how they would leave it. It's an experience he hasn't had in over ten years. Their conversation had been so easy he could have been talking to Mort. That she was oblivious to his scent was a godsend. They'd both unloaded their baggage, so there were no surprises. Something about this just felt right, and it had been a hell of a long time since anything felt right to Jonah. Even rehab felt like he was hurting himself. This didn't feel like that.

June noticed both coffees were empty as well, slid out of the booth, and stood. "It's been great getting to know you, Jonah. Can I give you my number?" She pulled a large Motorola flip phone from her small purse and read off her number.

Jonah was impressed with her tech and figured she must make good money as a dancer. He did not own a cell phone, so he gave her his landline number. June punched it into her Motorola, and they walked each other out. "Can I walk you home?" Jonah asked.

"Nah, I'm good to pick up the bus from here and ride it the rest of the way," June replied, placing a stick of gum in her mouth. "Coffee breath," she stated.

Jonah nearly gasped at the thought she might lean in to kiss him next. *Drip, drip, drip,* went the armpits. Jonah walked her to the bus stop and stayed with her until the bus arrived, which, to his relief, was just a minute more. "Okay, safe trip," he said, and then she pulled him into her and kissed him deeply. She was a pro. Jonah kissed her back, their tongues touched and probed. She pulled back hard, smiled, chewed her gum, and got onto the bus. "Same time tomorrow?" She asked.

Jonah nodded, smiled, and waved.

1994

Out of the City

"Mort, I'm telling you, man, this girl is like no one I've ever met," Jonah explained excitedly to his best friend as they played video games well into the night.

"And *how* many people have you actually met?" Mort's voice rose in pitch as he responded with a light-hearted jab. They laughed. Jonah knew how true a statement that was. He'd done his damnedest to avoid people most of his life.

"She just... ah, I don't know, Morty," Jonah threw his head back and stared at the ceiling, "she was the *aggressor*, you know?" He rolled his head to Mort. "She didn't see me as the creep watching her on the bus. She saw me as *interested...*" Jonah sat up, realizing the game had not paused. He jerked his controller into his body as if the act would help his avatar avoid Mort's attempt to trap him in a headlock.

"And then she just like, laid herself bare..." Mort recalled from Jonah's earlier description of the event, tapping madly at his controller to secure the headlock.

"Exactly," Jonah replied, pulling his controller into his body. "Her whole story; as if she were in a hurry to unload her baggage."

"That's a good thing, I guess?" Mort hadn't had a girlfriend since high school but seemed to understand what Jonah was relaying.

"Made me want to tell her everything too," Jonah confirmed Mort's suspicion. "And the Bromhidrosis - she *likes* it..." Mort paused the game.

Morty looked at Jonah and smiled a genuine smile full of empathy, knowing how bad it had been for Jonah once they'd transitioned to high school. His unique scent kept everyone at a distance. He was bullied relentlessly over it and developed a traumatic association with it. "Then you hold onto this one, man. You hold onto her like you got her in a *sleeper hold* finishing move." Mort's wrestling metaphor was not lost on Jonah.

"I plan on it, trust me." Jonah's attention returned to the screen. "Did I tell you how *hot* she is?"

Mort laughed and nodded. "First thing you said. I can't wait to see her some morning in just her panties." Mort filled his right hand with cheese puffs and shoveled them into his mouth. Jonah restarted the game and leveled Mort's avatar with a dropkick while his friend rubbed the orange dust from his sweaty hand onto his track pants.

"Any interest in going to the river tomorrow with me?" Jonah asked quietly. The river which ran along the west end of his city traveled much further south, where a substantial, federally funded, and protected forest and wildlife preserve stood. Jonah loved it there. It allowed him to connect with nature, which offered him a kind of inner strength. Six months earlier, when he'd decided to abstain from drinking again, he visited the place to experience the power of nature. It rarely failed him.

Mort, aware of his friend's needs, nodded. "Sure, it'll do me good to get outta the house."

* * *

Jonah slept better than he had in years. At 11 am, on Saturday morning, the two caught the bus heading out of the city, following the river route. Mort had packed a bag of snacks in a backpack, which Jonah carried. After the thirty-minute trip, their stop was just a block from the park, and Mort had already begun rooting through the pack for a granola bar. Once inside the preserve, Jonah walked Mort to his favorite spot overlooking a gorge. Far below their dangling feet, raged the river. The moisture from the water beating against large rocks and other debris sent a cooling mist up to meet them.

"Hot for June," Morty explained, struggling to pull his sandals off swollen feet. Jonah raised his chin and closed his eyes against the bright sun penetrating the canopy. Impossibly bowed trees lined the cliff, reminding him of a tower of Giraffes kneeling awkwardly to sip at the river's edge. They could tumble down the sheer rock wall and crash into the river at any moment, Jonah surmised, but through sheer will to live, they hung on. This prospect had always excited Jonah.

Fingers dragging along the forest floor, he gripped an exposed root the thickness of his forearm and tugged.

Not much could deter the good vibes he felt over the incredible events of the night before. He seemed to want to share that feeling with the world - the natural world - to thank the universe. Besides, he loved forests, and trees were generally kinder than people. When he was a kid, the family never really ventured outside the city limits. It wasn't until the rehab program took the residents on a bus tour during his seventeenth year that Jonah discovered nature's beauty and developed empathy for the natural world.

After that trip, he had visited the same location for years whenever he felt overwhelmed. He's not surprised he needed to come back. June, the girl, not the month, had pulled him out of a possible relapse he'd sensed gripping him after his latest rejection letter. But more than that, she'd given him a reason to exist. He felt rejuvenated by her presence in his life, her shining personality, her interest. What other benefits might reveal themselves? *She's a stripper,* his mother's voice reminded him. *What does it matter what she thinks of you? She obviously has no morals.*

Jonah knew he hadn't heard the last from his ego on this topic. *I'm no better than her.* He reminded himself. *Don't let her in, Jonah. She can only hurt you.* His mother assured him. *No, I'm done not letting anyone in. June thinks I'm attractive. She accepts me for who I am. She's funny and witty, and I've been so lonely for so long. She could help me. Help me be a better person.* He argues. *A stripper is going to help you be a better person? Do you hear yourself?* Ego attacks. The inner dialogue begins to irritate Jonah, and he stands to shake off the anxiety rising in his chest.

"We on the move?" Mort asks, hopeful Jonah's answer will be no.

"I just need to walk for a bit," Jonah replied, shaking out his arms. "If you want to stay here, I'll see you in a few." Jonah started to walk away, and Mort called after him.

"Can you leave the backpack?" Jonah removed it and tossed it to his friend. "Thanks."

Jonah's walk proved healing the further he marched into the denser forest employing mindfulness into his regimen. He ignored the voices in his head and focused on the sound of his breathing. He took deep inhales, pulling in the cleansing atmosphere of the woods. He coughed out his exhales, wondering when he might quit smoking for good. But that was against the doctor's orders, for now. Still, he doubted very much that he would ever manage to quit cigarettes.

The day improved the more he practiced his mindfulness, the very same tactics he'd had trouble believing in the day before. The world seemed suddenly to make sense. The trees were taller, their crowns fuller, the sky more prominent. His heart was bigger, his mind more accepting of the good the world offered. *Could one person change me so quickly? Was it so easy for a complete stranger to accept me for all my faults? Was it so simple to appreciate the good because someone else saw the good in me?* Jonah allowed himself to sink into this attitude of gratitude, as one counselor had put it. He'd laughed that off when he'd heard it the first time. He had rarely seen the good for all the bad in his life. But here he was, accepting the teachings and putting them into practice, all for the affections of a girl.

* * *

That evening he received a call from June to meet up at the coffee shop again, and he set off to see her at 8:30 pm. He smoked a cigarette on the way and stopped to watch her in the window of the cafe. He watched as she pulled her shiny, long hair into a high ponytail, watched as she wiped off whatever makeup she had on and reapplied a lighter lipstick. She snapped her compact closed and ordered a coffee from the waiter, who was admiring her a moment before.

She seemed in complete control of her surroundings, confident and gracious – *graceful* even. The title of stripper definitely did not define her. Jonah put out his smoke and joined June at the table.

"Hi, good-looking!" June said with an enthusiastic grin. "I ordered us both a decaf."

"Super, thanks," Jonah felt nervous, half thinking last night was a dream or that June would have thought better of coming or her attitude toward his looks would change. "You look beautiful," he said, ignoring the nonsense bouncing around inside his head.

"Aww shucks," June replied, her chin sinking into her chest, big eyes blinking comically up at him.

"Ah, you probably hear that all the time," Jonah waved off his compliment, not sure why he'd said that.

"Yeeeah," June replied, looking a bit disappointed, "but I don't hear it from anyone who matters." She accepted her coffee from the server and stirred some milk into it.

"I shouldn't have said that. I don't know why I said that June, I'm sorry, I didn't mean anything by it, I..." Jonah sighed heavily. He looked into his black cup of coffee, lamenting his observation, and trying to breathe.

June placed a hand on his, and he met her gaze, experiencing the calm she projected. "Jonah, it's a common enough thing to say. I'm sorry if I seemed put off by it. I just, I know you didn't mean it like it sounded. At least, I hope you didn't."

"Jesus, *no,* June," Jonah's hand squeezed his cup a little tighter. "I just meant to recognize that *everyone* must see you the way I see you, not just..."

"My customers," June finished his sentence. "I know, Jonah, I'm *not* mad. But I want to know you're okay with what I do before taking this any further. You seem like a really great guy, and I'd like to explore possibilities with a really great guy."

Jonah could hardly believe what he was hearing. Such a dipshit thing to have said, and she's taking it in stride. *She wants to explore possibilities!* And all of a sudden, the diner smelled better than he remembered, the waitress' prettier, the lights a little brighter, and the place generally cleaner. Why was he noticing so many details at that moment? *Had the world righted itself? Had it lifted the veil of fog he'd been squinting through all his life and showing him what it was like on the other side?* Perhaps the world was opening up to him because he was open to the world of possibilities presenting themselves through June.

"I'm *excellent* with it, June. It's not an issue." Jonah flinches at 'excellent' as his descriptor, his hands, spread across the table, curl into fists to emphasize the awkwardness of his reply.

"Okay, okay," June laughed a little at his obvious discomfort. "Just checking."

The evening saw two more decafs and a shared piece of lemon meringue pie. Conversation flowed smoothly after the initial and unintentional backhanded compliment. Jonah described his day in the woods with Mort and the excitement of witnessing a tractor trailer tip over into a ditch on the bus ride home. He explained the origins of his alcoholism and the struggle he had growing up in a home with an addict for a mother and a father who showed no interest in him. He even mentioned Jack, his dead brother. Through it all June listened intently, squeezed his hand when he needed to collect his thoughts, and even kissed away a tear when he relived his mother's death. She was nothing less than a miracle.

The evening concluded with a longer kiss at the bus stop than the night before. Jonah was a new man.

2020

December, Severn at Sixty

The smell of lavender sets the mood. Combined with the furnishings' warm brown leather tones and rich accents, thaw Severn's detached response to her lost past. Dr. Sturgis has run through several sessions with Severn, dropping hints from each discovery, pointing her toward the full picture of her horrific past. It has been no easy feat, but Severn is strong and willing and accepting. But she is also somewhat withdrawn, and this final session of remembrance has left her at a loss for words.

Still, Sturgis presses. Severn cannot be lost to her past now. Not now that all has been exposed. Sturgis shifts in her seat to ask again, laying a hand on Severn's hand.

"Severn, life, as I understand it is to live and to learn - to experience all the highs and lows. After everything *you've* discovered of your lost years, what *one* thing do you feel you've learned from this exercise?" Sturgis asks, offering closure on Severn's rediscovered trauma.

"What - have - I - learned," she repeats, sounding detached, apathetic, the final effects of hypnosis wearing off. She considers this carefully. She's learned of her forced captivity, a descent into sexual slavery, the devastating experiences that accompanied those years, the emotional fallout, and those responsible for her escape. Severn clears her throat and takes a long drink of water.

"The truth," Severn says, looking up at her therapist, head shaking almost imperceptivity. Her eyes dance in the mid-day sun as it pours through the office window. They are full of answers.

"And what do you think you've *gained* by knowing?" Sturgis isn't done asking difficult things of her.

"Gained?" Severn smiles despite herself. *"Everything."* She admits through a sigh, becoming more animated. "I've gained my life, myself, just... *everything.* I–I can look at myself without wondering. I can see the victim and console her. I see the survivor and applaud her. I can control my anxiety because I know where it originates. My life is my *own."*

"Do you truly believe that?"

"Oh, *yes*, I believe it, doctor," Severn assures her. "Over the past few weeks, the creeping dread I felt in certain situations has diminished because I understand where it's coming from. The debilitating heartburn is gone. *Knowing* has given me back my life. It's a late start, but it's *my* life now. How you've explained it to me today was like placing the final piece of the puzzle. It's still unnerving – what happened to me."

"Good, Severn. And what emotions are at the forefront of these discoveries?"

"I'm *angry*," Severn admits immediately, her head nodding. "I lost eighteen years of my life. I'm furious about that." She sits up straighter and continues. "I'm *sad*, too, for the trauma my mother and friends suffered. But I'm *grateful* for being alive."

"You should be *very* proud of your progress." Sturgis certainly is.

"Thank you for insisting I go through this step. My life makes sense. I even went on a date three nights ago. I've been *dying* to tell you."

"Men don't terrify you anymore," Sturgis states confidently.

"Not at all, and he was a very nice man. *Kind*, you know?" Severn's cheeks redden. "He bought dinner, he delivered flowers the following day. He has a daughter and three cats. Divorced five years ago. He's a professor at the college."

"He sounds like a real catch." Sturgis smiles brightly at her client. "I'm so *happy* for you, Severn."

Severn's expression languishes, and she looks down at her hands, fingertips tapping one another. "I feel a pull to thank those involved in my rescue, *our* rescue."

"You want to connect to those responsible for your freedom?"

"Yes. I'd like very much to express my gratitude."

"I think it's a wonderful notion, Severn. Keep expectations reasonable, though. The first responders involved in the operation may have trauma themselves over the condition in which they found you and the others." The doctor urges Severn. "I understand it was quite a devastating scene."

"Yes," Severn goes quiet a moment. She resists the magnetic pull of reliving the horror of sinking the knife into Dominus and watching on as he was torn apart. Is it any wonder her sub-conscious delivered her from those memories? "It was a terrible place," she admits. "I will tread carefully."

* * *

Since Severn's mother convinced her in '94 to forego discovering what had happened during those missing years, Severn had no idea of the generosity shown to her and her peers. After accepting Dr. Sturgis' recommendation, Severn joined the group developed to assist in her healing, listened to what the others had to say, and immediately emailed her benefactor and an appointment set up with Darnell Lincoln. A local philanthropist whose charity Severn and those in her group had been a recipient. Armed with this new information, she knew tomorrow would bring her that much closer to the whole truth.

2020

Severn Meets Darnell

Severn approaches the handsome brownstone in a less than affluent neighborhood mid-town. She passes three homeless men wheeling their overflowing, appropriated grocery carts down the wide sidewalk. As Severn is prone to, she gives them each a dollar. She has, for all her struggles, retained the spirit of that thirteen-year-old girl.

The breeze is anything but tropical, and it forces Severn to pull her coat closed. Snow accompanies the wind, and she looks down at her feet where a used syringe has rolled to meet the toe of her boot.

The brownstone building has been revitalized with newer windows, sandblasted brick, front gardens, and trees that will bear fruit in the summer months. It is the crown jewel of the neighborhood. Standing in front of the building, Severn's hand falls on her heart as a sense of excitement mounts. That she would soon meet the man who had played such an integral role in helping those freed from Dominus and his wicked trade makes her dizzy. She takes a deep breath and straightens her posture, lifting her chin and rolling back her shoulder, then makes her way up the short stairs and through the double doors.

At the front desk she is directed to the fourth floor, where Darnell greets her with a firm handshake and a glowing smile. He is every bit as handsome as his brownstone, Severn thinks, younger though, much younger.

"Severn," Darnell's voice is smooth and inviting, guiding her into his expansive office with the wave of his arm. He's tall and slender, dressed in slim-fitting

slacks and a white, button-up shirt. A brown belt matches his shoes to complete the outfit. His dark skin is radiant. He exudes joy.

Severn feels safe in his presence and takes a seat as Darnell effortlessly rounds his desk. He sits and leans over the desk, the wheels of his chair barely audible as they draw him closer to her. His elbows bend on the desktop, and hands support his square jaw as he stares at Severn a moment, smiling all the while.

"So, you're the one who got away," he says.

"Well, was *kept* away, I'm afraid," Severn knows what he means. That she was the one shielded from her time with Dominus. "My mother said I was better off, not knowing."

"You can't really blame her," Darnell says, leaning back into his chair. "Your memories were lost the moment you laid eyes on her; I'm told."

"Yes and thank you so much for your support arranging my counseling and that for the others over the years. You also arranged our group meetings?"

"You're very welcome, and *yes*, I saw a great need for group therapy. I contacted your mother twice over the years, asking whether she thought you were ready to know the truth." Darnell opens a file folder and lays it on his desktop. "There's something else I wanted to explain to you, Severn." He slides over a photocopy of a newspaper clipping from the folder and turns it for Severn to read.

"This article includes a photo of the man you and the others called Dominus. I didn't want to cause any triggers, so I've scribbled him out. Still, the article itself mentions him." He pauses and turns the paper over.

Severn's heart does a flip flop as her eyes land on the scribble of the man who had tortured her all those years; allowed children to die in his care, murdered innocence, and used up lives as if they were his to do so. The scribble is successful in hiding the monster's features. Severn's hand goes instinctively to her stomach as she reads the article.

"It... it says he left a son -" Severn states without looking up from the article. "The caption is highlighted, a seventeen-year-old son." She feels a slight pang of guilt over this information.

"That's right," Darnell hadn't let the other victims in on this secret but wants Severn to know everything.

"He was found dead at the time of law enforcement's arrival." Severn reads, remembering the graphic and horrific scene of Dominus' violent end. As deserving as it was, it seemed surreal, like a scene from a slasher film.

"Yes, his victims had already done him in," Darnell says. "You were there." Severn nods, eyes still on the article. "No doubt it was a long time coming for him."

"It couldn't have come soon enough for any of us," she admits, sniffling and accepting a tissue from Darnell.

"I couldn't agree more, Severn," Darnell slides the article back into the folder. "You see, your *Dominus* was my father."

This new information floors Severn, forcing her back, pressing her full weight into the plush chair while her fingernails dig into the armrests. She's frightened. The sensation is so contradictory to what she'd experienced just moments ago that she suffers something akin to an out of body experience. It's overwhelming. Her head floats and the balloon bursts plunging her back into Darnell's office. "*You?* But... you're the benefactor to so many," she's shaking her head. Her whole body shakes.

"*Please,* Severn, I'm nothing like my father," Darnell begins, realizing he's been too forward with the shocking information and chastises himself for his insensitive approach. "I'm telling you this because I want your *complete* trust. There are things you should know, all of you who suffered through those years at my father's cruelty."

"I'm listening," she breathes a shuddering breath, moves a rouge strand of hair from her face, wearing a less than friendly expression now.

"I'm so sorry I've upset you, it wasn't my intention. I too was on the wrong end of his abuse, nothing like what you and the other's endured, but abuse, nonetheless. I *hated* the man. I was getting ready to leave him when the police announced he was dead." Darnell is leaning on his desktop again, hands clasped together.

"That same night, I found a bounty of cash under our floorboards, fled, and found unconventional ways of making that cash grow. A year later, when I learned of the sexual slavery my father was involved in, I began my outreach program. I researched the victims of my father's brutality and tried to make amends."

"With all the good work you've done," Severn is warming up to him again.

"I know nothing will ever be enough, but I had to *try*."

"You've done more than most would have."

"Maybe. This is a truth I've hidden from everyone. But there is a deeper truth to my story and yours."

Severn is growing more and more intrigued as Darnell continues his confession. She shifts in her seat to prepare for this next truth. He's redeeming himself.

"What I've managed for the victims, the growth of my organization, and our accomplishments in meeting the needs of so many – I take very *little* credit for."

"How can you say that? You used that found money to rebuild lives. Who else is as deserving as you?" Severn asks, now leaning in as well, feeling the pull of Darnell's energy.

"That's why I'm so excited to have you here with me, Severn. I've someone I want you to meet. Someone *I* have yet to meet. But during my research so many years ago, I uncovered a truth I have sat on until now. But I'm ready now, and I'd like you to join me in this discovery."

1994

Talking it Out

"Jonah, I want to approach your anxiety over situations next," Dr. Sturgis began. This was Jonah's first session since meeting June and the fourth since the theatre shooting. Today he exuded a refreshing sense of confidence.

"Sure, which situations: being near people, people being near *me*, people pointing guns at me, doing shit alone,"

"You mentioned the shooter again," she pointed out. "How are you coping?"

"I have nightmares. I don't see myself going to a theatre anytime soon." Jonah explained candidly.

"Yes, the nightmares will diminish with time, but they're not keeping you from sleep?" Sturgis studied his reaction as Jonah shifted in his seat.

"I get to sleep alright. It's when I wake up at 3 am and can't shake the image of that fucker eyeing me down... *that* keeps me up. I try not to think about him otherwise."

"Don't forget to use the exercises we've gone over when that happens. You have the tools. Please use them. Your subconscious is still replaying the event in its entirety?" The doctor asked.

"If that's where my dreams live, then yeah."

"And how have you been otherwise, since our last session? You seem almost *energetic* today," she smiled at him.

"Same shit mostly, another rejection letter for my *non*-book. That sucked, as it does. I did meet someone, though, a couple nights back." He scratched at his eight o'clock shadow. "A girl. Name's June." Jonah explained how they met and under what circumstances, June's reaction to his condition and history in general.

"She sounds wonderful for you, Jonah," Sturgis said with a sense of foreboding in her tone. "I would encourage you to discover where this could go. No self-sabotaging. No negative self-talk. You *deserve* happiness, Jonah, every bit as much as June does. Give it room to grow."

"I'm doing that," Jonah assured her. "She's too good to be true." His head shook.

Sturgis lowered her glasses and offered a sympathetic smile. "That's just a *saying*, Jonah." She said, sensing his distress over the phrase.

"I know," Jonah's hands formed a tight ball on his lap. "It's just how it all happened and how well it's going. It seems almost like a set-up, *you know?*"

"Keep your ego out of it this time. Be cautious but be agreeable to wherever this goes. Let it happen without doubting yourself at every turn. Block your mother's voice using the techniques we've discussed and put into practice."

"That's never worked," Jonah said, dejectedly with a short, sarcastic laugh. "I can't block her."

"If you tell yourself you can't, then you *won't*. Remember what we've discussed. *I AM* are the two most powerful words in the world. You're telling yourself and the universe what you're capable of by uttering those two words."

"I know, *I know*, but then I get a lot of flak from the self-talk, and I give up. I feel weird reciting affirmations." Jonah's just tired of having to fight for space in his head.

"I can't make you do it, Jonah. This is one of those things you need to do for yourself. I want you to use this technique when thinking of June. Say *'I am going to see where this goes without interference.'* She suggested. "Say *'I am in a loving relationship,'* if that's where *you* want it to go."

"Love," Jonah said back with a smirk. "I've never been in love. Wouldn't know it if it happened."

"Trust me, you'll know. It will come so quickly and take you so far out of your comfort zone that you *will* know it."

"Sounds terrifying," Jonah admitted.

"In a good way," Sturgis smiled, and Jonah didn't spend much time fantasizing over what that smile meant. *Was he over her? Had June replaced Dr. Sturgis so quickly?*

"Your condition, have you found it lessens each time you meet with June?"

"Yes, actually, last time I barely dripped at all."

"Do you think it's because she so readily embraced it as non-threatening?"

"I haven't given it much thought – didn't want to jinx it, but yeah, maybe. She was good with it; liked it even."

"That must have come as quite a surprise. There's science that back it -"

"*I know*, June said the same thing." Jonah cut in. This is something he's never done, and Sturgis noticed with a pleasant grin. "Do you think she could be like my support animal or something?" Jonah laughed to himself over the thought. "Like, I take her everywhere and don't offend anyone within a few feet of me?"

"You said *support animal.* Why did you choose that term?" Sturgis crossed her legs and leaned forward.

"What? No, it's just, you *know*, like a support person, she's obviously not an *animal.*"

"Is that *obvious* to you, Jonah? You said she works as a stripper. That's not a highly regarded career. Do you feel at all uncomfortable with it?" Sturgis sizes him up with those giant, unblinking eyes framed by long, black eyelashes.

"Look, I just, I *misspoke*, that's all." But he knew Sturgis might consider a slip of the tongue. "I didn't mean it, *really.*" He pleads.

"You're fighting for her now, so I believe you. Not everything is a Freudian slip." She winked, and he felt that familiar rise in his groin.

"Remember what I said," she stood, announcing his session was over. "Use the '*I AM*' mantra and tell yourself all the positive and uplifting things that you are, for you are *many*, Jonah."

Jonah thanked her and left the office with a sense of progress. He really liked June and would continue to fight for her.

1994

A Walk in the Park

Jonah and June scheduled a date in the same nature reserve Jonah had taken Mort several times. Summer was in full swing, and the weather was perfect for a walk within the shaded trails under the watchful gaze of the trees. Jonah felt complete as he held June's hand, and a breeze carried his scent into the woods. He felt normal. He felt... *good.*

"If you want, you could join me tomorrow," June said, her eyes turned upward to appreciate the negative space of blue sky beyond the crowns of the Birch and Maples. "I'm tree-planting."

Jonah looked to her, surprise sending his brows hurtling toward his hairline. "Tree-planting... *wow,* you're full of surprises." Jonah neither loved nor hated the idea.

"I do it every year, well, for the last *five* years," June replied, looking to Jonah, who was smiling down at her. "Ever since my uncle died, he was a Forest Ranger. He died in one of the wildfires out west."

"I'm sorry to hear that. Were you close?"

"Until he went west, yes, we were very close. He'd taught me everything about the trees, the soil, animals, insects, and ecosystems that made it all possible. He was a good man with a lot of good to do." June seemed deflated talking about her uncle.

"Doesn't seem right taking a man like that out of the world," Jonah said, shaking his head at the ground.

"Right? We're losing nature to deforestation, all of it; the animals, the bugs, the... *everything.* He was here protecting all of that, educating the rest of us *morons* on how to live with nature. Now he's gone five years."

"It's like there's no point to any of it - life," Jonah said, angry for June's loss. "Wouldn't it make sense that if there were some grand scheme to see us all through this that your uncle would survive?" Frustration entered his tone while twigs snapped loudly under his feet as they continued their hike.

June shook her head solemnly and looked up at Jonah again. "Maybe that was the *point,* you know? My uncle died but left me a love of nature. Maybe he'd left that same impression on everyone he met." She shrugged, pulling up some of the forest floor with the toe of her boot. "He probably did."

"Well, if it worked with you, that same inspiration most likely manifested in others," Jonah agreed, and June finished his sentence. "And now more trees than he could have ever protected are being planted by the people whose lives he touched." She looked up at him again with a knowing smile. "*Thank you* for that, Jonah," her hand closed around his. "You've given me a new perspective."

"I'm glad," Jonah said, squeezing back. June pulled him to her level and gently kissed him on the mouth.

She pulled away, then in a more vibrant tone, said, "It's like when a squirrel or Jay bury a seed for the winter, you know?" June had become reflective on the subject. "If they die before retrieving it, they've seeded the next growth of forest without even knowing it. Like a blind affect."

"Blind affect?"

"Yeah, spelled with an 'a' not an 'e.' Is that bad grammar? Call it poetic license."

"Oh, you're a poet now?" Jonah said, teasing.

June laughed, "I don't know if it's a saying or not, but it's like when you do something, and it affects someone else's life in some way you'll never know. *A blind affect.*"

"I like it," Jonah said, considering its deeper meaning.

* * *

That night Morty met June for the first time and made a better impression than Jonah thought he might. Mort was dressed in what would pass as his Sunday best, which meant no tracksuit, a button-up shirt he must have just picked up from the Salvation Army, and a pair of slacks.

"Socks, too," Jonah teased and introduced June. They ate together and played video games until June announced she was heading to bed. Jonah looked at Mort and Mort at Jonah, savoring the moment. *Better Man* by Pearl Jam ran through Jonah's head like Self-talk was DJ'ing his inner monologue. *She's only here, with you, because she can't find a better man.* You know what? Jonah said to himself. *Fuck off!*

When June had gone into the bathroom, Morty held his hand up to receive a high-five. Jonah felt awkward over the gesture but eventually gave in and offered a light slap. To Jonah's mortification June caught them and said, "Just a *high-five*, boys? Get both hands up! Jonah's getting lucky tonight." She winked, laughed openly, and delivered herself into Jonah's bedroom. Neither man pretended not to see the lingerie June was wearing under her see-through nighty.

Mort and Jonah shared another look, this time both men's mouths were agape. Mort, with one hand still raised, slowly lifted the other. Jonah, feeling nervous and excited and oh so grateful, connected his palms with Morty's and didn't hold back. Mort wailed from the sting. Jonah rushed into the bathroom, brushed his teeth, and took a quick shower. He suffered anxiety over his inexperience. Jonah looked in the mirror; and for what might have been the first time in a long time, he actually studied himself. Jonah wasn't a bad looking guy. He had his hair, a strong jaw, a petite nose, brown eyes, and... no, *hazel* eyes. He wasn't overweight or underweight. He didn't have bulging muscles, but most guys didn't. He saw himself differently as a man with someone who appreciated him. It was June he had to thank for that. June was making things happen. June would deliver him from himself.

* * *

The following day, after breakfast, June and Jonah invited Mort along to plant trees on the outskirts of the very same forest they'd all experienced. Mort begged their forgiveness for opting out as he had three levels left to conquer in his new first-person shooter game.

Jonah was okay with this as Mort would only serve to slow them down. Besides, he knew what it felt like to be a third wheel. He'd been there with Mort through high school. As much as the couple denied it, the third wheel knew they weren't really welcome. Mort was a smart guy. He got it.

* * *

Moving through the woods, following the brightly marked path to the planting site, June pulled Jonah behind a huge boulder where she dropped her shorts so Jonah could enjoy her again - and she, him, as if three times the night before weren't enough. They were smitten.

That day they got their hands dirty and planted over one-hundred trees between them. A total of 3,000 were put in the ground. BBQ dinner was served to the volunteers at the end of the day, and June and Jonah caught the bus back to his place. She stayed the night again, having taken the weekend off from work to spend with him.

As they lay in bed after another long stretch of lovemaking, Jonah admitted his overriding fear to June. "It's like I'm waiting for the punchline, you know? Like this is some elaborate set-up."

"Oh, you need to think more of yourself than that," June said, her hand caressing his chest. "You've more going for you than most of the guys I've known. You're employed, kind, intelligent... *handsome*. You have a past, I have a past, we all have them, but they don't have to define us any more than our jobs do."

"We both appreciate nature," Jonah offered, June's head nestled into his shoulder. Her hair prickled his skin terribly, but he refused to admit it for fear of losing the connection. She smelled of earth and outdoors. "I think we'll discover that we like a lot of the same things."

"Maybe," June agreed with a tired sigh. "I *like* you; I know that much. Maybe that's enough."

"Maybe," He kissed her forehead and shifted enough that June's hair moved with him, and the itch was gone.

1997

Christmas

Christmas wasn't something Jonah had looked forward to since his mother died. Even while she was alive, the whole idea of faking the *spirit* of Christmas made him feel like a phony. He remembered being ten. Even his father would be at the house for three days straight. That was enough of a Christmas present for him. He wanted to like his father. He loved the man, he knew that, but he cherished the additional time at Christmas to get to know him and perhaps understand him. They would share a couch, all three of them, Jonah in the middle. Mother smoking with one hand and an eggnog occupying the other. Father half reading the paper and half watching *It's a Wonderful Life* on T.V. The tree up and decorated with a dozen presents wrapped neatly beneath it. This was family time. This was what Jonah expected families to do all the time, so he took advantage of the fictitious family life and reveled in it at Christmas. Christmas Eve, they attended the late church service, came home to hot chocolate and a present to open. The following day he would rush to his stocking, filled with comic books, candy, and a single clementine. Dinner was as festive as any he might imagine the neighbors enjoying, and the day after, they played with his new toys and consumed books and chocolates.

With the church and its self-soothing celebrations little more than an ever-eroding memory, Jonah worried about his first Christmas with June. Now, he was on his third. Sobriety had never felt so good. Three years behind him, June in front of him, *Christmas* upon him.

"Were you a good boy this year?" June asked playfully as she set the table to receive friends. Mort would arrive soon, a bouncer from June's work, and two of the dancers, Tiffany, and Leslie would complete their table. No one drank around Jonah. He encouraged them to do whatever they liked but was always relieved when they insisted on a *dry* night.

"You'd know best," Jonah replied. He'd been a very good boy, though. He'd experienced no relapses, no temper tantrums, no nothing like that on account of his many addictions. It had been an outstanding year. "Did Santa bring me what I asked for?"

"I guess you'll find out tomorrow morning." June reached across the table to place the final glass.

"You know, I get to open a present tonight."

"And you will. One of *my* choosing, *not* yours."

"Ah, good, you *did* get it for me," Jonah said, laughing as he basted the young turkey. "Otherwise, you wouldn't have put it like that." June hated, *hated* how he could guess every gift under the tree.

"You think you're *sooo* smart. Well, maybe I've outwitted you this year." She poured tap water into a jug and placed it on the table. She'd taken such care to set the mood in the apartment, wreaths, candles, lights, the works. June's Christmas spirit reanimated the ten-year-old in Jonah and let him revisit long-dead emotions attached to the season. He was grateful for that.

"My *Spidey sense* is tingling," Jonah confessed, comically wiggling his fingers at his temples. "There's a *Nintendo 64* in one of those packages." He gestured to the tree.

"If you think I'm spending good money on another gaming system, you're out to lunch, Jonah." She said it so convincingly Jonah felt a pang of loss.

"Nah," he brushed it off, "I'll be playing Mario Cart 64 by morning." He winked and accepted a slap on the ass as June passed through the galley-style kitchen to get the front door. "You're *impossible*," she said, feigning frustration.

The door opened to greet Morty and his gift of dessert. He was the dessert-bringer to any social gathering hosted by June and Jonah. "Made it myself," Mort declared as he handed over the premade, prewrapped and pre-purchased cake in a box.

"At least it's not missing a piece this year," June replied, accepted the cake with a smile, and placed it on the counter.

"If I'd had the time, I would have honored that little tradition, but I came straight from the store." Mort jams his two index fingers into the deep dimples on both cheeks, and June takes the opportunity to wrap her arms around the big man's waist in a hug. Mort hugs her back and pats her on the shoulders.

"Alright, alright, you two, get your meat hooks off my girl," Jonah teases Mort, and they hug. Pulling away, Mort announces, "Place looks shiny, June."

"Thank you, Morty. I appreciate your noticing the shiny things. You're like a bird." The three laugh, and Jonah invites Mort to sit.

Moments later, the bouncer named Sid is welcomed, with Tiff and Leslie close behind. "No gawking this year, Mort," Jonah whispered with a good-humored jab at his friend's belly.

"Get outta here," Mort replied, slapping Jonah's hands away. "Which one is June setting me up with?"

"*Neither*" Jonah said back, amused. "If you wanna talk one of them up, I'll be your wingman. But first, you need to figure out which one is with Sid."

Mort sized up the big man up. "*Jesus*, the guy looks like he's got his own finishing move," Mort said. Sid was built to intimidate. "Maybe I'll just let the girls do the work."

Jonah slapped Mort on the arm and couldn't help but snort out a reply. "They'll be fighting over you by the end of the night."

"If I have to throw down with Sid, what do you suggest?"

"No high-flying maneuvers," Jonah supplied the wrestling jargon straight-faced as he poured himself a soda water. "That will only serve to work against you. If you can get him on the floor, pull a *Hogan* leg drop."

"*Niiice,*" Mort said. Jonah enjoyed watching his friend playing out the fantasy. "I was thinking into the rope body slam, but the leg drop is more me."

"Do you see any ropes in the apartment, Mort? *Come on*, man, you gotta work within the parameters of the ring." Jonah missed the nonsense conversations he'd had with Mort throughout his life but found them all the more endearing when they got together for celebrations. He loved Mort. He couldn't say that about many people. Two, in fact. He and June had exchanged '*I love you's*' in '95, barely a year after being together. Then there was the discussion about moving in together and the need to do it without Mort. Initially, Jonah had invited June to live with them. She didn't want a roommate. Jonah also liked the idea of living alone with June. Like a real relationship. Something he'd never truly experienced. Mort took the news in stride. He never once argued against it. He'd only had Jonah's best interests in mind.

When introductions were made, and everyone felt at ease with one another, Jonah and Mort learned Sid was in training, and so a dry night was exactly what he needed. Tiffany had been a ballet dancer before an accident changed the course of her career, and Leslie abstained from alcohol as a general rule. June had cherry-picked her friends for the night to meet all of Jonah's requirements to stay sober. She was always looking out for him. She truly saw something in him worth saving.

The night was a success, and as everyone filed out, Mort received a kiss from both Tiffany and Leslie, and, to everyone's surprise, Sid! Mort hung back a moment after they'd left, flush faced. "Well, at least now we know Sid's finishing move," he stated, receiving a kiss from June and then landing one of his own on Jonah. They laughed.

"Yup, that would finish *me* off!" Jonah bellowed and accepted a middle finger from his friend as he passed into the stairwell. Shaking his head, he turned to June, and she caught him in a passionate kiss.

"I *love* our life," she proclaimed, fingers laced together behind his neck. Jonah nodded and exhaled shakily. "Are you okay?" June asked, her dark eyes reflecting in the candlelight.

"Oh, *June,* "Jonah declared, "I've never been better."

1999

Dinner

May of 1999 would mark five blissful years of June. He coined it the perpetual summer of Jonah. June lived with him in the apartment above Morty, who had remained in their rental with foreign exchange students paying the bulk of the rent. For four years Jonah and June had lived in relative peace; planting trees annually, going to work, and coming home to each other. Jonah was grateful for every day he had with June – but never had he been so manic to think he might spend years with her. It had happened so organically he could hardly describe the ease in which they managed it all.

June remained a dancer during this period at a semi-reputable club not far from their home. Jonah had been several times to escort her home and had stayed to watch more than once. Never did he take advantage of his status to indulge in a dance from one of the girls. Through his voyeurism, he realized that June was an artist on stage. No touching, no grinding, nothing too lewd but wow, did she entertain. June manipulated that pole like a gymnast. No wonder she had a six-pack! Hanging horizontally with her legs wrapped around the pole was impressive enough to put her in a Cirque act. It doesn't pay what a dancer can make, she'd reply, and she was right. June brought home enough and had saved enough that they had begun discussing *owning* rather than renting.

During a walk in the same forest they'd helped revitalize, Jonah kicked at a burnt-out campfire. "They know they shouldn't be lighting fires in this park," June said, glaring at the blackened wood and lazily placed circle of stones. "Yet the evidence of their ignorance remains," Jonah added. June hated the idea of humans starting forest fires. That was how her favorite uncle had died, defending a small town against an ever-intensifying blaze.

"So, few spaces like this left and still human stupidity somehow overrides sense." June kneeled down to investigate the scene.

"Just some kids having fun," Jonah suggested, changing his tune when June's glare fell on him. "But that doesn't give them the right."

"No, it *doesn't*," June stood up and sighed. "But we were all young once, I suppose." June wasn't a saint in her youth either. She wasn't an alcoholic or drug-addicted fiend. Still, she'd had destructive relationships and been a part of the cocaine crowd in the '80s. During a challenging time in her mid-twenties, she found dancing. As she'd explained it, dancing found her. Not Jazz, or Tap, of course - Exotic dancing. A boyfriend suggested June's work as an office assistant wasn't paying enough to afford their apartment and his addictions, so she started one night a week at The Strip.

She was a headliner within months of starting her new career and hadn't looked back since. Jonah never asked what she made. She covered her half of the rent and groceries, and that's all he ever expected. They had enough to enjoy dinners out and new furniture once they'd moved into the apartment. June even treated them to a 27" Sony Trinitron TV.

Jonah and June kept mostly to themselves. Jonah had kicked his habits, save smoking. June didn't really drink alcohol as it was considered unnecessary calories. In her line of work, there was no room for excess calories. They were happy and considering adding on to their family.

"I don't think Mort would go for it, June," Jonah would say when she brought it up. "He's a big boy; he can live on his own." They would laugh, and she would tilt her head and smile that whimsical smile at him.

"Seriously though, Jonah, don't you *want* to have kids?" She pulled her ponytail tighter, her biceps flexing. "We'd make a good-looking kid."

"Honestly, I'm afraid of passing my defective genes onto a child of my own," was Jonah's argument against children.

"There's no guarantee our kid's gonna have *your* faulty genes," June winked at him and threw a soft elbow into his ribs. Jonah grabbed her and held on. "Besides, you beat it. Who's to say they won't?"

"Why put a kid in that position? Why fuck with perfection?" Jonah was serious; he loved his life for the first time. He liked himself and felt accomplished after a day of work. Coming home to June - if she wasn't working late - was a treat.

Making her a meal she could enjoy with him or when she returned was enough for him.

"I don't want perfection to become complacency," June wrapped an arm around Jonah and pulled him even tighter. The woods smelled of rich of flora and she breathed it in.

"Do you worry about us?" Jonah's expression fell. The day was so warm and the air so fresh he had hoped the conversation would remain in the realm of nonsense, as they were prone to.

"I don't," her free hand slid up his chest, and she pulled his chin down to kiss him. "I just wonder what it would be like. I'm thirty-six. You're forty. If we were going to do it, we'd need to consider it in the next year."

"Tick tock, eh?" Jonah squeezed her ass. He sighed as she pushed his hand away. It amused Jonah endlessly that in a public place, she could become such a prude when her job demanded she be the polar opposite. It seemed a recent change in her.

"Yeah, *tick-tock*, old man," June replied. They continued to walk the woods, June pointing out the mosses and foliage growing along the forest floor. "Sometimes I think I should go back to school for forestry."

"Bit *long in the tooth*, don't you think?" Jonah said to sustain a reaction. She slapped him in the nuts. It stung a moment, but she was a pro; she knew where and how hard to hit. It was like a superpower or something- knowing exactly where the left nut hung. June kissed the top of his head as he lurched forward to instinctively cover his groin.

As the day went on, they sat where a spectacular vista availed itself to any who dared to venture onto the protruding stone, some two-hundred feet above the valley. They sat without a millimeter between them. They were one with nature and with each other. The wind picked up and began to move through the trees along the high cliffs which bordered the valley below. A strong wind was not welcome on the protrusion, and Jonah pulled June to the safety of the woods as the wind gusted. It was a cool breeze, announcing the evening's arrival. They gathered themselves up and decided to go to dinner at a restaurant not far from the park.

June had purchased a new car a month earlier and loved to drive. She had acquired her license the moment she was legal, in stark contrast to Jonah having never gotten his. Jonah preferred the car to public transit. He never had to feel uncomfortable with his Bromhidrosis when removed from others. His world was getting bigger.

Michael Poeltl

Say My Name by Destiny's Child on the car radio demanded June turn up the volume. "What do you think of this song?" Rhetorical question. "It sets a nice mood for a final dance in my routine, wouldn't you agree?"

Jonah's mind goes to the last time he watched June work the runway. This time he imagined it to *Say My Name*. On all fours, her knees pressing against the blanket, moving her body up, down, up, like a feral cat on the hunt, propelling her along the stage and then rolling over onto her chiseled back with her muscular legs up in the air. Her hands float over her torso and stretch out over her head. Next, she rolls up on her shoulders, legs wrapping around the brass pole, and she pulls herself up into an arched position. Arms reach behind her to take the pole next. Legs release and she pushes herself, ever so slowly into a horizontal position, the strength in her upper body revealed. Her body on display. She was a master of the tease.

As they drove down a busy street, June took his hand, and he squeezed hers back, studying her long lashes. "I'm looking forward to dinner," June told him, eyes wide and brows lifting in surprise. *Why were they surprised?*

The answer came immediately as Jonah's body was hurled against his seatbelt. Pain radiated from the sudden and violent motion. Simultaneously an explosion deafened him, and something punched him square in the face. The sound came almost after the jolt; a crashing sound of metal on metal, plastic snapping, components bursting, bones cracking, blood pounding in his head. None of it made any sense. They were just going to dinner.

* * *

Jonah awoke in the hospital to Mort. His unmistakable form looked as though it'd been poured into the small chair at Jonah's bedside. Jonah's glasses were held together by epoxy and resting on his chest. He managed to place them on his nose, wincing from a sharp pain in his shoulder. The room was quiet, the door was open, the drapes were drawn. It was night. The lighting was dim, and the scent in the room was a mixture of his Bromhidrosis and that sickly sweet smell of disinfectant. Next, Jonah assessed his situation. His left leg was raised on pillows, not broken, but sore. He felt around his face and flinched where he remembered his nose had been pushed sideways. His forehead felt pockmarked. *Shrapnel from the windshield? I'd been in a car accident.* He was wearing a neck brace as well. *Jesus,* had he broken his neck? He wiggled the toes of his right foot. Seemingly not.

His thoughts turned next to June. *Why weren't they in the same recovery room?* It would have been nice to be together for however long it might take to get back on their feet. Jonah scanned his room for a button to call a nurse. He secured his glasses behind his ears and watched Mort snore from what must have been an exceptionally uncomfortable position. "Mort," Jonah didn't recognize his own voice as it cracked. *How long had he been like this?* He cleared his throat and tried again. "Morty," he called out, jarring the big man awake.

A startled Mort rubbed his eyes and smiled at his friend. Mort pulled himself free of the chair, pushing off the armrests, and stumbled over to Jonah, careful not to disturb the tubes running in and out of his friend. "Jonah, you're awake." He said as if Jonah were unaware.

"What's happened, Mort? Where's June?" Jonah was getting his voice back. Mort scrambled to give him an ice cube. Jonah let the welcome moisture into his mouth and sucked.

"She's uh, in another room," Mort explained, nodding. "I'm supposed to alert the staff when you woke up. They'll, uh, they can give you more information -"

"Mort," Jonah locked eyes with his best friend, conveying the lifetime of trust that existed between them, begging for the truth. *"Where. Is. She?"* Jonah's heart fluttered; the rhythm interrupted by the distress which manifested in Mort's expression. Mort's face collapsed into a grimace. Jonah's head began to shake side to side. *"Don't.* Don't tell me she's -"

"Jonah, I *need* to get the doctor in here," Mort said flatly. "It's not my place to -"

"To *what*, Mort?! What the *fuck* is happening?" Jonah's voice fizzled out, and frustration morphed into a pained moan. He began to sob uncontrollably, his hands clasping and pulling at the sheets beneath him. The thought June might be gone began the involuntary rise of anxiety in his chest, triggering fear, paralyzing both arms with pins and needles. His breathing became erratic, and his whole body began to shake.

Mort placed panicky hands on Jonah's torso in an attempt to stop the trembling. Jonah's voice was raw, guttural as he called out June's name. Mort began to tremble himself. A nurse appeared at the door and rushed in to assist.

Mort, with tears streaming down his round, red cheeks, apologized for not following protocol. The nurse asked him to move to the side and then administered something which seemed to calm Jonah considerably.

"He can't thrash around like that," the nurse told Mort. "Not in his fragile condition."

"H - he asked about June, about his girlfriend." Mort wiped his face with the sleeve of his shirt. "I didn't tell him anything, but I think he figured it out."

The nurse nodded and placed a sympathetic hand on Mort's shoulder. Jonah was still conscious and heard every word; he was just incapable of responding save the tears, which blurred his sight and stung his eyes. He closed them hard and, as the calming effect of the drug overtook him, dreamed of June.

1999

They Say They Come in Threes

There was no waking up from this nightmare. Nothing anyone could say would make it better or force sense into it. Jonah had taken one giant leap forward when he'd met June, and when she left him, he felt like he'd taken a dozen steps back. He felt hollow, insisting the nurses increase his morphine drip as he continued to complain about pain. Of course, the physical pain was manageable - the drip dulled the emotional trauma. Jonah was an addict without a support system. Morty had visited daily for the first two weeks. Jonah's refusal to contribute to a conversation or speak at all kept Mort at a distance on the third week.

Jonah descended into self-talk and allowed it to berate his feelings and question *every. single. moment* that had made up the day of the crash. It wondered things like *why hadn't he gotten his license? This accident might have been avoided. Maybe it's your fault. Keep asking for morphine until you feel nothing. You didn't really expect Happily Ever After to go on predictably? Not for you. Here's how you can end it all and join June in the nothingness.* Then ego made itself known and Jonah's mother's voice explained how the world exposes weaknesses, targets them and endeavors to crush those who dared to live and to love. *It's not your fault, but you shouldn't have tried.*

Jonah had attended June's funeral with the assistance of Mort and a single crutch. He'd spoken to the few family members who had attended, a cousin, aunt and uncle from June's hometown, and her estranged father. The girls from The Strip also showed their support. There were lots of tears and sympathies unloaded on Jonah. Though they were offered with the best intentions, he felt heavier for accepting them - as if each *"I'm sorry"* somehow remained with him as the grieving parties made their exit. He would live with this loss forever. They would all go back to work and back to loving the living in their lives.

It was an open coffin. June looked nice, but not herself. Jonah knew what they did to the dead in the basement of funeral homes. *Vampires. Seamstresses. Painters.* The bodily fluids drained and replaced with formaldehyde-based chemicals. Mouths sewn shut from the inside, and plastic inserted behind the eyelids to maintain their natural shape. Color reintroduced to their faces using an airbrush because the skin becomes too tight for conventional makeup. It was something he'd learned at Squid Ink as a fellow customer - a mortician - explained the process to their tattoo artist. *Thank Christ they didn't use her headshot from The Strip to go by.* They must have pulled a pic from his apartment. June never needed makeup, and they seemed to get that. Just enough blush to raise her cheek bones and a clear lip balm to brighten her smile. Eyeliner and mascara compliment her long lashes. Tiffany, June's friend from the club, had volunteered to do her hair once they'd washed it. It was the most authentic part of her, Jonah thought, and thanked Tiff for her kind gesture.

Jonah had approached the coffin with the assurance that the act would offer him closure. At least that's what they say. See the body, accept the fact. He didn't want to accept it. But that wasn't his reality. It was a fact. June was dead. And so, a part of him was gone, his favorite part. He trembled upon seeing her. Hands gripped the coffins edge. Ego pleaded for him to run while self-talk screamed in his head that this was avoidable. Jonah did his best to bury the voices. His mind wandered. The coffin wasn't what she'd be buried in. June had requested something far less ornate. The outfit was one he'd purchased for her birthday two years earlier after she'd carefully selected three dresses for him to choose from. He smiled at the memory. She knew him so well. No one had ever known him like June had. Countless memories assaulted Jonah's heart and he bowed at the weight of them. Tears fell effortlessly into the coffin as his body jerked to repress the sobs. Mort gathered him up and took him to another room. Jonah obeyed. There he stayed until it was over.

How could he recover from such a loss? How would he ever face another moment without her?

* * *

June and Jonah had made Wills two years prior, so Jonah inherited all of June's worldly goods. The money she'd saved had kept him going while he'd taken an extended leave of absence from work. It kept him in the drink. Another loved one dead, and yet somehow, he kept on living.

Morty had tried to stop him. He'd pleaded with Jonah not to take the familiar path. It's not what June would have wanted. *Well, June would want for nothing anymore.* His self-talk supported his decision to go back to the bottle, his ego just repeating, *'I told you so,'* over and over again in his mother's fragile voice. Alcohol and Mort were the only two who'd stuck it out with him. They'd always be there.

Jonah was heartbroken. He was weak and tired and sick over the choices he'd made. *Guess I'll never learn.* He took a deep drag from his cigarette and blew the smoke across his living room. Night had crept in. *Had he been sitting on the loveseat all day?* The bottle of Vodka on the coffee table was nearly empty. Had he eaten anything? Who had the time? He tried to stand and immediately fell back into the loveseat. He was in no shape to move. He stubbed out the smoke after three attempts and laid down. *Bad things happen in threes*, self-talk reminded him. If that were true, then, by his count, one more must be waiting in the shadows. Something terrible delaying its arrival until he was sober enough to appreciate it. But Jonah never expected to be sober again. In this, he would outwit fate. Thunder rolled across the city, and flashes of lightning lit the dark corners of the apartment, igniting the baubles and trinkets June had purchased over the years. She wasn't a shopper, but when she really loved something, she incorporated it, adding to the comfortable ambiance she'd created in their living space. Jonah had considered packing them up and moving on, actually beginning the process under the manic influence of cocaine one night but couldn't bring himself to do it. And so, they remained a reminder of better times. *Times you'll never know again.*

* * *

The following day Jonah woke to the sound of rapping at his door. It continued unabated until he managed to move across the room and answer it. His head pounded, and his body trembled. Through chattering teeth, he asked who was there. "It's Mort, Jonah, open up." Mort – Jonah gave this special consideration. How often had he ignored his best friend from downstairs since June's passing? Many times. *Would he do it again?*

"Not feeling well, Morty," It seemed he would. "Just making some soup -"

"Oh, *bullshit*, Jonah," Mort retorted, his tone one of mounting frustration. "Just open the fucking door. I'm tired of waiting you out."

"I'm not interested in anything you have to say to me," Jonah explained.

"This ain't about *you!*" Mort fired back. "Jesus, *Jonah*, are we still friends or not? *I* need to talk to you!" Mort's head could be heard to thump against the door. Jonah unlocked the chain and pulled the door open.

"Thank you," Mort said - a wall of smoke and stink meeting him upon entry. He waved both hands in front of his face and ran to the window, which he cranked open. "Jonah, man, are you *seriously* living like this?"

"If you can call it living," Jonah replied, wandering into the kitchen, searching out bottles to drink from. As one bottle touched another in Jonah's bleary-eyed review, it seemed to Mort like an ensemble of singing glasses played in a chorus of the absurd. Clothes were everywhere, and the ones on his back were stained with sweat marks. Take-out food containers were competing for dominance over the liquor boxes that intruded upon every corner of the apartment.

"I got *cancer*, Jonah," Mort hoped his announcement would stay the clanging of bottles. Jonah looked up at his friend and noticed him for the first time in several days. Mort had lost weight. Mostly in his face, it seemed gaunt in comparison to his usual robust and rosy cheeks. His skin was pale, and his eyes bloodshot. The grimace he wore completed his tale of tragedy.

"Don't *you* fucking die on me too," Jonah said in a commanding, raspy voice, an accusing finger pointed at his friend from across the room. Jonah's hands flew up, and he let them fall heavily at his sides. "How do you *know* you have cancer? Why is this the first I hear about it?" Shouting the last sentence in frustration forced Jonah's fingers to his temples.

Mort sat at the kitchen table June had ordered for the couple from her favorite store. He studied the finish on the tabletop and shook his head. *"Fuck you, "* he replied softly. "I found out *days* ago. I've tried to get in touch with you, but work says you've taken extended leave, and your phone goes right to voice mail. I've knocked... I don't know how many times and heard nothing back. I've been to the two places you might have gone. You've been impossible since the funeral."

Jonah nodded and sat across from Mort, falling hard into the designer chair. If Morty really had cancer... then he was a bad friend. "I'm sorry, Mort," he offered, elbows on the table, shoulders aiming skyward and head drooping. Jonah's hair hadn't seen a comb in a week. "I'm caught up in my own shit."

"No, kidding. June's going to take a long time to get over... and that's okay, she *should*, but you have to give yourself that time." Mort raised a hand at the plethora of bottles lining the kitchen's breakfast bar. It could be a scene from a bachelor party. No one man should be capable of consuming so much alcohol in such a short time, Mort thought. Jonah offered him the obligatory nod. "Seriously, Jonah, this *isn't* okay. June would hate what you've done to yourself. *I* hate it. I *need* you now. I need you, man..." Mort looked devastated. His jaw went slack, and his eyes stayed fixed on the tabletop as if still processing his own news. Jonah placed a hand on his friend's thick forearm.

"You selfish prick," Jonah mumbled as a sarcastic smile inched up one side of this face. "You *would* fuck up my misery with a dash of your own just to keep me sober." His tired body jerked as a hollow laugh escaped him.

Mort snorted at this. "That *is* something I would do," he admitted. "Still, I'm not that creative. I'd have faked a suicide or choked on a ham sandwich." The laughter grew, and before long, both men were incapable of stopping. Something in them had snapped. Something wonderful perhaps – perhaps not, but as Jonah saw it, what harm could it do?

Eventually, the laughter had slowed, and tears were wiped from weeping eyes. Jonah lit a cigarette, and Morty asked him to put it out. "Cancer? Remember... *asshole?"* This began another fit of laughter, and Jonah put out the smoke, chuckling at his own ignorance.

"I *am* an asshole!" They laughed through this and several more realizations until finally, the apartment fell quiet. The men were exhausted, and their stomachs ached from the workout.

"I need to go take my meds," Mort remembered. "Want to come down and play a round of RAW with me? You can have The Undertaker." Mort stopped at the front door.

"I'll be right behind you, Morty," Jonah told him, waving him off. Then he lit another cigarette and allowed the reality of his friend's illness to sink in, sobbing at his window over the news. Jonah hated how the universe seemed to target the good people for extermination. First, it was his grandma Anne, then his parents, June and what now? Now it wanted his best friend. Jonah had earned a place amongst them. *Christ, I'd practically begged to be taken, and yet I remain while those I love leave me. What possible point was there to my existing? To suffer, of course.* Self-talk. It was beginning to feel more like truth-talk to Jonah.

Mort wouldn't appreciate where Jonah's head was going. So, he sucked it up and spit it out the open window, shook himself off, and rolled his head over his neck, prompting multiple snaps and cracks. He threw on a hat and drank a glass of water, then chased that with a couple shots of whiskey. He would game with his friend and try to be in the moment. He would be Jonah, and Mort would be Mort, and their shared history would see them through the day. He had to believe that. He couldn't lose Mort.

* * *

Sobriety was disorienting. Too many thoughts made it past whatever gatekeeper materialized during his binges. Without drugs and alcohol, it welcomed them with open arms and offered them a seat. Memories too, *"stay as long as you like,"* the sober gatekeeper announced, *"Put your feet up. Tell me a story."*

The thoughts were often murderous. The memories supported the demons he'd let in his head by losing himself in gaming rather than maintaining a level of drunkenness. Jonah flinched at the truths his memories revealed to him. *She's gone. Forever. You're alone. Again. It's not worth it without her. She gave your life meaning. Now you have none.*

Torturous thoughts rushed in, and he was defenseless against them. The bottles on the counter beckoned. The framed picture of June caught his eye, and he stopped short of a bottle of vodka. "I have to, June," he explained hastily. "I'm no good without you -" Jonah's voice caught in his throat, and he steadied a shaking hand. Tears followed the pained announcement. He'd never been enough by himself. *Never.* June had given him everything.

He broke from June's glare and, in a blind rage, charged into the bedroom. There he began to yank clothes from hangers and pull drawers from the dresser, grabbing handfuls of June's belongings, thrusting them into a black garbage bag. "You're *gone*, June!" He shouted into the bag. "We're *done*. You *died.*" His thoughts returned to the accident, the joyful moments before it happened, but even those memories sparked a storm he could not quiet.

Jonah spun on his heels in the small bedroom and, taking inventory of what was June's, snapped up items large and small and pushed them into the garbage bag. Jesus, even the bedsheets were hers, or, at least, she'd bought them. He couldn't possibly erase June's memory altogether without leaving with the clothes on his back, and even then... she'd picked out everything he was wearing.

Jonah collapsed on the floor next, crying hysterically into June's belongings. Her scent wafted up from the bag to slap him in the face. His hands formed fists, clutching at a bra, a toque, and a plush toy rabbit she refused to part with. Snot and tears smeared on the rabbit's fur, matting it down as Jonah's face rubbed across the length of its back. For this, he felt guilty. He was demeaning the stuffed animal June had carried with her for decades. He stood, made his way to the bathroom, and rinsed the rabbit gingerly under a warm stream of water. This I'll keep, but nothing else, he told himself. It was her *Rosebud*, the rabbit. From *Citizen Kane*. Like the teddy bear in the movie, it represented simplicity and comfort. She could take her childhood with her wherever she went, wrapped up tidily in a plush toy. That's how June had described it when it first presented itself to Jonah, and he'd teased her for it. Jonah immediately rented the movie to understand her attachment. He felt sad he hadn't anything like it to recall his youth. *For the best, perhaps.*

Michael Poeltl

2001

Of Loss and Lessons

Morty, also known as Mortimer Edward Gladstone, died peacefully on November 22nd, 2001, while undergoing cancer treatments at St. Joseph's Hospital, surrounded by family and close friends. In lieu of flowers, please donate in Mort's memory to the Cancer Foundation's ongoing work to end this brutal disease with the family's thanks.

Jonah didn't really like what his parents had written for Mort's eulogy, but he was their son. Jonah had written his own for consideration, which actually spoke to Morty's personality and humor. What they put in the newspaper was about as generic as the beer Jonah drank before returning to Squid Ink.

"Honestly, Mort, I thought it would be your heart," Jonah recalled saying as Mort entered his second week at the hospital. They laughed. Months earlier, they thought they'd gotten all of the cancer. Mort had lost at least a hundred pounds for the surgery and had begun to look human. He'd lost more over the course of the continued chemo. Then a new tumor - a much more aggressive tumor, made its appearance, announcing his death sentence.

"Cancer hurts," Mort replied, drinking water from a straw, "but there's something to experiencing it that I'm grateful for." Mort looked serene, accepting of his pain. "Like, a heart attack would be quick, but you'd have no time to contemplate your life or say goodbye. You'd just drop, and the cats would get your eyeballs before anyone noticed."

"I get it," Jonah said, wondering whether he did. The year leading up to the two weeks of constant care had been hard. In the end, it was all for nothing. Mort would die anyway. It sucked. It more than sucked; it shattered Jonah. "I'm just glad I could clean up enough to see you through it."

"Fuck'n guy," Mort teased, "always has to come back to you, man." More effortless laughter from both men and Jonah stymied a tear. Mort looked contemplative. "I made peace with my father, you know? We had the heart to heart. He apologized."

"That's good, Mort," Jonah said, wondering why it took the end of his son's life to extract an apology for his abuse all those years ago.

Realization took the place of contemplation on Mort's expression. "Well, at least I did everything I wanted to."

Jonah laughed again, confused over the comment. *"Like what?!"*

"Fuck all and nothin, man. *Fucking nothing."* Mort admitted showing no bitterness over the fact. Jonah looked defeated by it. "Seriously, Jonah, I had *no* ambition and have *no* regrets. I did exactly what I wanted to."

"Nothing," Jonah repeated, the word pulling him down.

"Yep," Morty agreed. "What *did* I do? I completed a couple dozen video games, dated a couple girls, went to college. Worked at what, twenty jobs? What else is there?"

"I'm not the one to ask, Mort," Jonah confessed, his voice betraying his exhaustion. He was always so desperate for a drink or a snort when he visited Mort. It sounded shallow and even selfish, but he was anxious for it all to be over. He'd been given a month. He had a week left. Having the shadow of death hanging over you like Mort had was heart-rending to watch. Plus, he was slightly ashamed to admit it - but - he wanted that drink, and Mort's death meant he was back off the wagon. Addiction was a powerful thing.

Mort did die, of course, and there was a funeral and everything. Jonah hugged Mort's mom and sister and glared at his father, regardless of his apology to Mort on his death bed, he couldn't help remembering the tales of beatings at the man's hands. Mort's life wasn't particularly special. He was the first to admit it, but he was Jonah's best and only friend, and that had to mean something. *Didn't it?* He was always there for Jonah, even when he wasn't there for himself. Mort was kind and easy to be around and funny. That had to stand for something. *Right?* Jonah never looked at Mort and saw the fat, social outcast. He saw the kid he grew up with who'd struggled with his weight and put up with the cruel ambitions of others designing ways to make him feel like shit about himself. At some point, he'd just stopped caring, but Jonah never doubted that he'd ever stopped hurting.

As he collected the gaming systems from Mort's apartment at the behest of his grieving mother and sister, Jonah locked himself inside his apartment. He began binging on alcohol and video games.

"Mort, you prick," he said aloud as he reviewed the wrestling game's avatars, "I *hate* playing against the computer. Why did you have to fuck off on me like this?" Jonah inhaled and stubbed his cigarette out in the overflowing ashtray. He lobbed the game controller at his TV and picked up a bottle of beer. A long drink from the bottle drained it, and he reached over the arm of his couch for another. *Hash Pipe* by Weezer played on his CD player and Jonah felt the warm tug of his addictions.

"I know, I know," he said with venom on his tongue to his now invisible friend, "you *hate* I'm doing this to myself, but there's no one left to give a shit, Mort." Then an idea began to percolate. He had more than one addiction he could satisfy tonight. Mort's passing was an important life event for Jonah. It needed to be documented in something more permanent than the printed program he'd received at the funeral. He gathered himself together, threw on a jacket and marched out of his apartment to Squid Inks. Mort's end, like June's, demanded a tattoo. This time it would be *The Undertaker.*

"Nearly completed this sleeve, Jim," Sid said, still oblivious to Jonah's actual name. "We gonna start the other soon?"

"Just the one, I think," Jonah replied, not expecting to live long enough to begin the other arm.

"Wrestling fan, eh?" Sid asked, always trying to make conversation and distract from the needle.

"Not actually," Jonah confessed. He only liked playing the game with Mort. The Undertaker was his favorite. It was something in the name.

"Are you an undertaker? Like a modern-day undertaker? What is it called - a mortician? Working at a morgue?" Sid looked up a moment to wink at his girlfriend, who was working on another customer.

"Nope," Jonah closed his eyes and tried to relax into the chair and just meditate on the buzz of the gun as it tattooed another memory into his flesh. "Not as obvious as all that."

"You like to keep to yourself," Sid was tired of the games. "Cool."

Jonah let it go and breathed through the pain, allowing himself to feel something other than grief and self-loathing.

After 45-minutes in the chair, his arm bandaged and enjoying a smoke on the street, Jonah watched as a transport trailer rushed past him. *How easy would it be to just step out in front of a truck and join June and Mort and Mom? Apparently not that easy, or he'd have done it by now. Fair enough. Still, why hadn't he tried suicide? Too messy?* He'd hate to fuck it up and end up a cripple or vegetable or something.

Was it cowardice? Maybe, or was suicide the coward's way out? None of it was easy. Not anymore. Not since June. Jonah took a leisurely route home and ran into a group of men huddled around a garbage can they'd lit on fire. He made eye contact with one man, who then asked for a cigarette. Jonah gladly offered him one. While still experiencing the adrenaline from the new tattoo, he decided to join them around the burning circle as homage to his past.

"Ya look older," the wrinkled little man with dark eyes smoking his cigarette commented. Jonah looked at him a moment later, realizing he was speaking to him. "Yes, *ya*, scruff."

"Me?" Jonah pointed a thumb at himself and blew a billow of smoke from his nostrils. "We don't know each other," he said dismissively.

"Ya don't remember, but I gots a steel trap of a memory." The older man claimed, tapping his temple with a fingerless gloved hand. His beard was long and gray, and his hair seemed to pour out from under a ratty-looking toque in greasy curls. His face wasn't familiar to Jonah. *Could he be from my past?*

"Why do you think you know me?" Jonah took a step back from the roaring fire.

"Must be ten years gone," the older man contemplated, "twelve, maybe." He dropped his cigarette into the trash can and stepped away from the fire as well. "Walk with me," he said, and Jonah caught up in the curiosity of the moment, saw no reason not to.

"Ya were a young lad last we stood 'round a fire like that," the man pulled a small bottle of something from his ragged jacket and took a swig. "I had hoped after what ya saw then... that ya would have cleaned up and gotten yer life in order."

Jonah laughed at this. "I had my opportunities," he put his hand out, asking for the bottle. If he remembered right, a cigarette would afford him a shot of the drink—hobo rules.

"And ya wasted them," the old man said back, reluctantly handing Jonah his prize. Jonah drank from the bottle, undeterred over what might be in it or who had drunk from it. He flinched at the strength of the hooch. At least nothing could live in it.

"Yes, sir," Jonah said, a little more animated than he meant to. "And I'm right back where I started."

"Why would ya want that?"

"I don't want that, old man; it's just my lot in life," Jonah laughed to himself. "Why do you want to live out here dodging all the homeless and addicts and gangsters?"

"They are the *meek*. They are my people," he announced with his head held high.

"They'll inherit the earth?" Jonah said sarcastically.

"That's what they say," the old man smiled a toothless smile. Jonah looked at him worryingly. The old man laughed at this.

Jonah figured him for mad and went to return to the path home, but the man grabbed onto his shirt and spun him around with a show of surprising strength. Jonah was terrified for a moment, and then his eyes again caught the old man's hardened gaze.

"Good things still happen to good people, Jonah," he explained aggressively. "No one's out to get ya, son. Ya always thought the world had it out for ya. Only one who has it out for ya... is *ya!*"

Jonah pulled his arm away, and the old man's grip failed. "You don't *know* me."

"But I *did* know ya - when you were one of us," he told Jonah, voice raised. "Ya filled yer nose and yer lungs but never yer veins. Ya were cautious. Ya were in control. Ya didn't belong here. Don't let despair settle in, boyo. Remember who ya were. *Remember,"* the old man shooed him away and returned to the fire.

Jonah was shaken by the exchange and lit another cigarette on his walk home to rid his mouth of the distasteful hooch he'd swallowed, listening to the old man's final warning repeat in his head, *'remember.' Was it a warning?*

At home, Jonah couldn't sense June's presence near him or smell her scent as he sat polishing off another bottle of vodka. She wasn't haunting the apartment. It's just as well, Jonah thought, how depressing would it be to find your spirit attached to anything less than an ancient country mansion or castle? Never mind that, what if she'd attached her ghost to him! That, Jonah decided, would be most depressing of all. He didn't want to be attached to himself, not anymore, not now that she was gone.

The Blind Affect

Though she wasn't felt in that ethereal way, there were many reminders of June woven into the place's fabric. Physically, in the couch, and curtains, and the dust bunnies collecting next to the return air registers. Long, black hairs which didn't know enough to fuck off; to die with their owner, littered the place. Jonah was endlessly pulling them out of the sheets and towels and every surface that didn't repel them. They were all at once a comfort and a constant reminder of his loss. If he could *Weird Science* her back from a strand of her hair, he would. He'd dreamed that very scenario several times. But science wasn't the answer any more than summoning her spirit through a séance. She was gone, and he'd been forced to move on. Of course, a few steps backward are expected after tragedy strikes before one can take a step forward and mean it.

2003

An Attempt at a Normal Life

It's fair to say Severn had terrifying nightmares – some psychoanalysts labeling them *night terrors* but careful not to mention childhood trauma as the trigger, understanding Severn's situation, and wishes. Severn had never had to pay for a single session with any of the numerous therapists she'd seen upon her return to life in 1994. Her mother told her it was taken care of, but nothing more.

The night terrors frightened her the most. The only control she had over those was to secure one wrist to the bedpost. Living alone had been a big step after spending a year with her mother. Hoping to re-enter society fully, Severn had to silence her mother's pleas to stay to become a self-sufficient woman. After that, she'd gone to school, received her high school and then college certificates, and secured a career in social work. Severn was proud of her accomplishments and being able to pay her own way in the world. Still, the nightmares continued.

She took drugs to help her sleep through most of the dreams, remembering very little once she'd awoken. The rim of her wrist was usually red, and the skin dry where she'd thrashed in the night. Severn wore a watch in an attempt to hide this aspect of her life. She ached for normalcy, she craved it, and nine years removed from her missing years, she thought all the Romcom's she'd watched with Mary and the romance novels she'd read had prepared her for the possibility of dating.

Mary set her up with her first real date. He was handsome enough, she told Mary as they reviewed his pictures during cottage weekends and nights out with Mary and her husband. Severn always worried about her baggage with the nightmares and missing years and how a conversation might lead her down that path. It had given her bouts of anxiety over dating before, which kept her single. This time she knew she had to try.

The afternoon was pleasant, and the sun warm enough to keep them outdoors but not so warm as to illicit shade. Birds chirped excitedly in Mary's expansive backyard, nearly drowning out the water feature in the large Koi Pond at their backs.

"It's now or never," Severn told her friend as they sat out on the new deck sipping lemon coolers. "What was his wife like? Am I his type?"

"Jesus, Severn, you're *everybody's* type!" Maribel explained, looking her friend up and down in her fitted, yellow summer dress and short cut blonde hair with hints of grey encroaching at the temples. "I don't know *anyone* who wears their forties as well as you, honey."

Severn blushed, wondering why she couldn't take a compliment like that. It had always been a point of confusion for her. She'd mentioned it to a therapist or two before, but they could only comment on what she could or would tell them. The missing time never really came up because of her fear of releasing it into her conscious life. *Sometimes we bury things to protect ourselves,* her mother would say, and that comment had stayed with her through all of her therapy sessions. Still, if she wanted to move on with a normal life, she would need to learn how to accept a compliment.

"You're kind," Severn laughed it off, but Mary looked at her, frustration in her expression, and said, "You're *hot.* The sooner you realize that the sooner you'll find a man. Remember when we were in grade seven and that kid - that boy Jesse James or something - he bought you those flowers or did he pick them, I don't remember, but he was so smitten with you. He's just one example, though. You had all the boys cooing over you. I was so jealous."

"Oh, come on, now you're being ridiculous!" Severn felt strange that she couldn't remember that detail about her life. What else was her subconscious hiding from her?

Mary set her jaw and put her drink down. "Severn, if you see anyone but a beautiful woman in the mirror, I'm sending you to *my* shrink!" Mary softened and, with her free hand, gently brushed the blonde hair from Severn's cheek. Of course, Maribel knew what had happened to Severn all those years ago and wanted to build up her confidence, but she wasn't just being kind. Severn was beautiful and always had been. Sure, a few greys were replacing the brilliant blonde, but she wore them well. She wore everything well. What had happened to her was cruel and unfair; it made Mary sick. This was a girl who had everything until her father died, and then still, she somehow carried herself with grace.

"I've seen my share of shrinks," Severn looked thoughtfully at her best friend and tilted her head slightly in contemplation of asking the question *what happened to me?* But she didn't. It was too much to ask of a friend to do that to her. "So, this guy, Brian, he's a nice guy, right? He didn't cheat on his wife, and that's why they're divorced?"

"No, he's the good guy in this story," Mary assured her. "No more bad guys for you -" Mary had slipped. She cursed herself for it but recovered with another story of their pre-teens. Bobby Hastings had pushed her repeatedly through the whole sixth grade, determined to win her over through violence. It was hard knowing what she knew and not occasionally slipping like that. Severn seemed to accept the story.

"Anyway, I think you two will get along. That you're willing to give it a shot is all this is really about. Get some experience behind you. We'll double date, you and me and Richard and Brian."

"Does he... know about me?" Severn asked cautiously. "I mean, I don't even know about me, so he should know what not to ask."

"He knows enough not to ask," Mary replied, took a sip from her drink, and placed her glass on the table. She leaned in to offer encouragement to her friend with a comforting hand on her forearm. "I know it's weird, honey, but you made a choice to leave those years where they belong. I support that. We *all* do."

"Weird, yeah," Severn agreed, staring off into the distance. The idea that everyone knew, and she didn't made her feel vulnerable in every social engagement. It made her skin crawl. And that she might never know what had happened all those years ago would sometimes usher in a panic attack, and so not knowing became her norm. "It's my secret, but not mine to tell. It's so *fucking* bizarre, Mary." Severn placed her hand on top of Maribel's - tears streamed down her cheeks. She wiped them away quickly and apologized.

"Oh, Severn, honey, you don't *ever* need to apologize for wanting to know. I'm sure it's a terrible burden, not knowing. I guess we all assume it would be worse to know." Mary's strong façade disappeared, and she, too, shed a tear.

"I imagine it's pretty awful - what happened to me, and so I get not reliving it, but I don't know if I can *never* know." Severn's bright features began to transform, to darken, like storm clouds casting heavy shadows on an otherwise perfect day. The idea she would forever be shielded from eighteen years of her life seemed an insurmountable obstacle in becoming the person she was meant

184

to be. Still, it terrified her to know. How could it not with so many loved ones vehemently against it?

"It's your choice, Severn, you know that. What your mom wanted for you – maybe it's not enough anymore. I just... I don't want to lose you again. I don't want you to lose yourself." Mary was visibly traumatized by the conversation and worked a finger under her eye in an attempt to push back the tears.

"I'm sorry you have to know what you know and don't feel you can tell me," Severn said gently, looking at her friend. "That I'm so torn over it. It must be difficult for you -"

"Oh, honey, don't *worry* about me, please," Mary was crying. "We're so happy to have gotten you back. We count our blessings for it. But if you want to know, I mean *really* want to know, then you need to do that with a professional who has the training to walk you through it."

Severn felt better for the candid conversation, worried Mary would suffer the effects, but happier for the exchange. She was blessed to have such a friend. Severn blew her nose and wiped her tears. Hoping to put the afternoon back on track, she said, "You've been wonderful with me, Mary. You have; you and your family. And I would like to set up the date. Are you thinking next weekend?"

"If that's not rushing it," Mary replied, sitting back in her chair and wiping her eyes.

Severn chortled at that. "*Rushing it*, no... not after all this time, I don't think we can call it that." The women laughed and returned to their lemonades.

* * *

The afternoon of the double date, Severn did several mental checks. She also ran through things to discuss and what not to bring up. *Don't bring up his past as that might lead to yours. You don't have a past. Don't bring up the ex-wife as that may lead to trauma talk. No prior relationship talk as you have none. What will you talk about, work? Yes. Family? Maybe. A dead father and a recovering alcoholic mother... maybe not. Shit. What is there to talk about? The weather? I'm going to bomb this. But I have Mary there for support.* She'll dominate the conversation. *That's a good thing.*

Next, Severn tried on several outfits. It would be a warm evening, so she decided on a summer dress with a heavy sweater should it cool down. They were meeting Brian on a patio at a popular pub on the West end.

When the knock came at her door, she invited Mary and Richard in for a drink before leaving. This was when a system was refined as to how the evening would play out. They each agreed on Maribel leading each topic, and should Brian ask something unanswerable, Mary would try to answer it for Severn (being best friends since grade two) and lead him down another rabbit hole.

At the restaurant, Severn noticed the many couples and groups of friends enjoying themselves. *What traumas might they have suffered before reaching this happy moment?* Tiny lights rimmed the umbrellas, and flameless candles lit the tables. The ambiance was warm and inviting. She hoped it would set the mood for easy conversation. A captivating tune played on the patio's speakers softly, *Bring Me to Life* by Evanescence. Fitting, Severn thought. *Could Brian do that for me?*

Seated on the patio, Mary sat next to Severn while Richard sat opposite Severn so as not to create too much angst among the potential couple. When Brian arrived, everyone stood to receive him, and even Severn managed a light hug. Brian was dressed in a button-up short-sleeved shirt and light blue trousers with Birkenstock sandals and no socks (thank God). He was pretty close to perfect with his straight, white teeth, chiseled features, and thick, dark hair. He wore an expensive watch. The cropped bit of chest hair visible through his open collar felt like an invitation to Severn to explore further. She felt a rush of excitement.

Richard looked old compared to his friend. The non-threatening, loveable devout husband to Severn's best friend was cute but didn't possess the rugged beauty Brian oozed. Richard had never made Severn feel uncomfortable, and for that, she was thankful. Brian made her slightly nervous. Most men made her nervous, though. The *why* of it was the question. The nervousness had to be put to bed. The trick of it, though, was deciding whether she was experiencing good nerves - where butterflies fluttered or bad nerves where you sensed danger lurking just around the corner.

The conversation began immediately with Brian leading, as Severn knew he would. She answered a question about where she lived. Then Mary began to rhyme off a few facts about Severn to sidestep any questions that might make Severn retreat into herself. All in all, the evening was off to a good start. Severn smiled a lot through dinner and even laughed at the stupid dad jokes between Richard and Brian.

Brian had two children finishing high school who lived with their mother full time. He saw them every weekend. Beyond surface details, not much more was revealed. Without digging into someone's past, Severn thought it was difficult to really get to know them. She felt cheated in knowing herself, having lost so many years to forgetfulness. *Would Brian be put off because of her short answers?*

At the end of the evening, Brian volunteered to drive Severn home. She looked to Mary for instruction and took her emphatic nod to mean yes, take him up on the offer. She did and hugged her friend's goodbye, Mary whispering in her ear, "Don't be intimidated, just have fun. He's harmless."

Brian drove a shiny new **BMW M-class** convertible he couldn't hope to fit two teenage sons in. The top was down, and Severn enjoyed the warm breeze on her face. She felt a bit tipsy from the two bottles of wine shared at dinner and found it made her less inhibited. It was a nice feeling. The thought that maybe she might make something of her personal life actually seemed possible at that moment.

She invited Brian in for a nightcap before he headed home, as she'd seen in so many movies. She wasn't sure he'd accept but felt she didn't want the night to end. Brian happily accepted her offer, and the two sat on her couch with a glass of scotch each, staring into each other's eyes. The scotch was a gift she'd never opened. Brian took Severn's glass from her and placed it gingerly on the coffee table. Then he leaned in to kiss her, and his hot breath tickled her lips, making her shudder. The reaction wasn't alarming to Brian, but he began to pull back. Then Severn reached out and, with one hand wrapped around the back of his head, pulled him into her. The kiss lasted a long time. Before she knew it, she had unzipped the top of her summer dress and let it fall to her waist, pushing herself down on him. Satisfied moans from Brian made her even more aggressive, owning the act, and unzipping his pants.

Brian slipped out of his trousers and lifted her sundress. Severn kissed him hungrily, and Brian let her grind against him until both were naked, and he was scrambling for the condom in his discarded pants.

"Forget it," she told him in a frantic voice, and he did. Brian flipped their positions, caught up in the moment, placing himself on top, and pushed himself inside her, thrusting his pelvis against hers. This triggered something in Severn - a terrifying sense of foreboding. She began to struggle against his repetitive motion. Soon she was pushing against his chest and then pounding her fists on his shoulders and crying.

Brian, confused and frightened by her sudden change of heart, backed off and pulled out, taking Severn's wrists in his hands. When he'd cleared the couch, he released her and watched as she curled up in the fetal position sobbing. Brian was stunned into silence, standing naked in the dim lighting reliving the last twenty minutes in his mind. *Had he forced himself on her?*

He couldn't comfort her. He called Maribel and explained the scene from Severn's kitchen. "She's, uh, I know you told me some things about her, but it was her idea. I was just following her lead," Brian managed. "She's been crying for half an hour curled up on the couch. I - I don't know what to do, Mary."

"I'm sorry it went that way, Brian," Mary said apologetically. "I'll be right over. It's not your fault. Believe me when I say that. Severn is - she's just - *complicated.* But she's worth it if you ever decide to try again. Stay put until I get there."

Brian hung up and watched as Severn's slender body convulsed on the couch. It was the most unnerving experience of his life, and one he would never revisit.

Mary arrived and hugged Brian goodbye. She approached Severn as one would a wounded animal. She pulled a blanket over her fragile body and kneeled down, whispering to her that she was safe. It was a long night of this, and in the morning, Mary suggested a new therapist, a Dr. Sturgis.

2003

Dr. Sturgis

Two days after the unfortunate and embarrassing experience with Brian, Severn found herself sitting across from yet another psychiatrist who would try to make sense of her life. Dr. Sturgis came highly recommended by Maribel, who knew her from their college days.

"I don't know what Mary told you about me," Severn said awkwardly, the doctor's obvious beauty an intimidating factor in revealing her ugly past. "There are things I won't discuss, I can't discuss. I recently had a traumatic experience that should have been an empowering one."

"Let's start there," Sturgis slipped a pair of reading glasses on and reviewed whatever was on her clipboard. "Maribel did describe your recent experience, so now I'd like your account."

Severn explained the date and the good feelings that accompanied it. In the retelling, it seemed picture-perfect. How had she let it all come undone so easily? She described her bold move in inviting Brian in for a nightcap and her strategy to seduce him. It had all gone to plan. "Kissing him was magical," her face scrunched up, and her head shook anxiously, regretting the childish description. She kneaded her thumb into the palm of her hand. "I don't think I'd ever kissed anyone like that before, so it all felt new to me." Admitting this made Severn feel like the unpopular girl at a slumber party, being in her forties and having never experienced a real kiss.

"Were you also a virgin, then?" Sturgis asked plainly.

"Uh, yes, as far as I know, I've never participated in sex of any sort." *Was she an old maid? Would she start collecting cats?* "It's the missing time," she disclosed, "that makes me wonder. I could have been married and had a dozen children for all I know."

"And you've no interest in knowing? Never been to an MD to make the discovery?"

"My mother told me my Hyman broke when I was twelve."

"Your mother, who doesn't want you to remember your past," Sturgis said it like she was throwing knives, albeit in a practiced, professional manner.

"In not so many words, I've been told its better not to know."

"In my profession, I can tell you that's the polar opposite of what *I* believe."

"Yes, well, I've gotten the flak from some of the other therapists I've seen over the last nine years, too."

"Still, you don't *want* to know?"

"I wouldn't say I don't want to know, but I would say I'm terrified to know. There was a time I tried to find out but was blocked at every turn. Our entire community was working for my mother, or so it seemed."

"Then I won't push you right now." The doctor shifted in her seat as though her statement made her uncomfortable. "Let's consider your reaction to sex two nights ago."

"It surprised me, I can tell you that. One minute I was controlling the action, the next, not."

"Did it hurt you? Is that why you pushed him away? Were you in physical pain from the act?"

Severn thought about this a moment. "No... no, it wasn't like that. It was more... *instinctive.* I don't know." She surprised herself with that account.

"That's an excellent descriptive, Severn," the doctor seemed pleased with her efforts. "Instinct runs deep in the human psyche. Tell me, did you experience a panic attack while you were caught up in the moment? I understand you have had them in the past where men were concerned." Severn watched the doctor's eyes scan her clipboard and was sure she read from notes sent to her by Severn's prior therapists to prepare for this session.

"Yes, and I cried for hours after."

"Then you felt threatened. Do men or the idea of a man in a power position make you uncomfortable?"

"Yes... definitely." On this detail, Severn had no question.

"But in all your sessions with other therapists, you've never discovered the *why* of it." It wasn't a question but rather felt like a judgment to Severn.

"We've worked around it," Severn explained, "uh, using situations to build defensive techniques like tapping or mindfulness."

"Those weren't a consideration when you took this major step in sleeping with a man, though?"

"Well, no, it happened so fast, and I thought I was the one controlling it until," Severn stopped herself as she felt her heart begin to race with the memory.

"It's okay, Severn, you're safe here. You need to know first and foremost that you did *nothing* wrong. What you set out to accomplish was brave and consensual. Something triggered your deep anxiety, and we're going to discover what that was. Then we're going to help you understand it and deal with it. Take a few breaths, and I'll try to fill in the blanks." This doctor was good, Severn thought as she inhaled through her nose and out through her mouth. *Breath in, breath out, and repeat.* "You said you thought you were in control, and then he jockeyed for position and took your control away. Do you feel you could have completed the act were you the one controlling the action?"

"Maybe?" Severn thought long and hard about this, and the doctor allowed the silence to linger, coaxing more from her. "Impossible to know, I guess." Her left thumb continued to work the palm of her right hand.

"Like your missing years," Sturgis suggested.

"I don't know if those are *impossible* to know. Others know about them. I could know if I wanted to."

"But you don't want to."

"I guess not."

"It's obvious to me, and I think to most of your therapists, that you have suffered some serious anxiety over a relationship or relationships to men. Perhaps an abusive relationship, or a string of abusive relationships. If gone untreated, it will continue to arise in situations like the one you experienced two nights ago." A pause and Sturgis looked directly at Severn. "I'm happy to take you on as your therapist. I will suggest therapies you can do to get through some of the lessor triggers, but don't expect much to change with physical acts if you're unwilling to discover what happened to you during those lost years."

"I understand." She doesn't.

"You're not taking any medications for your anxiety," the doctor said, the tip of her pen tapping at the clipboard. "Are you self-medicating? With alcohol or recreational drugs?"

"No, I mean, I have a drink once in a while," She remembers the bottle of wine she drained the night before. "I try to be careful. My mother is an alcoholic."

"Alright, sometimes we fill emotional gaps with substance abuse. I'm happy to hear you're not. I suggest you not see this man again and consider your mental health before attempting another pairing like this. Nothing good will come from a physical relationship right now. We need to consider therapy to address it. I will suggest treatments for you and see you in a week."

"Thank you, doctor," as tough as Sturgis was, Severn liked her. She thought maybe she could discover her missing years with someone like her leading the way. But for Severn, that was still years away.

2013

Doing Good

Nearly twenty years after Darnell's hair-raising escape from his father's house - swarming with police and under cover of night - he shoveled a heaping spoonful of lasagna onto the waiting plate of a homeless man. The interior of the shelter smelled of something rotten despite its scrubbed appearance. Darnell put that on the unfortunate patrons. The lasagna at least covered the odor enough that he began feeling a rumbling in his stomach as he spooned out the meals.

This charitable nature came after recognizing the damage his father's clandestine business had done to so many. Initially, he'd considered just handing the money he'd found under the house over to the victims and their families but felt there wasn't enough to go around to make a real difference. A better idea would be to invest the money and make more so he could do more—a business relationship with the right man at the right time afforded Darnell exactly that. Technology companies were making major advancements in 1994, and one investment paid out more than 440% while another yielded an over 1,200% payday. He was an instant millionaire many times over.

The money offered him the opportunity to help many more than just those affected by his father's cruel enterprise. Still, they were his focus, and through some new connections, he located all of the victims. He arranged for their counseling and created a joint Trust for each to make up for the years of loss spent satisfying his father's wicked ambitions. Never would Darnell make money on the backs of others. He would help. He would ask himself how, and he would make it happen. He lived in a humble home within the city limits and took public transit. He managed various government contracts through healthcare initiatives, many of which he'd proposed, and continued to do good in his city.

Darnell had never married, rather wed to his work. He did hobnob with the elite and held multiple fundraisers and Gala events for inner-city projects to secure funds that would benefit the underprivileged. Everything he did was to combat the evil his father had done and divorce himself from that legacy. He'd felt guilt over being in the dark all those years, spending his father's money on food and basic life necessities. Hindsight is 20/20, so they say. It haunted him. He saw therapists himself to help understand his lineage. *How could anyone be so cruel? Could he? Was it in him to be like his father?*

Thankfully he didn't believe that, nor did the doctors. On his return to the office, he felt nostalgic for that time in his life when everything changed. He removed his earbuds and placed his iPod on his desktop. *Super soaker* by Kings of Leon was barely audible through the buds. He pulled the paper file - one of his first - and flipped it open on his desk. There they were, photographs of each woman, man, and child his father had recruited into his den of inequity. Darnell's hand instinctively covered his mouth as he moved from one picture to the next. He sighed heavily at the one who'd refused to know. The one who had apparently, unconsciously compartmentalized the trauma once she'd laid eyes on her mother. All of it... gone. All the suffering and the cruelty pushed to a dark corner, never to be revisited. Darnell likened it to a room in a house with a barred door adorned by many locks and chains, where a traumatized and frightened little girl sat huddled in the corner hugging her knees up to her chin. Her mother had accepted the free treatments for the woman, but with the caveat that she would never be asked to relive the two decades she'd suffered.

"Eighteen years," Darnell said to himself, looking at the photo of a frightened Severn captured hours after she and her peers were liberated from the brothel. She was thin, like death camp thin. Her hair was matted to one side with blood - his father's, he guessed, and her eyes stared at the photographer with an unsettling sense of grief. Another heavy sigh, and Darnell reviewed her contact information. There was little doubt she lived with her mother still. He wondered whether she had taken the step to learn about her past.

"Why wonder," he told himself and picked up his office phone. He called his reception area and asked to speak with the caseworker for the group.

"Margery," Darnell greeted the employee who'd been with his organization the longest.

"Mr. Lincoln, what can I do you for?" Marg was always in a good mood. It amazed Darnell considering the horrors she'd witnessed on the job. She was the office morale officer, among other things.

"Marg, I'm just caught up in some nostalgia here and wondered about the case on my father's victims." Darnell had never shied away from his connection to the worst sex trade scandal his city had known. "I'm looking at Severn Holmen and wondering what became of her."

"Severn, yes, uh, just a sec... she moved to a private psychiatrist ten years ago on a referral," Margery's voice trailed off. The satisfying clicks of her keyboard kept Darnell entranced as she typed out search information. "We'd managed to work out payments with the therapist, a doctor Sturgis, and she sees Severn once a month now." Marg was on top of her game this morning, Darnell thought.

"Excellent, thank you, and this Sturgis, she's good then?"

"She's excellent, yes. I remember being surprised she took her on when I explained compensation. Sturgis is an exceptional therapist."

"Could you send me her contact information? I'd love to drop her a line and show my gratitude." Darnell's head filled with possibilities. Though the doctor couldn't give him any specifics on the patient, he wondered if she might tell him whether Severn had relived those years yet and, if not, the importance of doing so.

"I've emailed you the doctor's info," Marg said.

"Thank you," Darnell said thoughtfully.

"Good luck getting anything out of Sturgis. She's as to the letter as they come as I understand it."

"Noted," Darnell said. "Thanks for your help, Marg." Darnell hung up and pulled Severn's photo from the file. "The one that got away," he said aloud, placed the photo back in the file, and made a call to Sturgis.

A receptionist answered, and Darnell asked to speak with the doctor. As luck would have it, she was available.

"Mr. Lincoln," Sturgis greeted him on the other end. "This is about Severn, I imagine." Her reply was terse, as though she'd been expecting someone to call for an update.

"Yes, as a matter of fact," Darnell replied, the tension the doctor brought to the call seemed slightly off-putting. "Severn's file surfaced, and I wondered how she was getting along."

"She's a very traumatized woman, Mr. Lincoln, but you know that. Incidentally, upon taking Severn on, I learned about your organization and your personal connection to the event that brought her here."

"I've never hidden the fact."

"And I was very impressed by your magnanimity."

"Yes, well, I'm calling to thank you for *your* generosity." Darnell hated receiving praise. "So, you know why I'm calling. Severn had refused to relive those memories. Has anything changed?"

"You know very well I can't go into details." From the sound of it, Darnell thought this was as far as he'd get on the subject.

"No, no, I appreciate that, doctor. I'm not looking for details. I only wanted to know she was progressing. It's been, what, ten years she's been in your care? You understand, like the others who suffered at the hands of my father, she's someone I feel a deep connection to."

"Shared trauma at the hands of your father will do that. Her not dealing with it likely has you in knots over the continued suffering she's experiencing on a subconscious level."

"Thank you for the free diagnosis, doctor, but I'm not calling to take advantage of your good nature." Darnell is caught off guard by the analysis but impressed by the doctor's obvious talent for deconstructing a psyche.

"Yes, well, she's a distance to go yet."

"Fair enough, and thank you for taking her on all those years ago. I know we don't pay your full asking per session, so I wanted to take this opportunity to say thank you."

"It's my pleasure, Mr. Lincoln. You take care." Then the line went dead. Darnell hung up on his end, and with a final look at Severn's photo, he closed the file.

2017

The Beginning of the End

Jonah found himself seated in a sparsely attended theater with a hundred others waiting for a movie to begin. It had been some time since his last attempt to go to the movies. June didn't like going to movies, and he still hated the idea of going alone. Of course, the theatre shooting he'd witnessed back in '94 certainly didn't fill him with confidence in a return to the big screen. Still, he wanted to see this movie, and something about being in your fifties and going to a movie alone didn't seem so pathetic. If he suspected someone staring at him, he thought they must think his wife had died recently; that maybe he'd had a life of some interest but found himself suddenly alone in his late fifties. Better to be viewed through the eyes of empathy than ridicule.

He'd been steadily drinking since Mort's death seventeen years ago. He'd remained working the same job, though he felt his company was becoming suspicious of his drinking, and he might not have a job for much longer. Still, he wasn't going to change his ways at fifty-eight. He brought a water bottle filled with a mixture of vodka and orange juice to get him through the movie. Paired with a slice of pizza from the concessions would keep him from stumbling out of the theatre.

Flashbacks made Jonah nervous still, and so his Bromhidrosis reacted. He was as secluded in the theatre as possible, with two empty seats to his right and the aisle to his left. Still, the technology to mask his odor had never been perfected. He still smelled satanic. Again though, being old offered a kind of confidence. Or maybe he just couldn't care less anymore. He'd battled the condition all his life. He was tired, and he looked tired. The alcoholism had pulled his face down, etched lines in his skin, brought burst blood vessels to the surface of his nose and cheeks, and given him a yellow tint. If ever he was an attractive man, it was not in his fifties. Thin and sporting a small potbelly, he fit the physical mould of a man who self-medicated.

The movie began without an incident involving anyone's shooting deaths, followed by a stampede of patrons vying for the quickest path out of the mayhem. Two hours and twenty minutes later, Jonah rose from his seat and then fell back into it as a distinct pain struck him in the chest. *Was it a panic attack?* Perhaps, though it resembled a panic attack, Jonah decided it was considerably more painful. He gripped at his chest and struggled for breath while sweat began to puddle along his shirt collar. Next, the panic. He felt invisible again as people stepped by so they could exit into the aisle he was blocking. Embarrassed by his inability to stand and in extraordinary pain, he shook his head and bit down on his lip. He rolled out of his seat into the crowded aisle in the hopes of making it into the lobby, where he'd noticed a defibrillator attached to the wall. He heard grunts arising from his throat, stumbled, his hand gripped his chest, and a small woman pulled him aside and called for help.

* * *

Jonah went to an intensive care unit that night via ambulance. It was a long night of confusing questions and multiple tests. At one point, he'd mentioned his alcohol intake, his Bromhidrosis, and his propensity for panic attacks. After some sleep in the hospital hallway, a doctor stood next to his bed to check on his vitals and explain what had happened at the theatre.

"Dilated cardiomyopathy," the doctor explained. "In your case, we've narrowed it down to your alcoholism." The man's dark eyes looked sternly at Jonah, omnipotent. "You have a serious condition brought on by your drinking, Jonah," he explained. "Your heart muscle has weakened due to years of abuse, and your heart is having difficulty pumping blood as a result." The doctor seemed unapologetically brutal about the diagnosis.

"Sounds serious," Jonah agreed in a small voice, incapable of expressing what the doctor clearly wanted to hear, regret. Jonah had been ready to die a thousand times before this had happened. Why it never seemed to take was the mystery of it.

"It's a severe and, as you've experienced, very unpleasant way to check out." He wrote something on his pad and left it with Jonah by placing it on his chest.

He was right about the pain. It was devastating. "What are you prescribing?"

"Therapy for the alcoholism, also two prescriptions to help avoid another surprise attack." The doctor's tone remained focused amidst all the chaos around him. The hospital was abuzz. "If you continue along this path, you will suffer multiple attacks before one finally takes you. That could result in stroke-like effects damaging your ability to feed yourself and on and on. There is a multitude of unfortunate symptoms due to a stroke. It won't be an easy out." The doctor studied Jonah's expression, reading his thoughts.

The idea that he'd nearly died had had an effect on him, whether he wanted to admit it or not. Regardless of the years spent wishing for death, the fact that death had just sent a warning shot across his bow was unsettling. *But why a warning shot? Why not just end him?* He couldn't let another episode like this play out without permanent damage if he heard the doctor right. A paralyzed face or throat muscles or anything like that would be a fate worse than death. It was all too painful, and Jonah abhorred pain.

"Maybe it's time," Jonah admitted picking the note up off his chest.

"Your choice, but I highly recommend you do the work and take the medications."

Yeah, sure, do the work - he said it like there was nothing to it. Sobriety didn't come easily. The work would be soul-crushing and physically wrenching. But if he would save himself the painful end of a heart attack or stroke, maybe he should consider it... again. Maybe he should consider many things; what his father had wanted, June had supported, and Mort warned against again and again.

* * *

After picking up the prescription at his local pharmacy, Jonah felt the familiar, seductive pull of his addiction. One more night won't make a difference. I'll start tomorrow. Up early and then focus. His ego didn't want him to suffer.

You don't actually think that after all this time, you'll stop? His self-talk chimed in. *Chances are your heart will give out quicker off the booze. But maybe that's what you want.* "Fuck off," Jonah said to himself softly. He was so tired of the constant drama self-talk brought into his life.

At home, he measured what alcohol he had left. There was half a bottle of vodka, seven beers, a quarter bottle of whiskey, and a single line of coke. He'd meant to top up on the cocaine, he remembered. Still, this would be an epic night. He would finish it all and then start fresh tomorrow. He snorted the line and, suddenly motivated, moved around the apartment, tossing bottles into the blue bin and cleaning countertops, vacuuming and dumping ashtrays. He lined up the bottles remaining and sat at the breakfast bar, cracked a beer, and poured a shot of vodka. He felt accomplished already. *Enjoy tonight. It's quite possibly the last night you'll ever enjoy.* Jonah's music couldn't compete with his upstairs neighbor, so he turned his off and listened as *Hard times* by Paramore blasted from above.

He drummed out every song his neighbors played - until he swallowed his final whiskey and dragged his polluted body to bed. *What horrors would morning bring?* Denying himself was not something he'd done in nearly two decades. He remembered the pain and nausea, and self-doubt that would follow. *If you can't, you can't,* ego told him, soothing him to sleep.

2020

Remembrances

It had been years since he had visited the forest where he and June planted trees. They were much taller. Lined up and spaced out unnaturally, row on row. The new forest had grown remarkably though, left to its own devices. Jonah couldn't make the same claim. Left alone, he had spiraled back into his addictions. He'd avoided the forest and the people who he'd gotten to know over his five years with June. Seeing them or being in the forest were emotional triggers that he knew he couldn't bear.

Clean for two years and feeling nostalgic over the timing, Jonah visited the forest on the very day planting was taking place. The woods continued to reclaim space from its past as industry left, and soil was remediated year after year. June would have loved to have seen the ground gained by nature, approaching the old-growth forest still intact along the riverbed.

Whether he'd planted a couple hundred trees or not, someone else would have. His personal contribution was overlooked and under-valued by the continued work going on. What the charity had accomplished was impressive. He'd insisted that June not receive flowers at her funeral but rather asked people to contribute to tree planting aid, donating their time in person or through a monetary contribution. He had accumulated over $3,000 in her name. For that sum, June had even been gifted an engraved plaque on one of the stone benches found among the forest's trails. He ran trembling fingers over the engraving as he sat to listen to the birds' chirping. He lay a handful of mixed seed on the bench next to him and smiled sadly as chickadees and even woodpeckers joined him to gobble up the nuts.

This return had been a difficult decision as he feared he might fall back into addiction merely from the memories the place would invoke. He still felt cheated out of a life with June, the plans they'd made, the way the world had opened up to him while she was in it. He pictured her seated to his right, her head on his shoulder and fingers entwined with his, her soft breath on his bare shoulder.

Jonah blinked away tears and forced a ragged breath, exhaling heavily. The cigarette between his fingers made its way to his lips, and he drew the tobacco into his lungs as if manufacturing a controlled burn to avoid a blaze. He wasn't allowed to smoke in a public park, but he rarely remembered where he could. The world was going smokeless. That was a good thing. If he'd had a child, perhaps he would have tried to stop.

June had talked about children once. She would have made a good mother, dancer, or not. She was a good person. Like so many who are reaped from the world before their time. Like Morty. Like his mother.

None of it is your fault, ego explained as Jonah wiped his eyes and placed the cigarette butt under his foot. Addiction ran in the family.

Jonah nodded over the fact. He'd loved his addiction. It had given him purpose. Maybe just to deal with a world out to get him - *where had he heard that before?*

That old man, the homeless guy around the trash can fire so many years ago. He'd told him that. He'd reminded him of the time Jonah had lived on the streets. He'd said he felt like the world was out to get him, and he *did* feel like that. He *still* felt like that. In fact, the only time he hadn't felt like that was when he was with June. Jonah hadn't remembered the old man from his youth, but he recalled how it frightened him the way the relic had recognized him. *Who remembers shit like that?*

Jonah considered returning to that trash can and seeking the old man out to ask him what else he thought he knew about him. *Who was he? Why would he remember Jonah? How did he recognize him?* The questions assaulted Jonah, and he lit another cigarette, to the chagrin of a family of four walking past. *Had the mother said something?* It didn't matter to Jonah. He leaned back and stared at the canopy overhead.

Without so much as a brisk wind as a warning, the sky opened up with a shock of rain the size of marbles teeming down upon him accompanied by crashes of thunder. Jonah pulled his hoodie over his head and tossed the cigarette onto the path. It was extinguished immediately. His shoulders rolled up in a protective stance against the rain, and he wrapped his arms around his torso, the rain falling hard and cold. He began to sprint to the Nature Centre and gave up midway, returning to a steady stride, coughing excessively. Soon the rain was cutting streams into the path, eroding the loosely packed dirt and limestone. Inside the building, people gathered with their families to escape the weather. Jonah found a bench and sat to catch his breath.

His thoughts returned to the old man and the trash can. A chill tore through him, and he visibly shuddered. Was it from the rain soaking him to the bone combined with the excessive air conditioning, or was it the image of the older man playing across his mind's eye whispering, remember? *Why remember the man's warning now?* Jonah was clean. Sure, he kept the cigarettes, but that was because it made him feel closer to his mother. At least, that's what Dr. Sturgis had said, and so he thought if he broke that tribute, he would lose the last of his mother's good memories, golden fingers and all. A taxidermized Beaver stared at Jonah with austere judgement in its marble eyes from a glass case.

Still, he wondered about the old man. The seed he'd planted so many years ago resurfacing - *remember* - what did he want him to remember? That he was cautious when caught up in his addiction? That he'd never once put a needle in his arm? *Was that really the line that separated a hopeless case from someone with a death wish? Had Jonah never really believed he wanted to sink into it? Had he always been just a nose above, treading the waters waiting to swallow and drown him? Had he been a victim of waterboarding all his life, having never delved too deep, saving himself from taking that final, frantic breath and filling his lungs with water?* Apparently so. *Why then? Why had he survived all his years? To what end?*

Jonah had no delusions of an afterlife; if anything, he believed in reincarnation. But even that concept he hadn't put any real thought into. *Had he lived a good life?* He felt that was true for his time with June, but the rest of it...

Too much reminiscing... Jonah knew this place would open old wounds. *Goddamn rain.* He wanted to charge out of the Nature Centre and run as far as his legs would carry him. His life felt like a short story. Not nearly enough to make up a novel like the one he'd written so long ago. His life had little to tell, almost nothing to hold onto. *What was the plot? Man lives, man dies: wasted breath. No wonder my book never saw the light of day.*

The rain tapered off, presenting Jonah his window to leave the increasingly claustrophobic space. He moved stealthily to the door and let himself out. The air was humid, with the scent of the forest floor hanging in the air. It calmed him. Jonah took three deep breaths, allowing for three extended exhales. His mind emptied, and he moved past the others exiting the center and down the path to the bus stop.

During the ride home, Jonah continued his breathing techniques to dam the flood of memories assaulting him. He was sweating, and his scent filled the cabin of the bus. His anxiety over it had been renewed after June's departure. When she was on his arm, people refused to believe he was the reason their airspace had been spoiled by the reprehensible smell. June had taken on the role of protector as well as redeemer.

When he returned to his apartment, he passed Morty's floor on the way up to his. More memories, more pain. Had he learned anything from all of it? Compassion, perhaps where Mort was concerned; something he'd never offered himself. Was that the lesson there? To know Mort was to understand compassion. *I'll take it.*

In his apartment, Jonah had attempted the minimalist lifestyle. Less stuff meant fewer triggers. That was a lesson from his most recent rehab adventure. Few pictures remained - one of him and June, another of him and Morty, and one of his mother and father on their wedding day. They all exacted difficult feelings when he looked at them, but they also gave him strength. Beyond those three photos, there was nothing else on the walls. He and his group from AA painted a bright, neutral colour throughout and had the carpets steam cleaned. June's scent had been swept away; save the perfume he kept in his medicine cabinet.

He bought a new bed and new sheets. He tried not to smoke in the house, which helped him smoke less and get out more. Sparkling water and lemon was his new drink of choice, but he couldn't get off the fast food. He hated preparing meals for himself and ordered in most dinners. His was a solitary life once more. More so than ever before, but he'd been here and done this more than once. The thought of meeting another woman was reprehensible to him after June's death. A few years later, he'd put himself up on a dating app but didn't bother to participate. After that, he decided to simply be alone.

Attempts to revitalize himself were few and far between. Sessions with psychiatrists dropped off altogether. He hadn't seen Sturgis since he and June moved in together. A few meditation classes, drum circles, and massage appointments made life bearable, but having nothing and no one to look forward to at the end of the day was difficult. Lately, it was more cumbersome as he'd removed his addictions save the cigarettes. He gamed and binge-watched seasons of shows he had little interest in. Work was work.

Life had become little more than existing. And to what end? He hadn't *lived* in years. Jonah questioned everything and had moments of frustration over his willpower. *One drink won't kill you,* ego whispers. *No one thinks you have it in you to stop anyway,* self-talk adds. Still, Jonah doesn't want to suffer another heart attack. Odds are he wouldn't die from it and be bound to repeat it time and again until one day it did take him. No thanks.

A collection of books had formed over the years after he discovered The Invisible Man comic. He'd been a voracious reader at times and discovered being clean gave him opportunities to do just that. Sometimes he would write, trying his hand at the art again but never completing anything.

Sitting on the couch June bought, he positioned himself for a night in front of the television when his cell phone rang. His cell phone never rang. No one called him. He didn't know anyone. He only kept it because work paid for it. He peered at the number showing on the display. It read *Outreach Centre.* He'd never been to one. His AA meetings, which he hardly attended, were held at the United Church. Probably someone was calling to ask for money. Jonah considered answering it and then tossed the phone to the other end of the couch. *What difference could I make?*

2020, August

Severn's Awakening

Dr. Sturgis has a tough road ahead of her. Severn had agreed to the hypnosis in May after years of avoiding the deeper issue of her psychosis. Now that Sturgis has discovered the devastating past Severn's unconscious has hidden from her all these years, it is time to release that information to Severn's conscious self. The doctor doesn't take this lightly and has discussed her patient's refusal to acknowledge the missing years at length with her colleagues. She was in denial and suffered the consequences in a myriad of fears and anxieties, and even night terrors, which could only be managed rather than cured, until now.

Sturgis's peers agreed that Severn would need to experience the trauma to progress and live a full life. What Sturgis was withholding would need to be brought to the forefront and confronted in such a way that the patient did not suffer undue pain. The emotional fallout could be catastrophic if the information was not presented just so. The patient might also slip further into herself as she had when she'd initially lost the memories. If this happens, she might never recover. Hypnosis was a tricky business when withholding information. The rollout of events should be managed carefully and mirror the timeline so as not to confuse.

Severn's mind had filtered out those eighteen years for a reason. Sturgis knew what that reason was, and so did Severn. The only difference was that Severn's mind had repressed the information to save her further trauma.

"Severn," the doctor's approach was comforting and supportive when she began the new treatment, "hypnosis is a tool and like any tool, it is designed to help. With this tool, I will guide you through your missing years."

Severn was a bundle of nerves waiting for the whole procedure to be over. Sweaty palms and a dry mouth accompanied the anxiety over discovering what everyone else already knew of her past. The office smells only faintly of lavender and the leather couches seem a little less comfortable. Even the pretty doctor manifests a threatening air. Everything seems slightly less conciliatory, and Severn trembles over the reality she will soon embrace her past. But she knows it's just nerves and reminds herself that she actually looks forward to the work that will see her through her past and toward her future.

"The missing years aren't the only memories you're repressing," Sturgis went on, "we all repress memories that do not serve us. Things we don't need to remember are discarded altogether. You're not alone in repressing memories, but your memories are preventing you from living a full life. So, you've bravely decided to face them." Severn nods, a nervous smile forming on trembling lips. Dr. Sturgis reaches out to take Severn's hand.

"I'm terrified," Severn tells her, "I'm still so fucking *terrified.*" She places her free hand on the doctors. She practices breathing and takes strength from Sturgis' gaze. A tear escapes and falls to her forearm. Severn releases her other hand to wipe the tear away.

"But you know you need to know, and so you're open to it," Sturgis reiterates, squeezing down on Severn's shaking hands.

"Yes..." Severn agrees. "And I trust you, doctor."

"And I will earn that trust today. You will only remember what I want you to remember until such a time as I believe you can safely know everything I know."

"Yes," Severn says again, nodding, tears stinging her eyes.

"Then let's begin. Lay back and close your eyes." Sturgis suggests in a calm and relaxing tone. "You're about to begin a transformative journey. You will understand why your memories were hidden from you and realize it was done so with compassion, but that to relive those lost years is integral to your being a whole person."

Severn let the doctor's words sink in, and her soft voice carry her away as Sturgis impressed her will upon her.

And so it went for several sessions. Each session was spaced out in days rather than weeks. The work was difficult for both patient and doctor - the details tough for Sturgis to listen to, while Severn remained consciously unaware of the work. Once Sturgis had learned all there was to learn, she developed the reveal. She gave Severn the command to *'know.'* She did this in phases, having left markers for the client to discover bit by bit the devastating life those eighteen years demanded of her sanity.

From the initial kidnapping through her peers' deaths in the soul-crushing sex trade to the victory over the man named Dominus and her reintegration. The counseling that continued long after the reveal dealt with all the demons that had emerged. Severn had suffered unimaginable horrors over decades. She felt sickened by it all. She felt worthless and unworthy and dirty. Sturgis pulled her out of all of that, and eventually, Severn experienced the weightlifting, as promised.

Severn connected the invisible dots as to why she'd felt compelled into a life of service as a social worker, but that was only after experiencing the five stages of grief over her losses. This took many more months of intense counseling with the doctor to overcome. She resented the fact that the man named Dominus had been murdered. In hindsight, as a victim, it would have been better to see Dominus and the others face justice and experience every victim and family member's personal trauma through open statements as the criminals sat chained to their chair. There they would have been forced to listen and understand the damage they'd caused. She felt cheated of that.

Not a month later, a documentary about a wealthy investor who had built a similar scenario to Dominus's, preying on children, but catering to the world's elite, caught her attention and pulled Severn back into her memories. Triggers were painful but necessary. She watched the documentary, relating to the now-grown women's testimonies. She trembled and cried through the program with Mary by her side. She felt pride in the women for coming forward. She felt the same over the *#MeToo* movement before any of her own experiences had come to light. The world seemed bent on destroying women. It was a troubling thought, but she was proud of herself for having survived and decided she would dedicate her life to exposing the monsters, her purpose discovered. Her life reclaimed.

Sturgis handed Severn a pamphlet and explained Darnell's institute's role in rehabilitating victims and their families. The LCPI or *Lincoln Centre for Personal Improvement* included a separate printout called *survivors.* This group was exclusive to her trauma and developed many years ago for the victims who had shared in her experience.

After three months of intensive therapy to deal with the fallout of what she had discovered, Severn left Sturgis's offices empowered to face her fears with a playbook of how to manage them. She felt grateful for the help and wanted to thank those who had given her the therapy and assistance through monetary means to return to school, achieving her high school diploma, and attending college. She would appear at the next meeting and hope for more healing.

2020

October, Group

Anxiety over joining the group of people she'd been trapped with all those years - all those years ago - grips Severn as she contemplates the move. The ordeal was decades ago, yet she had only just learned of it and how to manage the devastating feelings it provoked. It felt fresh, like an open wound. Still, those in the group had been gathering to heal since its inception, and Severn knew they could help her.

Who would be there, and what would they think of the girl who'd blocked them all out? It was a troublesome thought, but she couldn't let it deter her from further recovery. Besides, she thought, having lived the same Hell, how could any of them hold it against her?

Severn pulls herself together by practicing the skills she's learned through therapy to accept the world as it is presented to her. Whatever the outcome of group therapy, she would take what was useful and discard the rest. Besides, other people's opinions of her were none of her business.

Standing outside the dismal looking church designed in the '60s to reflect a community center more than a place of worship, Severn breathes deeply, releasing the stress and nervous apprehension she's experiencing. She feels lighter for it. The rain falling on her umbrella induces a calming sensation, and she allows it to envelope her, sending satisfying chills down her spine. She straightens her back and rounds her shoulders, watching the last member of the group pass through the double glass doors from her vantage point behind an ancient oak. She convinces herself that it is now or never, willing her feet to step over the puddle and her body to follow. Severn's breathing becomes more audible as she crosses the street, and she feels her pulse throbbing in her palm as her grip on the umbrella tightens.

She lowers the umbrella once under the church's canopy, feeling all the more exposed for it. But this is her decision, and she knows she would regret turning back. The door opens into a large foyer where several wet jackets hang. The sounds of laughter and quiet conversations emanate from within the building's basement. The smell of coffee and baked goods wafts up the tiled stairs on a warm current of air. Severn feels suddenly welcome as if the place were giving her an earnest hug upon entering. Her cheeks warm to the idea, and she places her umbrella in the appropriate spot and hangs her jacket with the others.

She notices a bathroom sign and hurries to find it. Inside she puts herself in front of the mirror and fixes her make-up. She's stalling, she knows, but she's here, and that's a big deal. Severn dabs a tissue under both eyes where her anxiety has produced tears. *Perhaps they're tears of joy?* She feels a lot of things right now, but anxiety is the wrong word to describe them. She's anxious, but not in a way that keeps someone from following through. She recognizes, rather, it's that anxious energy you experience when you're going on a first date or about to experience a roller coaster.

Another deep breath and steady exhale further solidify her decision to go through with the group. She offers herself a reassuring nod to the mirror, leaves the bathroom, and moves down the staircase into an open room with a low ceiling. Over a dozen people of varying ages and degrees are seated in a circle. Next, she notices the variety of races amongst them, recalling the cornucopia of colors collected for the pleasures of the *John's* paying for their company. It is a jarring memory that nearly sends Severn turning on her heels for the door. Instead, her feet have become frozen in place as she takes it all in.

"Oh, my God." A voice releases triumphantly as Severn debates what she will do with the memory; how she will compartmentalize it. Next, she finds everyone in the room turning to look in her direction. Absently, Severn turns as well expecting a giant cake or some other exciting feature, but nothing materializes. "Severn!" The same voice bellows, and she turns back, realizing it is she who has commanded everyone's attention. This sends her immediately into a cold sweat. She had hoped to just slip into a vacant chair and announce herself to the circle. This is not what she expected. A nervous smile and wave, and Severn is announced to her peers. They begin to approach tentatively.

"Guys," one of the men says in an insistent tone, "don't crowd her, please, this is obviously a huge step for Severn, and we need to respect her space," the small, slender man of East Asian descent with skin the color of polished mahogany

211

steps between the crowd and Severn, turning back to her and smiling brightly. "Severn, we were told you might make it to group this week but, we hadn't really believed it. Forgive the surprise; we're thrilled to have you here. You've been missed every month since its inception." He spoke quickly but in a low voice. His are kind eyes. Severn focuses on them, pulling from the strength within, and suffers another memory. This was a boy named Hiromi, who Dominus had named Beauty. He had been the last boy Severn consoled before they were freed. He was lucky. She remembered that he had only been raped a dozen times before their rescue.

As she fixates on Hiromi's face, more memories slip into the light. He was seven, maybe eight, when he was brought in. Severn was told to comfort the new arrivals and prepare them. She did this with as much compassion as she could muster. Hiromi had been drugged and still groggy from the effects when he had arrived. Severn cradled him in her arms, swaddled him in her blanket until he awoke confused and frightened. He spoke English, which was always easier than when they received a foreigner. His innocent eyes watched her, questioning everything that had happened. She cried every time, and though she knew this would terrify the child, she couldn't help herself - knowing what horrors awaited them. She recalls now how she'd fought with the idea of smothering him so he wouldn't have to go through the agony and constant humiliation and fear he would be subjected to.

"Hiromi," Severn spoke quietly, voice cracking and arms opening automatically to receive him once more. She was surprised by her sudden and jarring recognition of the man. It wasn't his face; it was his expression that brought the memory of Hiromi to the forefront. Her smile transformed into an expression Hiromi would have remembered awakening to in that basement all those years before. It is a benevolent smile paired with weeping eyes. Hiromi rushed to accept Severn's hug, and they melted into one another. Severn, losing the strength to stand, crumbled unceremoniously with Hiromi to their knees while still embracing. Severn wept into his shoulder, and Hiromi held onto her as if she were his lifeline once more.

The love shared at this moment surprises Severn. She feels everything, experiencing their connection as if she were still comforting that little boy, wishing she could protect him from his cruel fate. But she is grateful he has grown into a man with kind eyes. Severn pulls back, still grasping to Hiromi's shirt, eyes studying his face. The scar he'd been given on his third night by a wicked man remained as a reminder of his time with Dominus above his right eyebrow.

Severn's chin trembles as she looks from Hiromi to the others, who had grouped behind him on their knees. They share an expression of empathy and kneel beside them, arms wrapping around Severn and Hiromi in a communal hug. Severn is overwhelmed by the incredible display of kindness. The courage in this group of survivors could not be overstated, she thought. They'd lived with the knowledge of what they'd endured at the hands of Dominus all these years, whereas she had only begun to manage the memories. For Severn, it is an encouraging thing to acknowledge. They'd survived, and as she became reacquainted with each of them over the course of the evening, Severn heard stories from each that spoke of healing and lives reclaimed after the devastating acts against their bodies and minds.

"Not everyone is here tonight," Hiromi explained while the group was breaking up, "four had prior commitments and one, well, April left us some time ago." Hiromi's face falls into a grimace.

"April," Severn says, trying to remember which girl she was, "was that the girl called Squirt?" It still amazed her how much information continued to rush in from her subconscious.

"Yes, she - and this happened years ago... she couldn't manage the pain." Hiromi takes Severn's hand in his. "She fell from a height, from the old banker's building downtown." Severn's free hand darts up to cover her mouth. "There's only one reason to be on the roof of that building." Hiromi's eyes complete the explanation as a suicide.

Severn's memories rush in of Squirt and her auburn hair. The little girl she'd known was all curls and freckles. She hadn't deserved the life she'd been handed any more than the rest of them, and now she is gone. Severn is surprised she has any more tears to offer tonight, yet they stream from her swollen eyes, down her flushed cheeks. She feels Hiromi's hand squeeze down a little on hers to comfort her. She can see he's second-guessing himself for mentioning the suicide.

"She didn't attend many groups," he began, "April had made up her mind that as long as the *John's* were out there, she would never feel safe in her own skin. She'd declined the help we were all offered. She fell into a life of drugs to escape herself. We all feel for her and feel her loss, but April doesn't represent most of us. Like *you*, Severn, we're beating this, living lives, having families, being productive citizens, and giving back."

Severn's head nods. "Of course, Hiromi, you're right. I just... I remember her as a little girl."

A hand lands softly on Severn's shoulder as a woman named Debbie hands Severn her number. "If you've any questions or just want to talk to a friend," she tells her and leaves with a smile. Severn nods and smiles back, thanking her. Once everyone has left, she and Hiromi lock up the church and walk to their cars. The rain has tapered off, and the city smells of wet asphalt and congested storm sewers.

"You can't know how much it means to me to see you again, Severn," Hiromi tells her. "I've never forgotten you. You are the best memory I have of that time, as short as it was for me."

"I'm grateful to know so many have survived their memories," Severn replies. "You were such a dear little boy. That they took your innocence the way they did... the way they did all of us... it's a lot to bear."

"You don't have to bear it alone, Severn. Remember that. *Please.* You were the strongest person I'd ever known while we existed in that place. You still are." Hiromi's gaze never wavers.

"I will get through this, Hiromi," Severn replies, stopping under a streetlight and turning to her new friend. She is filled with courage after seeing and listening to everyone in group. "I'm just so happy to know you've done so well. We're all worthwhile, and that's an important thing to preach after experiencing what we have. So many of us can lose that connection to self-worth all too easily." She's quoting Sturgis now.

Hiromi stands back a moment from Severn and smiles brightly. "You've learned a lot since your reveal." He taps her shoulder and leaves his hand to linger. "You've inspired the group by coming. Where sometimes we forget why we're doing this, you've reinforced purpose."

"I'm so encouraged by it all – by all of you. I'll be a regular at group." She asserts, nodding.

"This is you?" Hiromi asks, motioning to the black Toyota. Severn nods. "I'll wait for you to leave," he tells her.

Severn hugs Hiromi and gets into her car. She rolls the window down and blows him a kiss. He does the same and watches her pull away.

2021

The Diagnosis

Not unlike prior years, January proves to be a brutal month of freezing days intermingling with mild ones brewing the perfect storm for a person to feel uncomfortable in their own skin. It also tends to breed the cold and flu season, and at this moment, Jonah's old bones ache as he suffers the clear indications of a worrisome cough due to cold. Every breath becomes labored, resulting in a hacking cough bent on bursting a lung or tearing his esophagus. He apologizes to his body for its susceptibility to catching the worst colds and flu known to man. Every year for the last ten, he has come down with a wretched virus that persists for months.

"Though you're clean now and been so for the past three years, your body may never accept it," Dr. Walsh explains, Jonah praying he is prescribed something to fight the infection. "You have a virus again, and as you know, there is nothing we can do about that. Your immune system is severely compromised from your unchecked addictions, and even now, three years later, it is hard-pressed to fight off any form of viral infection."

Jonah coughs violently in response to the ugly prognosis and wipes his mouth with a tissue. Seated on the high steel table, paper crunching under him on the vinyl cushion, Jonah sighs heavily. He's bent over and feels as though death were the foregone conclusion to his day.

"It feels like more this time, doc," Jonah manages, eyeing the opinionated young man in his long white jacket and stethoscope wound around his long neck. "I have pains I've never experienced before." He motions slowly to his abdomen

Michael Poeltl

and sides, and lower back with arthritic fingers. "My throat and chest are the least of my worries this time. Nothing feels right." He flinches as the doctor approaches and places his fingers on Jonah's side. He barely has to touch Jonah to know how bad it is. "Hurts every time I cough."

"Lay down for me, will you, Jonah," Walsh asks, and Jonah emits a pained cry as he shifts his weight, lowering his upper body and swinging his tired legs onto the cushion. Walsh motions for him to lift his shirt, and the doctor presses lightly along his abdomen, though it feels to Jonah like he is pushing with all his weight behind him. A more guttural groan escapes his lips this time, and he begs the doctor to stop.

"That's a lot of tenderness," Walsh says mostly to himself with a quizzical look. "It's not muscular, not with that reaction. I thought maybe because of your coughing fits...you still smoke?" Jonah nods, eyes shut, wishing away the pain. "We're going to send you to the hospital so they can run a few more detailed scans, Jonah. This may not be a virus."

Jonah is asked to pick up the paperwork being printed at reception and go immediately to the hospital's emergency room for further testing. He feels as if he's floating as reality is replaced by a surreal sensation. If it's as bad as the doctor's expression led him to believe... he knows he's done this to himself. If it's stomach cancer or some other death sentence, he's earned it fairly. He's abused his body from the tender age of ten, and that's nearly fifty years of damage to his organs. If he was accused of abusing someone else this long, he'd be given a life sentence and, in some countries, a death sentence. He wonders if this could be his death sentence.

At the hospital, they receive him after a three-hour wait. Typical. In the meantime, he'd been feeling more and more anxious over the possibilities, his mind running scenarios of every disease. Searches on his smartphone aren't helping. Dr. Google was a pessimistic son of a bitch. Once in the MRI machine, he began to relax despite the claustrophobic apparatus's obnoxious sound, *chucka, chucka, chucka.* More blood tests, and Jonah is asked to wait once more.

With no one to call and no one who could care if he lived or died, Jonah again assesses his life. This is a practice he tries to deny himself. It has been a lonely life - partly by his design and largely through genetics, upbringing, and conditioning. Oh! to have June here with him now. To have had June through all of the last twenty years of addiction... he wouldn't have gone back to it. He wouldn't be here now. He wouldn't have cut his life short. *But you did, and here you are.* Jonah only nods at his self-talk.

"Mr. Bishop," a woman calls his name for the second time. Jonah rises from his seat and lets her lead him into another room with a doctor or some health official there to deliver the news. He is asked to sit – never has anyone been asked to sit where a good prognosis was about to be delivered – and Jonah clasps his hands together on his lap while his heart races, awaiting the results. *Does it even matter if it's a death sentence?* Self-talk asks. *You've only been existing the past three years.* True, but to die is difficult to accept, says ego, *and I don't really want to die. I'm not prepared. Oh, how I wish you'd have listened.* His mother's voice still claimed his ego, tirelessly hoping to save him from emotional damage while soothing his nerves with alcohol. It has been a long three years trying to ignore her. Most people claim to have forgotten a loved one's voice when they die. It's the first thing they forget.

"Mr. Bishop," the official-looking woman says with her long nose buried in the computer print-out. "We are making you up a bed as we speak, sir. Your company insurance is taking care of the costs. You have sepsis and are currently experiencing organ failure. We've been in touch with your MD, and he's given us your history. You've been very late in coming to us with your discomfort, and now it seems you will be staying with us a good long time to get everything working again. We're going to place you on an aggressive run of antibiotics over the next few days, and if it shows signs of working we'll continue to monitor you. If not, the extent of the damage will be explored through surgery. It is my hope that the antibiotics will make a difference. Sepsis is not to be taken lightly, and we'll do everything we can to get you through this."

Jonah feels as though he's been slapped awake in the middle of a nightmare. *This is a wake-up call.* "What is... sepsis?" Jonah asks timidly.

"With your weakened immune system, sepsis is your body's reaction to an existing infection in the blood or other tissues. It shuts down organs and can lead to shock and then death. It is a severe condition that we hope we've caught in time. But as I said, we'll know more after we attempt the antibiotics. Our anesthesiologists are reviewing your case now, and a team being assembled for the operation if necessary."

Jonah isn't registering everything the lanky woman is telling him. His mind wanders as the information are delivered calmly and rationally. *How could she be so calm when relaying such dire news?* Though the words she is saying are very serious in nature, the woman's practiced delivery makes it seem like she couldn't care less about the operation's results. Jonah hates the idea of surgery. An open wound someone deliberately puts in you to play around with organs never meant to see the light of day. It's all very off-putting. Jonah feels weak thinking about it, and the doctor notices how his torso begins to bow.

"We're going to treat your pain as well, Mr. Bishop," she says, leaning into Jonah from across her desk. "There's no reason for you to suffer."

And there it is, Jonah thought, he'll be diagnosed and placed in palliative care hooked up to a morphine drip until dead. He'll die addicted to morphine. "I... appreciate that," Jonah manages gravely, standing when the doctor stands and follows her lead to what he can only assume is his deathbed.

It's not a private room, but it isn't hallway medicine either. He'll share his room with two others who seem equally fucked. Both lay motionless. *Great conversationalists, I'm sure.* Not that Jonah wants conversation. Monitors blink, and respirators hum. Jonah is given a gown and asked to change behind a curtain. Catching a glimpse of himself in the bathroom mirror, he wonders how it has taken so long to arrive at this prognosis. His bent form looks hollow and weak and withered. Were June here, she wouldn't recognize him. He is helped to bed, and immediately lines are run into his veins to manage hydration and the antibiotics through drip IVs. He hates watching his veins being penetrated like this. They experience complications - a nurse in training misses the vein altogether. Jonah swallows, shuts his eyes hard, turns his head away from the fussing nurse, and accepts his fate. He doesn't expect a good prognosis.

* * *

After a week of failed attempts with a number of antibiotic cocktails, exploratory surgery was next. Jonah wakes to confusion as half a dozen health care workers hover over him. All pain is gone, and he feels weightless. *Had it worked? Had they discovered a tumor or something and removed it?* It seems the morphine has acquired a voice to keep ego and self-talk at bay. But no, nothing ever kept self-talk from its harsh message. No, morphine is strong, but self-talk is stronger. *Look at yourself, you're all cut up, and these people are making an example of you. Don't do drugs, kids. Don't be like Jonah.*

Jonah turns his head to the side, alerting the group leader, and the woman who suggested the surgery speaks. "Jonah, you're awake," she says and sits on a stool next to the bed. The others watch and listen. "Surgery was successful in realizing the extent of the damage, and we removed a kidney and several inches of the large intestine." A long pause follows. *That's not good,* self-talk assures him. "I'm sorry to say, Jonah, discovery revealed extensive damage to multiple organs. What you've been experiencing this last week is much more dire than we'd hoped. Your tissues have begun to deteriorate, and the virus responsible has triggered sepsis." She looks up at her team, or pupils, or whoever they are and sighs. *Was that for show?*

"I'm sorry to tell you, Jonah, that with the assistance of machines and around the clock medical care, you are looking at about one month."

Until we're better? It is ego's last stand. *No mother, until we're dead,* self-talk corrects her.

This shouldn't come as a surprise to Jonah, and frankly, it doesn't. But that the time has finally arrived is still a difficult pill to swallow. His face feels wet, but he is too weak to wipe away the tears. "Thanks for the honesty, doc," he says, "so, what's my next move?"

2021

Walking the Talk

The streets fill with new snow as winter continues its assault on the city. To think all this time, the man they'd searched for has been living out his final days in such a stately place. Severn and Darnell navigate the sidewalk flanked by a cedar hedge which lines the acreage just on the fringe of the city's limits. The cedar scent mingling with the light snowfall is intoxicating.

Severn scoops up a pile of snow with the toe of her boot and kicks it into the air. "So, this is it?" She asks, folder tucked under her arm, staring up at the massive, century home. The sign on the lawn reads *Sunset Hospice,* a home for the dying. It crushed Severn to hear when Darnell first announced the man's whereabouts. He had proven a difficult person to find. No online presence of any kind. He'd vacated his apartment and had no forwarding address. His workplace explained he had quit several months ago and returned the company cell phone. For all intent and purposes, he had disappeared.

It wasn't until Darnell had managed to pull tax information that led to bank statements under false pretenses that he discovered Mr. Bishop's whereabouts. Severn was impressed; Darnell had deep connections within government, and law enforcement, and Severn trusted in his abilities explicitly.

"You're sure he's in there," Severn asks Darnell as they stand staring at the building.

"Only one way to know for sure," Darnell says, excitement building.

Severn sends him a harsh glare, eyebrows knitting together. "You said you'd called ahead -" she noticed right away Darnell was teasing and feels silly for the accusation. "You *did* call. *He. Is. In. There.*" Severn smiles and laughs over her gullibility. Working together the past few months, they have built an unbreakable trust and friendship that rivals any she's known. Darnel admitted the same one evening as they worked late pouring over a paper trail, which eventually led to this moment. In the days that followed Darnell saw great promise in Severn's abilities and offered her employment within his organization. She accepted.

"It was the only opportunity I was going to get," Darnell said back, mischief dancing in his bright, brown eyes, a smile revealing teeth as white as the virgin snow at their feet. "Shall we?" He extends an arm, and Severn threads hers through it.

Her eyes are glassy, mixing tears of happiness over this weighty moment with tears of sadness knowing what little time they must have. She blinks and they slip past her lashes and tumble down her white cheeks settling in her wool scarf. The tears track a warm glow over her cool skin. Darnell looks at her tenderly and retrieves the hanky from his breast pocket. Severn accepts and shakes her head, sniffling.

"It's silly I feel so out of sorts," she admits. "I've never met the man, and yet I'm crying already."

"Not at all, Severn," Darnell replies, "this man changed your life forever. You deserve to meet. I only wish it was under better circumstances."

Severn pulls in a deep, cleansing breath and wipes the excess eyeliner from her cheeks. "Thank you," she says, handing the handkerchief back, "you must be thrilled too."

"I am. The difference he's made in my life may not have been the difference between life and death, but it made me the man I am today," Darnell admitted, and Severn knew he meant every word. "To meet him is going to be a tremendous honor."

"I hardly know how to approach him," Severn confesses, looking up at Darnell through the thickening snowfall, "Where do I begin?"

"Lead with the photo and tell your story," Darnell suggests. "We don't want to alarm him. They'd explained to me over the phone that he is very frail."

"I wonder how much time he has," an inexplicable sense of loss enters Severn's heart as she gazes at the long, wrap-around porch.

"Well, it is a *hospice* after all, so we'd best make our way in," Darnell says, manipulating the mood before it gets too grim for both their sakes, inching Severn closer to the substantial entrance. They pick up their pace and enter the building where a front desk receives them.

They are greeted by a young man with a kind, round face behind the raised counter. The scent of cloves seems to permeate the foyer where a beautiful double staircase winds itself up on glossy hardwood to the second floor, and a massive chandelier hangs several feet overhead.

"Hello, I called earlier about Mr. Bishop, I'm Darnell, and this is Severn," Darnell tells the young man who is now checking his computer.

"Yes, please sign yourselves in and take a seat," the boy motions to the antique couch behind them. "I'll alert the head nurse, Mrs. Willoughby, and she'll see you to Mr. Bishop's room."

"Thank you, and how is Mr. Bishop faring?" Darnell asks as he scribbles his signature on the sign-in sheet.

"He's as well as can be expected," the boy answers, his expression of confusion over the question obvious. "I mean, you know, he's *here*."

"Yes, a silly question," Darnell apologizes. "I meant to ask whether he is awake and if we can see him now."

"Mrs. Willoughby can answer that and other general questions about the health of Mr. Bishop," the young man replies, "I'm really not supposed to comment on it. Sorry."

"Not at all," Darnell squints to read the boy's nametag, "Carsten." The boy nods and rushes off to page the head nurse, Mrs. Willoughby, who rounds the staircase and approaches.

"Well, isn't this a surprise!" She says to them both with a hand out to shake theirs. Willoughby's is a tight, sharp shake, one thrust, with the other hand closing around the top. Her smile is genuine, and her eyes alight with a kindness reserved for saints. Next, she snaps up a clipboard and reads their names.

"Is it?" Darnell says. "Does Mr. Bishop not receive many visitors?"

"None," she says, "this will be quite a shock for him as well," her voice thundering in the foyer, turning the heads of those moving past.

"Not *too* much of a shock, I hope," begged Severn. "We've waited a long time to meet him."

"You're relatives? He's never spoken of any family."

"Not related, no, but very close," Darnell offers.

"Not *lawyers* come to take what little he might have?" Willoughby eyes them suspiciously for a moment, and then her face softens. "I'm only joking, mind me, you must know Mr. Bishop's savings ran out a week ago, and we're keeping him on through our charitable donations."

"Oh?" This news came as a sad statement on the man's luck and Darnell acted, as he does, by offering to help. "I would like to offer you whatever compensation is required to keep Mr. Bishop comfortable for as long as is needed."

"*My,* that's very good of you, Darnell," Willoughby says, placing a warm, thick hand on his shoulder. "Any donations are always welcome and appreciated. Please speak with Carsten on your way out today, and he can explain."

"Wonderful, I'll certainly do that, Nurse Willoughby."

"I've just come from Mr. Bishop's room a few minutes ago, and he is quite alert. Mind all the tubes and fluids," Willoughby says, lowering her voice as she leads them up the stairs, "he's most definitely not a well man, as you will see. But he does have a sharp sense of humor. Oh, and if you don't already know, he suffers a condition which leaves him with a - shall we say, *distinct* odor - It's quite strong, but you do get used to it."

"Understood," Darnell said, and Willoughby stopped them at the top of the stairs. The smell of cloves had left them, replaced by the scent of death and the mess that goes with it. Air fresheners were littered throughout the hallway but couldn't mask the true scent of the place.

"As I told you, he's had no visitors during his stay here and is not exactly polished on social niceties. He'll likely be taken aback that he has visitors at all and could be quite closed off at first. Just remind him who you are and why you're here, and that should excite some recognition."

"*No one at all?*" Severn asked quietly, her expression falling. Willoughby shook her head. "That's so sad."

"It's a shame. He's a very lonely man. The nurses and I play board games with him occasionally and bathe and feed him... but he's waiting to die. He doesn't want to leave his bed."

Darnell and Severn share a look of empathy for the man they feel so indebted to. They nod that they understand, and Willoughby takes them to Mr. Bishop's room.

2021

A Reunion of Sorts

"Jonah, you have... visitors," Nurse Willoughby announces with a quizzical expression, standing in the doorway of Jonah's Hospice room. The two lock eyes - Willoughby's intense gaze and raised brows are designed to encourage him to recognize his visitors. Jonah's own brow furrows at the thought anyone would come to see him. After so long in the Hospice's care, Willoughby clearly shares his confusion.

Jonah just nods at Willoughby, scratching his beard, curious over the obvious mistake, but not about to turn away the opportunity to inject some interest into his day. His life here has been anything but interesting.

Nurse Willoughby nods and sees the two strangers in. One is a woman of, Jonah guesses, a similar age as him with long, white hair and an appealing face. The other is a well-dressed, tall black man, much younger than the woman. Jonah struggles to sit up in his bed, guiding the mattress upright with his handheld pendant. He manipulates his arm to avoid catching his intravenous tubes on the bed frame. He does not recognize either of them. Why would complete strangers come to visit? *Don't tell me it's some church group do-gooders hoping to turn me before I check out.*

"Jonah," the woman speaks in a soft sigh holding an intense gaze on him with a growing smile that strains against the tight wrinkles around her mouth. Jonah fears her delicate skin might tear. "Oh, Jonah, I'm so *delighted* to meet you."

Jonah's becoming increasingly confused, his hand rising to his gray beard again to scratch. She seems to think she knows him while he is certain he does not know her. "Yes," he replies, fascinated to know where this visit will go.

"We thought we'd never find you," she tells him, her head shaking almost imperceptibly side to side. "We're here to honor you, Jonah, you, whose life has had such a profound impact on ours." She looks nervous.

Jonah immediately goes to the dark side of this proclamation, assuming he's somehow wronged these people, and they were here for some sense of closure or to exact their revenge. "I - I'm sorry, I -"

"Please, there's nothing to apologize for, Jonah." The well-dressed man begins. "This is Severn, and I'm Darnell. When Severn says you've touched our lives profoundly, it's meant with the *greatest* gratitude."

Jonah likens the man's voice to a stream rolling over smooth stones. He feels safe under its spell. "I've never touched *anyone's* life," Jonah defends quietly. Over time Jonah had debunked any possibility he'd affected anyone's life in a manner that might command gratitude save June, and maybe Mort. "Why are you here?"

"Please, Jonah, let me explain. You were responsible for a series of events I've only recently discovered, which led to incredible outcomes." Severn says earnestly. "I have a photograph I'd like to show you from just this year," the tall, thin woman reaches into her purse and draws out an envelope. She passes it to Jonah, and he accepts it with a hand sporting far too many liver spots for his age.

"I don't recognize any of them," Jonah studies the photograph of over two dozen people. They are a multi-generational group - ranging from their late thirties to late fifties. He squints and finds Severn in the picture. He points to her image and looks up at the woman. "This is you," confusion still playing out across his face.

"Yes, me and those you pulled from the fire, so to speak." Severn again answers in a way Jonah cannot relate.

"Fire," Jonah's face falls. "You have the wrong man."

"She's using a turn of phrase, Jonah," Darnell explains. "We should have rehearsed our introductions. I'm afraid we're confusing you with our explanation. Forgive us. And forgive me if any of what I'm about to say is a trigger for you, but, in 1993, when you gave the police an account of the man in the theatre shooting and later identified him at the station, you set in motion a series of events that saved twenty-five people from a life of slavery and certain death."

Jonah runs his fingers along the tube, which hydrates him. His memories of the events of that night have never left him. "I remember them saying," he takes a hard breath, "I might have to point him out in a line-up... but never heard any more from them." He hates the feelings that surface with the memory. "I think you're stretching the truth a bit,"

"Jonah, you witnessed a double murder and fingered the bastard! You're a *hero.*" Severn jumps in. "You stayed at the scene. Your eye-witness report led the police to him... and to *me.*"

"Anyone could have singled out the shooter," Jonah suggests, remembering the event. His ego may like the idea, but his self-talk couldn't allow him to believe he'd made a difference. He'd been sheltered as a child and an addict all his life. He'd kept to himself. He didn't engage anyone if he didn't have to. He never felt compelled to stay in that theatre. He was terrified. *You're no hero.* "I'm no hero."

Severn's delicate hand lay on Jonah's shoulder; the warmth of her touch sends little electrical storms down his arm and into his chest. "Jonah, it doesn't matter *how* it happened. How you *responded* is what made the difference. You're a hero to me. You're a hero to everyone you freed through your selfless act. *One act* which resonated across so many lives." She taps delicately at the photo on Jonah's lap.

"I don't understand," a tear escapes and zigzags down Jonah's gaunt cheek lost to his gray beard. "I never made a difference. I've always been *no one.*" Why now is he hearing about this?

"And we're here to tell you otherwise. You're an extraordinary *someone.* To me, to the people in this photograph," Severn looks up at her friend and introduces him again. "To Darnell," she stands and invites Darnell to sit on the chair next to Jonah's bed.

Darnell sits. "Jonah, you can't know how privileged I feel to meet you. I thought my father's death was nothing more than a bad man being culled from this earth. But I was wrong. I discovered soon after that, he had been involved in human trafficking, where Severn and the others were being sold into sexual slavery." Darnell takes Jonah's tired hand in his. Jonah allows this.

"Who was your father, Darnell?" Jonah asks, his mouth dry from the conversation while a veil of serenity settled over him.

"He was the very man you fingered for the murders of the men in that theatre. They worked with him and had left to pursue other interests. It's said my father did not take that information well, sought them out, and murdered them in cold blood. I'm not saying they didn't have it coming. Still, I'm saying that your presence in that theatre and your testimony delivered me from my father and put a lot of money under my control. *Dirty* money: money which I have done only good with." Darnell looks up to Severn, who smiles and nods her head enthusiastically. The poor woman's face is wet with tears.

"Then it is *you* who is the hero of this story, Darnell, not me," Jonah repeats his self-talk verbatim, disappointed in himself for considering, even for a moment, that his life had been worth living.

"You're a humble man, Jonah, I can appreciate that, but you need to recognize your place in the series of events which gave so many their lives back," Darnell explains. "You've lived all this time not knowing the incredible effect you've had on hundreds, and now *thousands* of lives. It is a regret of mine that I did not seek you out sooner. I was young. I may have created something for the greater good, but it is because of *you* I'd been gifted the money to do so."

"Thousands," the number seems surreal to Jonah as he utters it thoughtfully, again drawn in by the man's soothing voice and the news he conveys.

"First, you helped those like Severn escape their captivity. Then you gave their families and friends back to their loved ones. Other missing children's cases were solved through your act from the names inscribed on a wall within the facility. For the last twenty-six years, the return on your single act of conscience has helped thousands through my organization." Darnell explained in an animated way.

Jonah can't quite believe what he's hearing. The history, the photographs, that they knew so much about him... it was unsettling. *He was no one.* He'd known that since he was a boy. He'd been on the losing side of life the moment his twin brother was stillborn. He'd been an addict. He'd made little of himself, yet these good people were here to tell him differently. A lump catches in his throat, and he tries to swallow it down. To feel pride over any portion of his life seemed manic. The sensation, though, is freeing. Jonah likens this news to a discarded film being pulled from its place in an unnamed warehouse, retouched, and reimagined as color floods into every scene of his life. As if every trial and triumph had been for some greater purpose.

"My life... it would seem, has meant more to strangers than it has to me," Jonah croaked, his fingers tracing his tattooed forearm where he'd had purpose inked after an episode with work. "I always assumed... I'd made no difference to anyone."

"That's what we want you to *understand*, Jonah," Darnell pressed, "and it's imperative now," Darnell looked worriedly at Severn and then back to Jonah, "that you *fully* appreciate your role. The changes for *good* you've set in motion." Darnell's grip on Jonah's hand becomes firmer with each declaration. "This world swallows people up every day, Jonah. It's a vast cyclical nightmare for so many, but there is always *purpose* awarded for all the pain and sacrifice. You have *never...* been no one."

Jonah is overwhelmed by this decree and cannot stop the deluge of tears that follow. The information he's received in such a short time and with such conviction has left him gob smacked. His head fills with the accounts of so many, their families and friends, and Darnell's own rise from poverty and abuse. The moments he could recall that paralleled the events evoked emotions he had repressed and denied himself his whole life. He was *proud*.

In addition to the blind affect he's had on these two, he wonders over his own life and the effect others had had on him. *Did his mother know she made it alright for him to become an addict? Did his father know he'd made it acceptable for him to be a recluse? Did Morty know he'd given Jonah a voice? That Morty was someone to listen to his grievances, ideas, and observations and make them real? Did June know she gave Jonah courage and the very best years of his life?*

Darnell, overcome by Jonah's emotional release, also weeps now with him, joined by Severn, who's taken the edge of Jonah's bed and places her hands on Jonah's and Darnell's. Shared grief plays itself out, then acceptance, and finally, closure. Jonah is beside himself with the knowledge these two have instilled in him in his eleventh hour. It is the blind affect in action June had once explained to him. He was moved through gratitude that they cared enough to find him and explain his influence on their lives. There could be no greater gift to a dying man. To have lived a life of worth and purpose and have *proof* of that standing beside him. Some find that in careers and children and faith. He couldn't boast those. *What greater purpose was there than to live a life in service of others?* He now knew that his life had been one of service even after his poor choices and familial difficulties.

"You... cannot know what you've given me," Jonah finally says, his attention focused on the two sets of hands holding his. "It's the gift of a life I did not know I'd lived."

"We couldn't be happier to have brought you this news, Jonah," Severn tells him through her tears. "I'm only sorry our time is so short."

Jonah feels light-headed now. "You've given me everything... that I will be remembered at all..." he manages through the wheezing, swallowing hard. "I *understand* now. I can go in *peace*. Thank you..." Jonah feels a sense of harmony and lucidity enter. Their warm hands on his icy fingers comforts him. There is a heightened vibration that radiates through his frail body. It is a new sensation, but not a frightening one. He feels as though he might vibrate right out of his skin. His eyes remain open, staring into a light so bright it blinds him to his physical surroundings. *Is something wrong with the ceiling lamp?* The light radiates warmth next, which quickens the vibrations under his skin. Not just under his skin, it underlies everything that he is. At first, it is a weighty sensation, quickly becoming lighter than air as the shadow he'd envisioned ever-present in his life retreats. Severn is saying something more at his bedside, but it is as if she is speaking from the other end of a long tunnel. It doesn't matter anymore. *None of it matters anymore.*

It is all so vast, he thinks, comparing this experience of slipping free from the material world to Darnell's explanation of life. *It is vast and beautiful.* As his eyes stare unblinkingly at the ceiling, Jonah quietly withdrawals from his known universe into something infinitely more meaningful. Space expands beyond his hospice room, and into the lives he's given back to those affected by his singular act. Expanding ever further from his center, Jonah feels everything; every sensation of every moment in his own life, taking responsibility for his actions and forgiving himself and others, viewing every moment with a new perspective; one of intense compassion. He is speechless, yet words do not escape him. He simply cannot speak. He is caught up in the reverence of his own life and the importance of life in general. He is caught in the extraordinary circumstances of being conceived at all, beating seemingly insurmountable odds, interacting with others who beat those same odds, and making a difference.

A short moment later, the heart monitor makes a noise neither Severn nor Darnell is prepared to hear - the long beeeep that accompanies a heart no longer pumping. They both stand up as the nurse rushes in at the sound. She takes Jonah's pulse and closes his eyes. Then she turns to greet them.

"I'm so sorry. I do hope your time with Jonah was productive." The nurse says. "He has a Do-Not-Resuscitate order. It's what he wanted... and why he's here."

"Of course. Of course." Severn replies softly, her hands over her heart, looking from the nurse back to Jonah.

"I believe we were able to convey what we needed, uh, what we all needed," Darnell says, his voice rattling. He feels a cool breeze embrace him as he studies Jonah's frail form. The small man looks smaller now that life has left him. He wears an expression of tired satisfaction, eyes closed but just ever so lightly. A lifetime cut short played across the landscape of Jonah's face. He studies Jonah's arm where a litany of words and phrases are inked into his flesh, telling the story of his life. Darnell leans in and places a soft hand upon Jonah's still chest. There is a soft bundle under the sheet. He rolls back the blanket revealing a small, plush toy bunny.

Jack, it's nice to finally meet you.

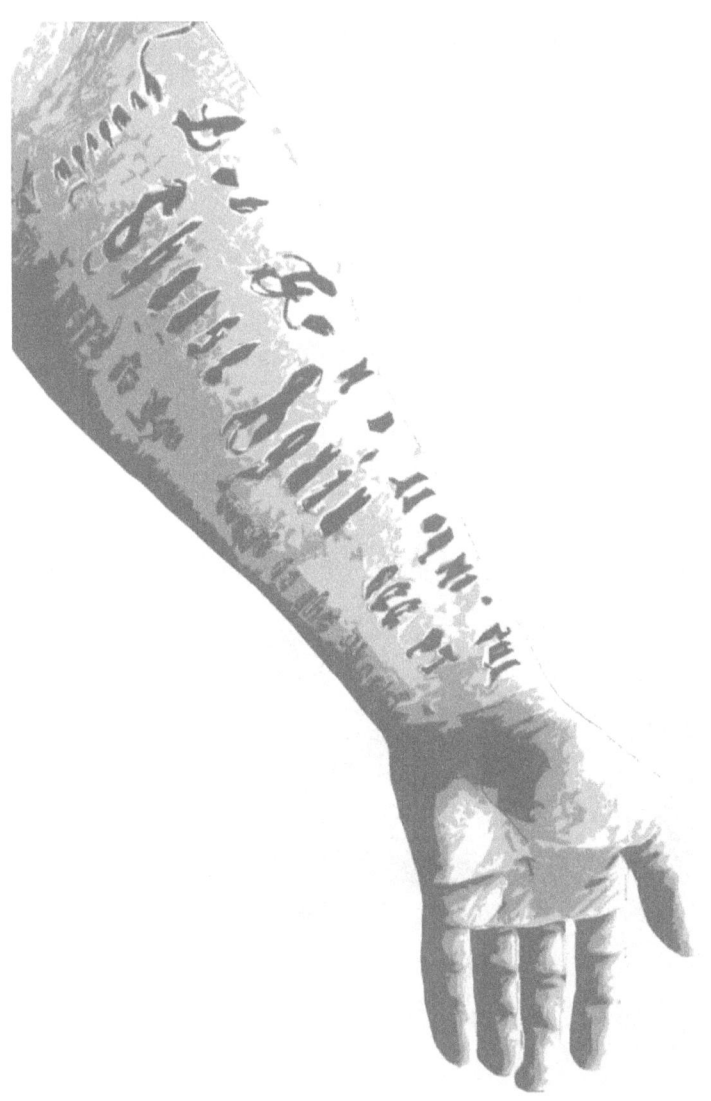

Enjoy the First Five Chapters from Michael Poeltl's, Her Past's Present:

Chapter One
September 15th, 2:00 am

It wasn't your fault. These are healing words, something Tess's therapist had her write out a thousand times when she was twelve. It became her mantra, a reassurance that what had happened to her baby brother could in no way be her fault.

Today, fifteen years after the suicide that had devastated her life and the lives of her parents, she finds power in those words once more.

"I'm sorry," says Sam, her husband, standing stock-still before her. All that separates them is the granite-topped island in the middle of a kitchen under renovation. It is the only working surface to lean on should he confirm her fears.

"Please," she pleads. "Please just tell me it doesn't mean anything. Tell me it was just the one time, and I can forgive you." She isn't hopeful for this outcome but can't bear the thought of the consequences of such an admission. To be a single mother amidst all the renovations, bills, contractors, and sleepless nights has overwhelmed her the past few days, and her already pale complexion is rapidly fading to a sickly, almost translucent white.

Sam's head drops slowly, his eyes studying the grout lines framing the new tile at his feet. His heart isn't in this. He was far from ready to tell his wife of five years he'd met someone else; he'd been seeing another woman since the last month of her pregnancy. Sam's decided that is a significant amount of time, and he is very much committed to this new woman. But not at all ready to tell his wife.

"Tess," he struggles with her name. His chin is beginning to tremble.

"Please, tell me it will be okay." She begs. "Tell me that you love me."

"I *do* love you, goddamn it," he manages through clenched teeth. His fist falls with a weak thump on the black granite counter while his other hand finds his face, defending Tess from his diminishing façade. He jerks and cries into his shield, turning away from Tess.

"Then why?" Tess begs, slowly sinking to her knees, coming to rest on the dusty tile, her back landing against the island's cupboard.

"I don't know why." Sam turns and slides down the opposite side of the island. "I don't know."

"Please don't leave me with nothing," she begs.

"If I had an answer, I'd give it."

"*Please.*"

"I don't have an answer for you. I haven't an answer for *myself.*"

Her voice cracks. "If you love me, be with me."

"Don't you think I want that? Don't you think I *want* to be happy here?"

"You're not happy?"

"You know I'm not."

"I'm sorry if I haven't had the time to put into you. We have a baby."

"Jesus, I know we have a baby, and I love her, but I feel like the walls are closing in on me."

Tess shifts uncomfortably, the thin fabric of her pajama pants offering little insulation from the cool tile. "It's okay to feel trapped, but you need to talk to me."

"It's not *you.*"

"Then what?"

"*Me.* It's me."

It's not your fault. She tells herself. *It's not your fault.*

Chapter Two
October 15th, Monday

Tess is up with her daughter. It's 3:30 in the morning. It is the second time tonight, and she only put Emilia down at ten. At six months old, Tess had hoped Emma would have gotten into a pattern of sleep that would take her through the night. Even if she weren't going to bed until later in the evening, at least sleeping through the night would be a blessing. But neither was happening, and now that she no longer has Sam to lean on, her days and nights seem to run together, one bleeding into the next.

Sitting in Emilia's room, rocking gently to the soothing sounds of her daughter feeding at the bottle, Tess wonders, as she does every night at this time, what next? It has been a month since Sam left. It was nearly that long since she'd heard from him, too. He left her with everything, including the bank account. She could complete the renovations on their apartment and live comfortably for the remainder of the year if it came to that. Still, Tess missed him endlessly: his presence in her bed, his turn with Emilia overnight, dinners, anticipating his return from work, adult conversation.

Tess cries silently over the baby, now convulsing to repress this reaction to her life. Every feeding ends up like this now - Tess crying over her infant daughter, a myriad of what-ifs tormenting her. *It wasn't your fault*, she reminds herself. *There is nothing you could have done to change the outcome.* Emilia is now sleeping, so Tess lays her in the crib. Careful not to make a noise, she sneaks out of Emilia's room.

It's now that the exhaustion of the day, both physical and emotional, hits her. With the last feeding of the night over, the long stretch of wakefulness begins until the morning light. Tess has not been able to sleep past four in the morning since Sam left, and with the relentless barrage of scenarios attacking her at her most vulnerable, there is no point in trying. Even lying in bed is a challenge. Reading a book is a lost cause; nothing silences the onslaught of questions. So, like every morning before sunrise, Tess drags her weakened spirit across the bedroom and into the nearly finished kitchen to begin her day.

After she makes a pot of coffee, Tess sits in front of a pile of bills she has had no time or inclination to pay. This spurs another panic attack. The first had happened the night after she and Sam had confronted his decision to leave. The experience was frightening, and this was no different. It comes without warning and starts in her left hand, travels up her arm, and attacks her shoulder. The feeling resembles a description Tess had read on heart attacks so closely that she immediately moves her right hand to her chest. Sure enough, the pain enters her chest, and Tess grips her left breast, willing the pain away.

Nothing can make you feel more confident that you're having a heart attack than a substantial panic attack. Even a heart attack either takes you within seconds or goes mostly unnoticed. A panic attack, on the other hand, goes on and on, and with each passing minute, your heart fills with dread that, this time, it really is a heart attack!

Tess fumbles with her tablet and punches in a search for panic attack symptoms. This technique settled her nerves enough to allow the attack to subside three days earlier. Finding the page again, she scrolls down, reading hungrily in anticipation of the pins and needles sensation in her arms dissipating. Breathing in and out slowly also assists in alleviating the building panic. Each breath is an exercise in concentration.

After ten minutes, the symptoms left as suddenly as they'd appeared. Feeling one hundred years older, Tess sits, bent over the dining room table, head in folded arms. Then, the baby cries.

It seems that she will be given no quarter today, and with the men coming to complete the kitchen in just a few short hours, Tess predicts a difficult day of electric drills and skill saws buzzing in her ear while she and Emilia shut themselves into her bedroom to watch cartoons.

* * * * *

As nine o'clock approaches, the buzzer sounds, and Tess lets the men in with all their noisy equipment. She's happy to know the work will end after today, or so she's been told, but the barrage of questions concerning the job's specifics is more than she can handle. This is their sixth time at the house, and Tess is well-versed in making small talk. She points out the coffee maker with a full pot brewed on the counter and relays her plans with the baby for the day.

The foreman assures Tess they will finish today and be out of her hair for good, barring any unforeseen difficulties. Tess nods and realizes she's been staring at the man. He looks inquisitively at her and asks whether there is something else. Tess, embarrassed, shakes her head.

"Sorry. Just tired, is all."

"If I have any questions, I'll knock on your door." He smiles and turns to accept a coffee from his apprentice.

Tess turns around and walks quickly to her room with Emma on her hip. It had been a long time since she'd even considered the company of a man, but fixed in that gaze, she suddenly yearned for the unshaven foreman dressed in a white tee, beige overalls, and steel-toed boots.

In her bedroom, Tess catches herself in the vanity mirror and stops. Studying her reflection, she chastises herself.

"Look at you. Nobody would want *you*." Her hair is in knots, and her face is blotchy from the embarrassment she felt from breaking eye contact with the foreman. She had done nothing to fix her appearance since waking up in preparation for their arrival, never even considered it. How could she have let herself go like this, she wonders. Glancing over at the collage of wedding photos still adorning her wall, she sets the baby down on her bed and pulls them down, lobbing them into the corner pile of laundry. The glass shatters on one of the frames, and she again berates herself. She had thought leaving them on the wall served one of two purposes: Either Sam would return, and everything would be as it was, or she was steeling herself against him. Nothing had changed, though. Not in the month since he had disappeared. He hadn't returned to them, nor had she felt stoic against the black-and-white memories. She lives in a Mausoleum, she decides, a sad memorial to a marriage that didn't work.

* * * * *

That afternoon, the work is completed as promised, and as the apprentice cleans up, the foreman knocks on Tess's door.

"All done," he says. Tess opens the door and smiles at him. She'd made herself up, put on something more appropriate than the tights and loose sweater she'd been wearing to greet them, and walked to the kitchen with Emilia, again resting on her hip.

"Wow, that looks really nice," she tells them. "I couldn't imagine it finished for the longest time."

As the men clear out of the apartment, tools in tow, the foreman hangs back a moment to collect his check. Tess places Emma on the floor in front of the TV and writes the remainder of what she owes him. She pauses, wondering whether she could ask him out for a drink sometime. She feels she needs to recover from the verbal beating she gave herself earlier in the day. A date would do that.

"Say, Remy, right?" She keeps her eyes on the check while she addresses him.

"Yes. Tess, right?"

"Yes, um, I was wondering if you wanted to; I mean, maybe you'd like to get a drink sometime?" Tess feels her face flush. Her gaze remains on the counter.

"Oh, uh, I can't, but I would like to." He pulls a ring from his pocket and places it back on his finger. "I, uh, I take it off when I'm working."

Tess glances over to see that his ring finger now wears a gold band. She stands up straight and hands his check to him, red-faced. "I'm so sorry. I mean, for me, not that you're married. I loved being married." She smiles awkwardly and walks to the door. "Listen, I'll, um, give you good references if you need them. Great work. Thanks again." She can't stop talking now, wishing the moment away.

"Hey, I'm honored, really," he tells her from the hall, quickly studying her decorated ring finger.

"Oh, you don't have to say that. I'm okay, I understand." She runs a hand up and down her arm nervously.

"Well, you take care and enjoy your new kitchen." He bows out and heads towards the elevator where his apprentice is waiting. Tess closes the door and sinks to the floor, humiliated.

Chapter Three
Tuesday, 3:00 am

Tess wakes with a start. Her heart is pounding, and she feels a chill on her back as she sits up. She's soaked through her nightshirt, and her hair is matted to one side of her face. She peels her shirt off and ties her hair back, lifting it off her neck. Looking at the alarm clock, she sees it's nearly time for Emilia to wake up for her feeding. It's not particularly hot in the house; in fact, it's quite cool, *so why all the sweat?* Bad dreams, she faintly recalls.

Tess moves to the other side of the bed, avoiding the sizeable damp circle, and lies down again. *Pathetic*, she thinks, that she still practices sleeping on her side of the bed, while *his* remains vacant. Then, the dream that woke her reveals itself in sporadic scenes; flashes of memory dance behind her eyelids.

There was a war going on outside her home. Not her current home, but her home all the same. It was dark save one electric light flickering with each vibration. Plaster fell on her each time a sound more threatening than thunder exploded overhead. The last thing she remembers of the dream was searching helplessly through the rubble of her home for her children, crying out to them, panic-stricken, wishing her husband was there.

I can't even escape into my dreams anymore, she tells herself, placing both hands over her face. The idea that she may find no peace in sleep now devastates her. Tess refuses to take anything to induce sleep for fear of not waking when the baby cries. She surrenders to the anxiety and turns to sob into the pillow, a pillow that still carries Sam's scent.

Emilia does not wake for her 4 am feeding on this night, and Tess manages to collapse back into sleep after an exhausting hour of crying. At 7 am she rolls over to look at the time. The house is silent. Tess is suddenly overcome by fear. *How could Emilia not be awake if she hadn't eaten in the night?* Tess hurries out of bed and rounds the hallway to her daughter's bedroom. She rushes in and finds Emilia on her stomach in her crib. She is still. Tess is afraid to touch her. She's afraid to know. She's heard of crib death in infants; she's heard of all kinds of awful ways a child might die.

Emilia coughs and Tess's heart leaps. She reaches down and pulls Emilia up to her chest. The baby is blurry-eyed and begins to cry. Tess savors the moment, hugging her and tearing up.

"Oh, Emma," she says over and over. "I love you. I love you. I love you."

Emilia settles down, and Tess walks her to the kitchen, opens the fridge, and retrieves a formula bottle. She had tried to breastfeed early on, but after a month of aggressive pumping, she became discouraged and decided to go with formula. This did nothing to encourage her that she was a good mother, and she scolded herself each time she prepared a bottle of store-bought baby formula.

Once the bottle is warmed, Tess sits on the couch and thumbs at the television converter for a children's show. Emilia is happily feeding on the bottle when the phone rings.

"Hello," she answers, more enthusiastically than she'd meant.

The other end is silent, so she repeats herself, this time with a hint of irritation.

Still, there is nothing from the caller. Tess listens attentively, furrowing her brow as she leans into the earpiece. The caller hasn't hung up. They haven't done *anything*. Emilia lets out a satisfied burp and goes back to feeding.

"Sam?" She waits for some response. "Sam, is that you?" The phone drops at the other end. Tess jerks back from the receiver and hangs up. She looks down at her daughter.

"Your Daddy says hi." She smiles sadly and brushes her thin fingers through Emilia's short blonde hair.

The phone rings again, and Tess checks the call display this time. *Unknown number.* Well, maybe it was, and maybe it wasn't. She would take some comfort in believing it was Sam and let it ring.

Chapter Four
Tuesday, 1:00 pm

That afternoon, Tess keeps a lunch date with a friend from her office. Amanda asked Tess more than once to bring Emilia in so everyone could ogle over her, but Tess found one reason after another as to why she couldn't. Now, a month into her separation, she couldn't imagine facing the humiliation of an explanation.

Sitting outside a trendy café, Emma rests comfortably in her stroller beside her. Tess waits for Amanda to arrive. Tess waves as she watches her friend approach from across the street. She stands to meet her, and the women hug.

"You look fan-*fucking*-tastic!" she tells Tess.

Embarrassed by the compliment, Tess waves it off, shaking her head as she sits.

"Shut up," Amanda continues. "I have to starve myself for a week to look like you. This is unfair. *I'm* having a baby!" She rounds the table and crouches next to the stroller. Looking up at Tess, she covers her mouth with one well-manicured hand. "Oh, she's *gorgeous.*"

Tess has always liked Amanda, who would often include her in group situations, pulling her into a debate and offering Tess up as an expert on something she barely knew anything about. It was all at once fun and frightening.

"Thank you." Tess tilts her head and smiles.

"So this is Emilia! I love the name too!" She reaches out to cup Tess's hand, and Tess closes her other hand over Amanda's. "Are you sure you won't bring her to the office?"

Tess shakes her head, her lips sealing into a tight, thin line. "Not a good time for me right now to face everyone."

Amanda's expression falls, but her beauty never diminishes. Just then, the waiter asks if they are ready to order drinks. Amanda asks for the house white, and Tess follows suit. Menus are left, but Amanda's gaze is too engaging for Tess to ignore.

"Sam left me," she puts bluntly. Amanda pushes back from the table, her brows nearly meeting her hairline. "About a month ago."

"Tess." Her friend is speechless. Her impossibly large eyes grow in size while her hands cover her mouth.

"It's okay," Tess tries to reassure her, shaking her head. "I'm okay, Emma's okay." She reaches into the stroller and pulls the blanket level with her sleeping daughter's bare neck. Tess had decided to share this information with Amanda, saving her the painful and repetitive discussions when she returned to work in a few months, knowing her friend would relay the data systematically.

Over lunch, Tess shared most of what she knew about what had happened and why. They break to eat quiche and sip their wine, but her sad news dominates the meal.

"You know, I have a friend who just went through something like this, and he went to a counselor and swore it saved his life." Amanda waves the server over and asks for a refill. Tess nods to another glass when asked and considers what her friend has suggested.

Looking past Amanda, Tess's eyes are drawn to the hospital, which sits atop the hill bordering the city's southwest end. "I hear the hospital has a new wing dedicated to psychiatry. I hear they design programs around a person's specific needs."

Amanda follows her gaze and then looks back in surprise. "You're not *crazy*; you don't need to go to a *hospital.* Just look into a counselor; they're a dime a dozen."

Tess smiles and nods, never taking her eyes from the hilltop. "Yeah, it costs like eight hundred dollars a day, but my insurance would pay a portion if my doctor signed off on the stay." Tess finds comfort in the building's architecture, and the idea that she could stay there for a time intrigues her.

"That's a LOT of money! Just consider counseling." Amanda cleans the lipstick from the rim of her glass. "This is one of those things that can play on your mind - you guys were together a long time."

Tess listens with a blank stare, watching Amanda's lips form word after word. She could never understand how anybody could talk so much about anything. Even in her career, Tess only spoke when absolutely necessary to get a point across or give direction. She nods as Amanda continues, undeterred, about how to deal with this challenging time in her life.

As Amanda gets up to return to work, Tess decides that therapy is how to approach the scenarios she's been suffering from lately and tells her friend that she will get help.

"It couldn't hurt."

Chapter Five
Tuesday, 3:00 pm

Tess walks Emilia back to the apartment after lunch. The October sun is warm on her face and feels invigorating. Waiting at a light, she closes her eyes and faces the blue sky, allowing the sun's healing properties to brighten her mood.

Since Sam left, she's been taking vitamin D, which promised to lift her depression, but she put little faith in herbal remedies and had always shied away from prescription drugs. Now, with the idea of therapy on the horizon, she can see an alternative to both.

But the pessimist in her finds new arguments regarding a shrink messing around in her head. She wrestles with the idea and confirms that it has worked for her in the past. When her brother had died, she was inconsolable. Therapy was right for her.

Deep in thought, Tess moves forward as a crowd passes her, indicating the light has changed and it is safe to walk. Unbeknownst to her, the group picks up their pace midway, as the light had gone from 'walk' to 'stop.' A car speeding toward the intersection, anticipating the green light, rushes through a red and strikes a van, making a right turn.

The sounds of crashing metal and squealing tires shock Tess, bringing her to a standstill in the middle of the crosswalk. The van careens into the light pole behind them, skidding within a few inches of her and Emilia. Tess's hair and dress lifted with the powerful gust accompanying the van's near hit.

A man rushes out to pull Tess and Emilia away as the van spills fluid from under its hood. Tess is frozen in place, but she completes the crossing at the man's urgings, her hands tightly gripping the stroller.

"Lady, if you had nine lives," the man tells her, breathless. Tess barely acknowledges him, staring at Emilia, still sleeping, secure in her stroller.

The crowd surrounding them moves to assist those involved in the accident while others direct traffic away from the scene.

"Thank you," Tess manages in a stunned whisper. The young man looks Tess up and down and guides her further away, distancing them a block or more. She allows him to lead her.

"Thank you," she says again, but the man does not release her arm. Tess finally looks at him and suddenly doesn't feel any safer than when she was standing in the middle of the street.

"I'm fine," she tells him, her grip on the stroller loosening should she need to defend herself. He looks at her and smirks. She wonders what's happening. *This isn't normal.*

"I just want to get you to a safe place," he explains. "I know a spot I can take you."

Despite her shock, Tess knows something is very wrong. Now she is frightened. Looking back, she sees they have traveled more than two city blocks from the gathering crowd.

"I'll scream," she tells him under her breath.

"You don't want to do that," he explains, showing a long knife at his belt, hidden behind his jacket. Tess can't believe her bad luck.

"What do you want?"

"Just to get you to a safe place."

"Is it money you want?"

"Yes, I want money," he continues to lead her along the broken sidewalk. "But I may ask for something more than money." A wink follows.

Tess is in no shape to fight a man with a knife. It is a seemingly impossible situation, and she is becoming increasingly alarmed as they travel into a less populated section of the street.

The man's hold on her arm is beginning to hurt, and she struggles weakly to shrug him off. He won't have any of it.

"I'll give you what you want; I will just promise me -"

"I don't make promises," he replies. "Too hard to keep."

"I have a *baby,* for Christ's sake!"

"So do I. Two, in fact, and they like to eat," he says matter-of-factly.

"So take my money," she pleads.

"I will," he assures her. "But you see, I like to fuck."

Tess goes cold. She was going to be raped. She was going to be raped, she says again and again to herself. But if that was all, then she could survive this, she rationalizes. If she cooperates, then he will let Emilia and her go.

As she tried to process what the next few hours might be like, two police officers rounded the corner and headed towards them.

His grip on her arm increases tenfold, and she winces at the pain as his filthy fingernails dig into her pale, soft flesh.

He leans toward her and whispers a threat. "Say anything, and I'll cut your throat, I swear."

"HELP ME!" Tess cries to the officers, pushing the stroller out in front of her. They eye the man and pull their weapons. He releases his grip and flees into the street. There, a tractor-trailer plows into him, sending his body dozens of feet forward as the driver slams on his brakes.

Tess watches on in horror as his corpse skids along the asphalt, and the truck runs him over a second time, pulling him under the right tire. The sound, the bursting and crunching, is unimaginable. Tess falls to her knees and crawls to the stroller where Emma is now stirring.

One officer rushes to Tess's aid while the other calls in the gruesome scene.

"Are you alright, Miss?" he asks, kneeling to meet her gaze. Tess pulls Emma from the stroller and hugs her tightly, leaning against a building to steady herself. She's nodding to the officer, her mouth open and debating whether or not to lose her lunch. Hiding behind the baby's carriage, Tess shields herself from the mess in the street. Two close calls, she thinks. *What's happening? Why is this happening to me?*

Pick up Her Past's Present at Amazon now!

Other Books of Fiction by Michael Poeltl

1. The Judas Syndrome
2. Rebirth (Book 2 of The Judas Syndrome)
3. Revelation (Book 3 of The Judas Syndrome)
4. Her Past's Present
5. Waning Metaphorically (14 Short Stories)
6. A.I. Insurrection - The General's War
7. A.I. Insurrection - Armageddon (Book 2 of the A.I. Series)
8. A.I. Insurrection - Exodus (Book 3 of the A.I. Series)

Young Reader Picture Books

1. West of Noreso
2. An Angry Earth

Educational Books by Michael Poeltl

1. If a Tree Falls in the Forest...
2. Energy is Forever, and so are YOU!

About the author

Author Website: www.mikepoeltl.com

Amazon Author Page: Michael Poeltl Amazon

Facebook Page: Michael.Poeltl.Author

Goodreads Author Page: Goodreads

Twitter Handle: @mpoeltlauthor

Further Acknowledgements

To whomever, or whatever is seeding my brain with these tales, narratives, and oddities: Gratitude.

Reviews and requests for interviews and guest blogs are always appreciated!